EVIL NOTIONS

EVIL NOTIONS

Suzann Smiley
and
Billy Smiley

To order additional copies of this book, contact:
Xlibris Corporation
1-888-795-4274
www.Xlibris.com
Orders@Xlibris.com
83191

CHAPTER ONE

In the summer months in Southern Alabama, the heat and humidity were always high until the sun went down; sometimes even after the sun had disappeared, it seemed to get hotter. All the folks would go to bed with their windows open, sometimes even the doors.

Jim and Mary Banks would be fast asleep in their bedroom when their daughter, Kate, would slip out into the night to meet the man of which she thought was her life. She knew it was more than just a desire that made her feel the way that she did; this time, it had to be love.

It was a useless, hopeless situation. And every night when she returned home, slipping back into the house, she would be deathly afraid that when she left him she would not ever see him again. Panic twisted through her. She became restless and hard to get along with, for she knew that her parents would not allow her to date openly. Knowing that, she was afraid that Bobby would become tired of her slipping around, for he was much older, an impatient sort, and Kate was too young.

She gave way to the tears that chased her checks, knowing that her mother and father were very stern and sincere about her not dating until she became of age; and she had a year to go.

Mary stood quietly and listened once again, glancing down the hall to Kate's room, seeing her slip back into her room, with her hair a mess and sometimes her walk wasn't so straight. It was easy to see, for the living room was always graced with a light.

Bobby Brent was an army man, tall, his shoulders broad, with a muscular build—any girl's dream. But for him, love was only in the movies. His line was find 'em, fuck 'em, and then forget 'em.

But little did Kate know, she fell right into his trap. When Bobby saw that she was getting serious, he got a case of the "gone ass," leaving her cold. He had gotten what he wanted from her anyway.

Kate felt the flash of apprehension tighten throughout her body and she tried desperately to combat herself. There was no need to worry about it now, the damage had been done. Lying across the bed, she closed her eyes, trying to escape the beginning of what was going to take a long time to fix.

Lying in the quiet, she heard the chirp of a small bird that was perched just outside her bedroom window. Its song called out for a companion. The lonely cry rang through her head as she opened her eyes. The bird sounded like the way I feel, she thought. Then she resolutely removed the thought from her mind, not allowing herself pity. She knew what she had done was wrong and against her parents' sole will. But that heavy feeling that she felt for the need to escape from the bond that they held so tightly over her had caused her to do foolish things. She was much too young to understand at the time, she felt that she was much more mature and deserved more freedom than her parents allowed her to absorb. This was exactly what her parents had tried to protect her from, but Kate's juvenile thinking and heart would never see or understand their love and true intentions. Her thoughts slapped and hammered her brain. She was now, for the first time, beginning to understand how cruel the world really was outside her sheltered home. But in spite of all the rights and wrongs, Kate ignored the intrusion that was now seeded inside her body. Her room had become her refuge from the outside world, and those around that loved her. However, the days passed quickly as Kate sat and watched her body being destroyed by the abundant swell that was taking place to her midsection. Even with that, she felt destined for the hands of the one who had betrayed her. Trying hard to ignore the time and the yearning for the man that she so desperately missed, she recognized that he had deserted, not the army, but her.

Pulling herself up to the head of the bed, she let her eyes glance around the room. The mismatched furniture gave off the impression that it was from Noah's Ark, and the almost rotted floor beneath showed a worn out but scrubbed look.

Kate fondled the faded fabrics of her dress, trying to control the trembling ends of her fingers, letting her hands fold up the ends of the material, wadding it tightly into her fist—a habit she had developed long ago. Looking across the way to the far end of her room, she saw the reflection of shame that stretched her body. Anger raised and spread throughout her, as she leaned over, taking a cup that sat by her bed, slinging it with the force of raging anger, shattering the mirror that hung on the wall. She was not expecting to start her life out like this. It wasn't a deliberate plan for her to betray herself. Kate shrugged, pushing herself up and off the bed. She made her way to the kitchen and poured herself a fourth cup of coffee. Through the kitchen window, she caught sight of the mail carrier whom she would look for daily, hoping for that letter from someone which never came.

Days, weeks, even months had passed, making her even more resentful of the situation at hand. She had come to enjoy taking advantage of her mother's nursing her hour after hour, in spite of the fatigue that was masking her mother's face. Kate only laughed and mocked her.

"You hate me, don't you?" Kate begrudgingly asked. "For all the shameful things that I have done and for the embarrassment it has brought to you. And I'm sure the church is running their mouth about it."

Mary stood a hand's breadth away, looking up at her, while Kate's dark assessing eyes waited for a reply.

"I'm not to judge," Mary answered, with a smile. "Only God has the right to judge what is right or wrong."

Contempt numbed Kate, as she tried to push away, sinking back on her bed, only for a moment, when she became restless, as she watched her mother close the door. When Kate processed a wave of anger that invaded her, then she lifted her hands circling her knuckles, with destruction on her mind, hating herself and having utmost difficulty holding on to any reason. Kate walked over to the dresser and took from a drawer a picture of Bobby that she had hidden there since the first time she met him. It was all she had to remember him by, but the phantom pain that gnawed inside her was more than she could stand. She took a matchbook from the nightstand. Placing the picture on the floor, she struck a match and held its flame to a corner. She watched it burn to a tiny pile of ash.

CHAPTER TWO

It was cold and frosty. It was not a typical night for Southern Alabama weather. It was worse than usual. The bitter cold matched the inner strength and coldness of Kate's heart, where she held anger and always a bad case of the nerves, knowing that the baby would be coming any time. Kate hated this place, herself, and the innocent life that lay inside her. Her plans did not include children and she wanted no part of this one. It was probably going to be a boy anyway. That thought depressed her even more.

Her body had been very curvy, and with her alluring ways, she had been able to entice any man she wanted. This miserable little bastard inside of her changed all that. No matter, she knew how to fix things, with that thought, she smiled Evil thoughts were her only means of happiness these days. It was a natural born gift that she had and she knew how to use, and had done since a child. Now that she was an adult, she had no qualms about doing or saying things that would shock most people, especially her mom and dad. Yet at the same time, she knew she had fooled a lot of people, making them believe that she was a good-hearted southern belle. She knew the words and mannerisms, but that was as far as it went. That thought caused her to smile again.

Kate loved deception. It had helped her survive. But now she had to face reality. The last few months had been hard. Times had been tough on the whole country, but she took it personally. Her mood was growing darker. She hated everything around her.

No money and little food had been her way of life. The old house they lived in gave no comfort. It barely stopped the wind but not the cold.

Yes, she thought, that damn howling wind is trying to haunt me. The wind became a momentary obsession. Each cold blast taunted her, laughed at her, and reminded her of the shape she was in. A slow hating rage filled her and she enjoyed it. It took her to even darker places. This rage caused pain, but it was pain she inflicted upon herself. Control was the key. Dark rage caused her to hate every minute of the life that grew in her. She had hit her stomach with her fists several times in these fits of anger, trying to stop the heartbeat of this new life, but had failed. Kate let the memory of the last time that she saw Bobby drift through her mind like cigarette smoke wafting through a still room.

Again, Kate was watching yet another sizzling sex—and profanity—packed action movie in the back of the bar that would make a blind man blush. She was not there to enjoy the flick, she was on a mission. Her mission would be the scene of an ambush. Her tactics had worked the first time, so she saw no reason to change her strategies; only this time, there was more at stake.

When a young man returns from the war, a part of it comes home with him. The destruction he lived with and witnessed can leave him somehow unbalanced and disturbed. Things that he had been a part of can leave him with confusing thoughts and ideas. Such a broken world and all the evil which men do to each other can overtake and ruin some warriors. Bobby was this person. He was struggling to live his life here on the home ground. The psychological trauma of the war haunted him, and left him with a bad temperament. Eventually, he became a fisherman; there he hoped he could find peace of mind on the lonely sea. He had just come in from a fishing trip to meet up with some of his comrades at the local bar. Then, after a couple of beers, he saw what lurked in the shadows that could sting with poison, with beauty that could destroy a conscious mind. There sat Kate. He walked over to say hello, like any gentleman would do. She boldly told him she was pregnant. Not believing a word she said, he refused to listen.

That news from her was a surprise in a full scale attack. Her words penetrated, but he was not prepared to defend himself.

Knowing that he was hardly capable of taking care of himself, he knew he did not have the strength or courage to play the role of a parent. Later in the night, his friends grabbed his limp passed-out body and carried him to his boat and flopped him onto the cold bare floor. In the bitter cold, his friends walked away. Hours later, he and his boat were gone from the harbor, and no one ever saw him again.

There was no attempt made for anyone to go out on the water and look for him. A town so full of good intentions, they gave him the benefit of the doubt.

Kate's thoughts tumbled over each other with frustration, anger and hate. In her frustration, she wondered if her future was cursed.

CHAPTER THREE

It was in the year 1950, on a cold November night, when her child was born, only a few minutes after midnight. The birth took place on a soft fluffy feather bed that Mary had prepared but there would be no doctor present to aid in the delivery. Mary was working so hard and praying that everything would be all right. The nine months had passed so slowly for Kate, who had had no intentions of this happening in her life. She hated its every minute of life inside her body, trying to take her life many times, but failing at each attempt. With luck, someone found her each time before it was too late. And for that, they were cursed by her. Bobby had left town, refusing to believe the child was his, believing that Kate was not even pregnant to start with. But even if the child did belong to him, he wanted no part of it. He had simply disappeared.

The place was in an old run-down house, in a back bedroom where the winter winds crept through the walls and around the window seals, where the dampness from the cold would chill a person to the bone.

Though the house was cold, it was filled with love by Jim and Mary who were soon to be grandparents. Their hearts were overwhelmed by the coming of this baby, but they were also saddened by the feelings that Kate had.

"Push," Mary said. "Now breathe, everything is all right. Push."

"Push? I can't . . . it hurts . . . do something," was Kate's screaming voice.

"Come on, you can do it. Push . . . push . . . that's it . . . Oh my god," and then Mary was very quiet.

"Fuck. What the hell? Is it dead?"

"No . . . it's a girl, and she is so beautiful." Mary had been so intent on looking at the child that she had not heard Kate's profanity.

Kate went back to her old mean ass, bad mouth, mocking Mary.

"No, it's a girl, and she is so beautiful."

"Let me finish up, so you can see her."

"I don't want to see her—I don't ever want to see her. Get that fuckin' thing away from me!"

Mary's heart just broke in two from the things that she was hearing from Kate. Mary's flash of anger at Kate for her curse words and actions was instantly stilled by the newborn infant cradled in her arms. "But you have to let her nurse; she needs your milk."

"It's not getting my anything, just take it and go away."

Mary went into the kitchen and fixed some goat's milk for the baby, for that's all she knew to do. But after doing that, the baby would not take the milk. Mary did not know what to do so she called for Jim. "Jim, please go and talk to Kate. if this baby doesn't get some milk she will die." But Kate overheard what was said and screamed out, "Then let it die," and slammed her bedroom door shut. Jim went to her door, knocking and calling out to her, but Kate was having no part of it.

With the sound of the baby's cry, it was like this newborn understood what was being said from her mother. Mary asked, "What do we do?" Jim said, "You know, try some orange juice, warm it, and I'll pray." Handing the baby to Jim, Mary fixed some warm juice and gave it to her. Their prayers were answered, the newborn nursed it, and in just a few minutes her little eyes were closed, and surprisingly, she slept through the night.

It had been two weeks now since the birth. Kate had not even looked at her baby, she refused, would not go near it. Her actions were as though nothing had ever happened.

At the beginning of the third week, Kate was still keeping herself locked in her room. All this time, she had been slipping out at night to get something to eat because she knew that Mary would leave food for her. Kate would not speak or talk to anyone; she just stayed in her room,

But Mary was not so worried, because every morning she would find that the food was gone that she always left for her. Mary and Jim hoped that by leaving her alone she would come around and be a mother to her baby, and change her way of thinking. They hoped that this would help her to grow up.

But what they hoped for didn't happen. When Kate regained her strength, she got up in the night, robbing her father and mother of all the money they had, taking the pocket watch that Jim's father had given him that belonged to his grandfather. It wasn't much, but it was a bus ticket without saying goodbye.

As Mary held the infant in her arms, accepting the tears that now run down her face, her voice trembled as she spoke. "You know, we have called her baby since she was born; she is three weeks old and doesn't have a name."

"Yes," Jim answered with a stern voice. "But that is going to change," Intentionally shocking her, Jim reached out, taking Mary by the hand. "I would like to name her Suzann Waycon."

"Why Waycon?" Mary asked.

"That means life from far away star, and I feel in my heart that is what she is."

"You're letting some of your heritage show, aren't you?"

Jim laughed softly in answer to her question.

A big smile showed on Mary's face. "I like that." Then there was a tear in her eye.

"Then why are you crying?" Jim asked.

"Oh," she said. "These are not sad tears; these, for once, are happy tears. Can we call her Suzann?"

"Absolutely. We will pick up our life and pray and give thanks to God for this gift that he has given us." Her eyes clouded as she moved forward to meet him. "I love you so much," she said, while biting her bottom lip to try to hold back the tears.

Suddenly both Jim and Mary were aware that they both were holding their breaths, as if the moment might slip away. As they stroked the tiny face that lay so innocently and so fragile beneath the blanket, their hearts swelled with love for the child and each other.

But down deep in their hearts, unspoken words did little to hide the hurt and shame they felt, knowing that their own daughter was filled with so much hate. They could not understand, for they had raised her with love and care.

They then decided that they would hold this secret from Suzann, for she need not know the likes of Kate. That would be heartbreaking to anyone and especially to a child.

CHAPTER FOUR

Times were very hard; Mary made all their clothes and all the food was raised from the garden. Hogs were killed in the winter for meat. The hams were hung in the smoke house, other meat was salted down. There was very little money and no car, so if they went anywhere they had to walk. Sometimes, they would get lucky and catch a ride, and of course, Suzann was always in the middle of everything. The closest store for them was eight miles away, a local general store that carried just about everything. Jim had credit there, which made it seem easy to get things, but it still had to be paid for on the first of each month.

But when it came time for a getaway, fishing was the trip. There were small creeks and rivers within walking distance. And there were those ponds in every pasture owned by neighbors all around, and they had plenty of catfish.

Jim and Mary loved fishing and would go every day if they could. There was so much fun and laughter in watching Suzann trying to learn to throw a rod and reel; needless to say, she caught more tree limbs and power lines than fish. When they returned home, there was always fish for supper. Everyone was so happy, Jim and Mary could not ask for nothing more than what they had. They knew that this child was so different, and she brought so much happiness to their lives, they could not imagine what they would do without her. And in their prayers every night was a humble thank you. Secretly and unknown to each other, they both hoped that Kate would never return.

CHAPTER FIVE

Suzann was now six years old, and it was time to start school. On her first day, she was so scared because leaving her mother and dad was something that she did not want to do. Not realizing that it would only be for the day and then she would be returning home, she was more than just a little excited.

That morning, Mary was getting her dressed with a brand new dress that she had made from a flour sack; it was white with little pink flowers on it. Putting her golden hair up in a ponytail that hung down past her waist, Mary said, "You look so pretty." Walking out the front door, she felt the tears that threatened her eyes. Trying to hold them back, knowing that this was something she had to do.

Jim took hold of her hand and they walked to meet the bus. When Suzann got on the bus, she watched her dad until he was out of sight. Then it hit her, that alone feeling, then realizing that this was the first time in six years that she had ever been apart from them. Looking around, not knowing anyone, but she was never one to be bashful. As she sat quietly, she began thinking, "If I can get up in church and sing in front of so many people that I didn't know, I can do this." With that thought, she began to feel better.

The school was so big, the classroom was large and filled with books, so many of them—books were everywhere. Never had she seen anything like this in her life.

And check this out, a big potbelly stove sat in the middle of the room, with pipes running out from the ceiling; there were tables and chairs that sat all in the room, with a big black board that hung on the wall. There was a lot of noise in the room when in walked an awfully big woman. And the room got really quiet.

"I am Mrs. Mullin, your teacher," speaking very loud as she stood behind her wooden desk. Everyone had that scared look on their face, but nevertheless, games were played, and when lunch was served, they had a banana sandwich with a bowl of soup. Mrs. Mullen handed out homework and then the first day of school was over. This is going to be easy, she thought because the home work she received, she had known since the age of three. Her grades were always great. Every time she made a hundred percent, she didn't get money or gifts, she got hugs and kisses and that was all she wanted, that was enough for her. Anything that made her mom and dad smile was all she could ask for.

CHAPTER SIX

The next two years came and went so fast, with school and work in the fields; it seemed that the summers were even shorter than they really were.

Mary sewed and made quilts for the public, a seamstress that everyone appreciated. Jim did all kinds of jobs, hoeing cotton, making chair bottoms and baskets from trees. Suzann always tagged along behind him as he made his way into the deep woods where he would cut down the tree that he needed. Dragging it back to the house, he would split it into long strands to fit whatever he was making. This work was time-consuming, but when it was finished, it had the constructed look like that of a picture in a Sears's catalogue. His designing had no limit, he worked hard and long hours; but aside from all the work, he always found time to take Suzann fishing.

The town they lived in was small, where everybody knew everybody, including the other man's business. Most of the townspeople's noses grew long. And when Sunday came, everyone went to church. It was a chance to catch up on the entire gospel. Jim was an old-time preacher, having been since the age of thirty-three when he had come to that place in life where he accepted the calling of God. Even being an older man now, he was still young at heart.

It was miles to the church where he preached, but the walk he was used to. He never took a dime, even in the times when he knew that they could use it, he always turned it down, asking them to give it to someone that needed it more. Going to church every Sunday and hearing Jim preach, God became a large mysterious presence in Suzann's life. Even though she had no proof that God existed, her dad and everybody said he did, and she had no reason to doubt them.

It was a small church that rested down by the river, where in the late spring there was always an annual Blossom Festival highlighted by some of the biggest gospel singers who would come in and sing all afternoon with dinner on the ground. Suzann could remember this event happening ever year and the same man with long hair and dirty fingernails who would pass the bucket for money to pay the singers. And thinking about how much she would like to someday be one of those singers. It was always good when Sundays came, all the townsfolk were like a huge family and involved themselves in each other's lives. Everybody helped one another—moms would mind little hurts, dads worked in the fields, mechanics would work under shade trees to fix people's cars, teachers would teach, little girls would play hopscotch on the chalk etched sidewalks at school, and the little boys would cut and balance bamboo and make spears and play cowboys and Indians. But then there were the bad days, when moms would go into a depressed daze and would continue to open the refrigerator door, then the stove, then the cabinet, and then do it all again hoping to find some food that maybe she had missed, but nothing would be there. There was always milk from the cow, eggs from the chickens, cresses from the spring, and the older hens, they were the ones that got their necks wrung. Rabbit or squirrel from a hunting trip was also a mainstay of their diet. It was a time when you could borrow anything from the neighbors but salt. That was a no-no because you always gave salt to someone who needed it. And when some got mad, they tried not to let it show, but sometimes you could hear the bitterness in someone's voice that cut like vinegar through a pleasant conversation. Even when things were bad, things were good.

Life was busy with work and family, and the days passed by.

CHAPTER SEVEN

Jim would say, "Sometimes you'll be going along in life minding your own business and then, all of a sudden, God will grab you and throw you into a brand-new world, then you find yourself wondering how you're going to deal with it." He would say, "You have to leave your baggage behind and get on with your life. For your destiny will not come to you, you will need to go to it."

So many people were so astounded by the number of times that Jim would preach on the course of your destiny. He'd say, "There will be so many times that you will put yourself in motion, thinking that the path that you are on is what you believe to be your destiny, but then something will happen, it may be as little of a thing as bumping into someone, that move's you into a whole new direction. Believe in the word, not in man," he would preach. Jim would read the Bible daily and do a lot of thinking to himself, sometimes even talk to himself.

"Sometimes we are the weakness of friends. We disappoint people, and when we see them again, we are embarrassed." He remembered one time he had a friend who was sick for three weeks and he didn't even call him and a friend that went through a divorce. "I was not there for him, friends who stopped by to see me, I was working somewhere, but I never got back with him, sometimes we are weak."

"Now that I am older and have this little girl, I pray to be stronger, for at my age I will never see her to become a grown woman. And I knew that she needs me, she has no one but us."

It was getting close to the school break, and there were a lot of plans being made for fishing, there was another plan being made also. On the last Friday of school, Jim and Mary caught the Greyhound bus and went into town, but that afternoon they didn't have to ride the bus home. That afternoon, when Suzann got off the school bus, Jim and Mary were sitting on the front porch swing. They were all smiles and she could tell that they were up to something.

"How was school today?"

"It was good."

"Did you learn something?"

"No," she answered.

"What do you mean no?"

"Well, Dad, I already knew everything that we talked about."

Her response brought a laugh from both Jim and Mary. Her answer had been stated as a matter of fact and very serious, like she really had the world by the tail.

"What is so funny?" she asked. "You both have a smile on your face from ear to ear."

"What do you think about not having to walk tomorrow to go fishing?"

"Are we going with someone?"

"No"

"Then how are we going to get there if we don't walk?"

"Come, Child," Mary said.

Taking her by the hand and walking behind the house, there it was.

"It's a truck, you got a new truck!"

"Well, it's not new but it's new to us."

"You mean *it's ours*?"

"There will be no more walking in this family."

Climbing in the front seat, "I love it," she said. "Does this mean that we are uptown?"

"Now, where did you hear that?"

"Well, most of the kids in school won't have much to do with me because they say that I am not uptown."

"Well, you can let them know that you are closer to being uptown now."

All this excitement made the night so long for Suzann could not wait for morning to come to take her first ride in their new truck.

The smell of sausage cooking from the kitchen woke her early, and as always, she could hear the coffee perking. With the appetite like she always had, no one had to get her up. As she walked toward the kitchen in her bare feet, passing the window, she saw the truck sitting in the front yard.

Forgetting all about the food, she decided that she would have a closer look. As she went out the door and walked across the grass, she remembered some of the things that she had heard other people say about her and her family. Some of the more uppity girls had informed Suzann that she and her family were poor people and had laughed about it. "I wonder what they will have to say about this poor family having a truck."

Mary and Jim came outside and interrupted her train of thought. Looking into their faces, it was easy to tell that they were on top of the world.

With her outstretched hand and her eyes flashing, Jim knew that Suzann was up to something.

"What you think you are going to do?" Jim asked.

"Oh, I just want to put the key in the switch and set behind the wheel for a while."

"You can't get anywhere like that," he replied with a laugh. "Come on, we might as well make the best of it. I think it is time for a candy bar and a Coca-Cola." Reaching in his pocket, Jim placed his fingers around the keys. "Come on, Mother," he said.

"No, I think I'll stay here, ya'll go on."

Every inch of his body was filled with excitement as they pulled into the parking lot of the general store.

The streets were filled with people shopping and doing their business, when everyone stopped to look and stare.

Suzann looked up at her dad and said, "Maybe we should give them a picture, Dad." And Jim laughed and pushed her into the door of the store.

The woman that stood behind the counter was tall, almost as tall as Jim. It was easy to see that at one time she must have been very attractive, but the hard work and long hours had worn away her good looks. She wiped her hands on the front of her white apron, brushing off the traces of grit from stocking shelves. Her sharp eyes rolled over and up as she looked in their direction, offering her assistance.

"Well, now," her voice loud and brisk. "What will it be for you folks today?"

Jim was overwhelmed by her charm in spite of himself,

"Yes, ma'am," Jim answered. "We need a carton of cokes and four Pay Day candy bars."

"Will that be all, Brother Jim?"

"Yes, ma'am," he said as he buried his hand deep into his pocket, withdrawing his wallet to pay for the goods.

Mr. Johnny was fixing to enter the store when he saw Jim and Suzann coming out; he opened the door as they approached, to let them out.

"You're looking well, Brother Jim, did anyone die today?"

He always teased Jim about his somber mood. It was a challenge to make Jim smile

Mr. Johnny had been friends with Jim for many years, and Jim was pleased to have him as a friend. He liked his dignity, his openness, his efficiency, and his jovial style. He had the kind of image that Jim admired.

Johnny smiled winningly at Jim and looked faintly amused, as though they shared a long standing joke. Johnny always danced to his own tune.

"No, Johnny, thank the good Lord that no one has died today. Besides, I wouldn't have time for a funeral today," he said jokingly. "I've promised this young lady a fishing trip, so I guess that we had better get on our way, if you know what I mean."

Johnny laughed heartily and replied, "I know exactly what you mean. By the way, if you catch more than that new truck can haul, then give me a holler. I sure do enjoy a good mess of fish, especially that deep fried catfish that Miss Mary makes." Johnny turned and started walking into the store when Jim said, "I'll keep you in mind."

When they returned home from the store, Mary was ready to go to the river as she stood on the porch holding the picnic basket filled with fried chicken and a few other goodies.

On the way to the river, Jim stated, "We're going where it is quiet and peaceful and some of the most beautiful sites you would ever want to see. Where it is pure and unchanged by human hands, where you can listen to the sounds of the birds and see all the natural colors that God has put here for human eyes to take pleasure in. Where we can swim, and of course, take in a little fishing." But of course, everyone knew that Jim was going to partake in some fishing anyway. As they arrived, only a few boats were out on the river, and most of those were on the other side.

"The fishing is the best over there," Jim explained. But just ahead is the best place for swimming. The bottom slopes gradually, the water is shallow, and there is a nice deep place there, for I know that you like to dive." They vacated the truck and headed to a tiny beach of white sand, just big enough for the three of them to stretch out on a couple of old quilts that Mary had made just for fishing.

Jim paused for a moment, and glanced at everyone meaningfully. "Well, here we are. Ain't it nice? Give me your hand, be careful getting into the water; the farther you go, the deeper it gets."

Weaving a little, Suzann nearly lost her balance but Jim reached out his long arms to steady her. They were having the time of their life.

"Race you back," he said, as he moved slightly ahead. By the time they reached the bank, Suzann was only a couple of strokes behind him.

"I should have let you win," he said.

"No, that would not have been very competitive!" she said, racing out of the water to the quilt that was spread out across the sand. Tossing Suzann a towel, Mary reached in her purse and pulled out a comb and began to comb Suzann's hair into place. That in itself was a job, for her hair was so long. Testing the quilt as she stretched out, resting her head on a cushion, she let her feet hang over the end digging her toes in the sand. The peacefulness she gratefully absorbed as the warm air was drying her hair, while her fingers riffed through it.

"Oh, Dad," she moaned. "This was a wonderful idea."

Seeing the gleam that flashed in his eyes, they all knew it was time to do some fishing. But for him, there were not many days that he couldn't find a little time for that. Watching him as he instantly baited his hook, as he had done so many times before, you could see the reflection of the waters dancing in his eyes caused by the bright summer sun. His eagerness to explore with his baited hook what lay below the surface of the water almost seemed like nervousness. He inhaled the sweet scented air along with stretching out his long legs. Excitement flooded throughout as the day for him had only began to come alive. For Jim, fishing was living life at its fullest.

It was like a vacation for Suzann and Mary as they lay basking in the hot summer sun, feeling the force of the heat that radiated through their bodies, relaxing the tight muscles from the previous week's work. Enjoying the pleasant surroundings, time had slipped by very quickly. After a couple of hours feeling the heat of mother nature as it burned their bare skin, offering the suggestion that they had had enough sun. They sat up admiring the beauty that surrounded them, watching Jim as he lingered patiently with the rod and reel in hand. He held himself ambitiously still, even though he hadn't so much as gotten a nibble in the time passed.

Jim noticed the perspiration on Mary's face as she wiped the moisture from her neck. Even though they continued their conversation with no complaints from the heat, he knew it was time to go. Starting to gather up his equipment, not noticing the sudden surge in the line, the reel was jerked halfway into the water. Suzann shouted, "Dad, your rod and reel!"

Jim turned quickly and pounced on the rod like a hungry animal grabbing for a piece of meat. Scrambling back to his feet, regaining his balance, he exclaimed, "My god, it must be a whale."

The fish was strong and unbending as it struggled notoriously to free itself from the life tugging snare that clutched at its body. His voice was sharp with pleasure as he vigorously worked the reel, simultaneously trying to talk the fish in.

The fierceness of his love for fishing, now more than ever, surpassed him. God's perfect beast fought so desperately against him. Jim had become obsessed, insane, or it could even be a little madness. Every inch of his body throbbed from the excitement that overwhelmed him. His patience was starting to run thin, for he couldn't wait to unveil his catch from the buttoned up waters. Then he saw it, staring up from the shadow of the deep blue water. It was magnificent. His impatience added to his desire, he could see the white of its belly as it reached its point in the air, then falling in the smoothness beneath the water. Jim struggled, pulling up on the line, holding it tightly, reluctant to let it go. The fears of losing this catch only strengthened him. His anxiety rose and his voice was but a whisper against his chest. Then Jim lifted his head and welcomed the mist-like rain that fell upon his face. Even though the sun was beaming hot and the sky was clear, the rain began to fall.

When Jim lowered his head, his feet slipped. The fear in his eyes was unmistakable for only a second as he thought he had lost his fish. But then he was satisfied at the comforting tug that he felt once again.

Just as suddenly as the fish had struck, the taut line snapped like an overloaded twig in a strong, fierce fall wind. Looking out across the now still water, with all the dismay of a man who has lost a great fight, Jim grunted, "Today you won but there will be more days to come. We just might tangle again, old man. The next time, I could be the victor."

CHAPTER EIGHT

The drive back home was a long one, with very little being said. Everyone was tired. When they pulled up into the driveway, Suzann pretended to be tired; with her own thoughts, she had something cooking. As they all walked into the house, Jim said, "Wait a minute, it seems everyone needs a little advice tonight." A frown lined his forehead. He walked across the room and knelt down in front of Suzann and Mary.

"Don't ever let a fish like that get away again."

Mary clasped her hands and held them together over her mouth for several moments before answering.

"Well, all right then," she said as her voice broke into a giggle. Then everyone broke down to laugh.

Suzann excused herself and went into her bedroom, realizing that she had to be the luckiest girl in the world. "Even though we are not what they call uptown, somehow, we always seem to get by and have so much fun doing it." With these thoughts rumbling through her head, another thought began to blossom. Silently walking over to the dresser, picking up a pad and a pencil, she began to write. Finishing her scribbling, smiling, she safely tucked the folded paper into her pocket.

Suzann had just walked out of her bedroom when she heard her mom calling them to supper. When they all sat down at the table, before the word of prayer, licking her lips to moisten them, she spoke softly.

"I have something I would like to read first, if I may, and it is dedicated to you, Dad."

She held her breath for only a second when she began to read from the folded up paper.

"Fishing

I went fishing the other day
Hooked a great big trout
I wanted to carry him home with me
But I couldn't get him out

I pulled and tugged
With all my might
But the harder I pulled
The harder he'd fight

Then all of a sudden
I almost had him to land
When my feet had to slip
And I fell in the sand

So I tied the line
To a great big limb
Said, now if you don't get me
I'll get him

Then he finally gave up
And I reeled him in
When I got him to the bank
Did I grin?

I said, when I get you home
I'm going to take off your hide
And how I'm gonna eat
When I get you fried

When the day was all through,
Jim was tired to the bone
He drove off in his truck
But the fish stayed home.
                    Written by Suzann."

Suzann slowly lifted her head, biting at her bottom lip anxiously waiting to see what Jim's reaction would be. His broad smile seemed to fill the air with mischievous magic. All harsh realities were forgotten for a few minutes as Mary began to laugh so hard that tears of happiness were streaming down her face.

Jim shook his head as he sank down in his chair, letting his shoulders bow slightly. He ran his calloused hands over his face. It had been a long hard day and the fishing trip had not ended like he'd hoped. But all bad things had been chased away with the reading of Suzann's poem.

"You know, sometimes it is hard to be the only man in the house but I feel that I'm the luckiest man in the world to have such a loving wife and such a smart daughter. But now we had better eat and get to bed because tomorrow is going to be a hard day."

CHAPTER NINE

Stella was very old and feeble, her head not always screwed on right. Her mind and way of thinking was in and out, spending the most of her last few years in the Leisure Nursing Home in Limestone County, Southern Alabama.

Some days she could remember things that she would rather not. But she spent most of her hours not even knowing her name.

"Hello, Stella," Rita the nurse said cheerfully as she handed Stella her meds. The rest of her arsenal consisted of a glass of water and a watchful eye, making sure that Stella swallowed the pills.

"Thank you," Stella said humbly, having not the slightest idea of what she was taking.

Her groaning began again, this time, louder.

"Please don't leave me," she said. "Please don't leave me," she repeated.

Rita answered, "No, I won't leave you, sweetie. Now you try to get some sleep for me, OK?"

Stella's breathing became faster, her mouth dry, blocked by a huge tube for suction to help clean her throat to aid in her breathing.

Rita had helped and worked with a lot of sick people, but there was something special about Stella. Rita often wondered what could have happened in her life that was so bad to cause her to be so afraid of the dark.

In Stella's profile and medical records, it looked as if there were few friends or family. She had four sons, two of them were killed in a car crash, and the third one, Jay T, survived. The paperwork had read, "Fourth Son," with no name being listed. Her husband Tom had been killed in their home late one night. The paper read that it was from someone who broke in their home while they were asleep. It was said that Tom went downstairs after hearing some kind of noise, to see what it was, taking his gun with him. There was a fight, loud voices and cursing, then a shot was heard.

Stella founded Tom on the floor, dead in his own pool of blood. There was no one there.

The gunshot had erased most of his face, but the shooter had fled and had never been caught.

There was a lot of talk that some believed that Jay T was the one that fled that night. But it could not be proved, and when questioned, Jay T said, "I know nothing, about nothing." But everyone believed that Stella knew, maybe that's why she was so afraid of the dark.

Stella was wide awake at half past nine to the sunlight through her window and the birds singing in the trees. For the first time in a long time, she remembered all. It was as clear as the ray from the sun shining in on her.

Rita walked into the room.

"Stella, there is someone here to see you."

Surprised to see something resembling fear on Stella's face that she had never seen before, Rita waited for a reply.

"Who?" Stella asked.

"He's a reporter; he would like to do a story on your life."

"What business is it of his?" Stella asked rudely.

"Maybe you would like to tell the truth about your son Jay T," a voice boomed out in the quiet room.

"Who do you think you are?"

"Why, I'm Mr. Brown, and I would like to write about you and your life."

And then she spoke as if she was talking to herself in a low voice. Just above a whisper, with a faraway look in her eyes, going back in time.

"Jay T could be a very dangerous man under the right circumstances, or any circumstance, as far as that goes."

"You mean like the night Tom was killed?"

"So you came here looking for that? Well, you came to the wrong place. That happened many years ago, may he rest in peace."

"Won't you tell the truth? Haven't you kept this horror closed up inside you long enough?"

"I'm glad, and I can appreciate your interest. But you see, it makes no difference anymore. For here, it doesn't get so dark, there's always a dim light on and my friend Rita is always nearby."

Mr. Brown asked, "Why you are really afraid of the dark?"

Not a word was spoken,

The light only showed the deep lines in her face and the sparkle in her long silver hair.

"I have nothing else to say to you!"

"But, Miss Stella . . ."

"You can go now," Stella said, in angry words with a tear that trickled down her cheek.

Rita escorted Mr. Brown from the room, closed the door behind him, and walked back to Stella's bed.

"You do remember, don't you?"

"I'm not much of a talkative person, but I want to thank you for being my friend and taking care of me during my stay here. But sometimes, things are better not said, better left alone."

Then all of a sudden, Stella had a scared look on her face that was mixed with hurt.

"I understand, Stella"

"Thank you for understanding. Now if you don't mind, I would like to be alone for a while."

"Yes, ma'am," said Rita as she walked out and closed the door behind her.

Stella lay there in the quiet, drifted back in time, and wondered in this, one of her few lucid moments, why things had happened in her life. The war that Tom was in and all the years he was gone away from home, not knowing from day to day if he would come back alive. Then, when he was home to stay, she lost him for nothing. Then she was forced to raise four boys on her own. The first two had grown up to be good men. They were, in the full sense of the word, gentlemen. The third child, Jay Thomas, known as Jay T, had been the source of agonizing pain and frustration. Even before he had started school, she had been able to recognize a mean and nasty streak in him. Even with that thought, she found a guarded smile as she remembered her last son, her "baby." He had only been a few years old when his oldest brothers had been killed. This had prompted her to send him away. She had sent him to distant relatives or boarding schools, whatever she could afford to accomplish two things. First, that he grow up with an education and be able to find a career and have a decent life. Second, that he would not know or be influenced by his only remaining brother, Jay T.

One moment that was frozen in time had seared a burning spot into the memories that she wished and prayed to forget. It was the evening after Jay T's thirteenth birthday. His huge hand had gripped her small chin and forced her eyes to stare into his. It was like looking into the coldest bottomless pit that she could have ever imagined. There was not even a hint of love, mercy, or compassion. His humorless laugh had only added to the cold chill that had overtaken her small body. The only thing that had kept her upright and standing had been the strong hold he had on her face. He laughed boisterously and shoved her onto the floor, where she lay in a quivering heap of terror.

His comings and goings had decreased with time; she did not know where he stayed or how he lived. Secretly, she hoped that he would move away or just disappear. Each time when he returned he would leave the kitchen in disarray. If she was up when he came in, she would simply go to her bedroom and close the door. She could hear him ransacking the refrigerator and cupboards but he would not even so much as speak to her, unless it was to threaten her if she ever told anyone. The little clay jar that Tom had given her as a gift when he got back from the war was where she kept what little money she had. He knew that she always put money in it, and when he came in, it would always be emptied when he left. Since the first time he had done this, Stella had purposely left some change in the jar so that he would take it and leave and not push the issue and not take all of her money.

Stella's normal sunlight-bright personality had changed since the birthday incident. His absence had helped her to recover some of her old cheer. But then, other things started happening that had darkened even her cheeriest thoughts.

She had walked into and overheard other conversations. Many of the townsfolk knew or believed that he was the culprit committing small to horrific crimes. This weighed terribly on her mind and way of living. Most of her former friends and other acquaintances seemed to look at her with a strange kind of pity in their eyes, very few even spoke to her anymore; and if they did, it was a short, sterile greeting.

As Stella walked through the small community, she kept her eyes on the ground in front of her feet. The same day each month, she made her way to pay her monthly debts. The only bright spot in the town and on these trips had to be Charlie Cox. He was the general store owner. He and his daughter, Sally, were the only people that treated her like a friend. She would stay in the store, even looking at things she couldn't afford, just to feel a bit of happiness and camaraderie.

As Rita came back into the room, Stella was sleeping peacefully; she adjusted the blind to block out some of the bright sunlight. When she turned back to retrieve the hardly eaten lunch tray,

Stella's face contorted horribly. Just as Rita was about to wake her, the awful look left her face. Stella's breathing returned to normal. So Rita did not bother her, but continued to watch her. All of a sudden, tears came welling from underneath Stella's closed eyelids. She did not sob or make any crying sounds, yet the tears continued to wet the soft pillow on each side of her aged face. Rita had never seen anything like this in her years of taking care of elderly people in rest homes.

In Stella's dreams, last night had been a harrowing experience for her. Jay T had come from nowhere. Instead of opening the unlocked door, he just kicked it open, sending the door banging loudly against the shelf standing beside it. She finished pouring her glass of tea, and walked into her bedroom, closing the door behind her. She listened as he rumbled through the refrigerator. She could hear jars breaking in the floor. Then there was silence for a brief moment. Then she heard the cupboard doors banging, as he rummaged through them slinging some of the contents across the room. She knew by his shuffling walk and muttered, unclear words that he had been drinking. This was the worst shape that she had ever seen him in.

All of a sudden, her bedroom door almost came off the hinges. Somehow, the hinges held, but were all twisted and grotesque-looking. The part of the door frame where the latch went was a jagged hole. The wood that had been there was now a splintered mess in the floor. She sat quietly and very still, not knowing what to expect from him now because, until now, he had never entered her sanctuary.

"Where's the damn money?" he said hatefully.

"I paid the bills today, Jay T, I have no money."

"Bitch," he said. He had never called her that, but yet it did not shock her. As she watched his face, she saw a flicker in his eyes. Those cold, cruel ports of evil seemed to light up.

As he leaned his huge drunken frame against the broken doorjamb, he started to rub his dirty semi-bearded chin, with his other hand he started rubbing his crotch in a foreplayish manner. As his eyes continued to stare into hers, she felt a sudden sickness in the pit of her stomach. What kind of animal had he become?

"Jay T, I AM your mother."

"Shut up, bitch, you ain't shit to me. Aw, fuck it, I'll find what I need. You'd be too damn old anyway."

He laughed an evil laugh, ending with a sick sounding giggle. Then he turned to leave. After taking a step, he turned and said,

"Next time, ya better have some money if you know what's good for ya."

She sat frozen on the bed and frozen in fear. The shock had left her momentarily paralyzed.

When she woke up the next morning, she couldn't remember lying down to go to sleep. There was no way she could remember fainting. She had just fallen over with her head hitting the pillow while her legs dangled at odd angles over the side of the bed.

An overwhelming feeling of being dirty filled her every fiber. It was as if evil had slipped under her unrevealing nightgown and painted her body. She glanced at the open door. She looked at it again, not in fear, but with the feeling of being trapped, with the need to run. "Yes," she thought. "Just get out and run, but run to where? To whom?" There was nowhere or anybody to run to. It took all her strength, but Stella, made herself calm down. She ran the hottest water she could stand and took a bath. When her skin could take no more of her zealous scrubbing, she got out and toweled dry. Only after the vigorous bath and fresh clean clothes did she feel somewhat better.

When she walked in the kitchen, the same panic almost took her again.

"I don't believe it," Stella said. "I don't motherfucking BELIEVE it." She wanted to close her eyes but could not, as she clutched her fists together. Only with an iron grip and steel will was she able to calm down again. He had destroyed most of her meager food supplies. Stella cleaned up the mess, concentrating on what she had to do, and not what had happened. It was all done except for the little clay money jar. It was in a hundred pieces. When she dumped the shards into the garbage, the panicked feeling tried to come back.

She just picked up her purse and walked out the door. This problem was not so simple, this was a big problem.

She had a little bit of money and a credit line with Charlie, and maybe getting out for a little while would help. Maybe.

Stella began to walk, moving slowly, trying to pull herself together. When she neared the center of the town, she noticed several groups of people standing around. Most were talking very low; the whole town seemed subdued. She continued to walk, and as she passed by, she heard some of the talk. "Raped," someone said.

"Is she gonna make it?" another said.

"Well, I heard when they found her, she was already dead," yet another voice added in.

When Stella finally rounded the corner and could see the general store, she saw Charlie sitting on the steps, holding his head in his hands. Standing around him were the sheriff, two deputies, and two men in different uniforms. As she got closer, she saw that those were Alabama State police. There were a few men of the town standing there also. One of them looked up and saw her and said, "That's her," in a voice full of hate, with a facial expression of open hostility.

The sheriff and a state trooper walked toward her.

"Stella," said the sheriff. "We need to ask you a couple of questions.

Have you seen Jay T?"

"Yes," she answered. "But he left last night."

"What time was this, ma'am?" the trooper asked.

"Well, I'm not exactly sure, but it was probably about nine thirty or ten. Why?" Stella asked.

"Stella," the sheriff paused. "Sally was abducted on her way to open the store. Charlie just got back from Birmingham getting store supplies. Anyway, Sally is gone, if you know what I mean. But who ever done this was cold and cruel. They done things that I wouldn't even tell a woman.

And another thing, a trucker saw a man headed out of town, said he was a big man. He said he had a beard, but what he noticed most was the guy's size and that he had scratches on his face. After all that, it kind of sounded like Jay T. But now, Stella, I'm not saying that he done anything, it's just that we need to talk to him."

"He only comes by once in a while," Stella replied. "I don't know where he goes or even where he's staying. Last night was the first time I've seen him in months."

"Well, thanks anyway."

"Stella, if you see him soon, tell him he needs to come see me, or better yet, just call me, OK?

"All right, Sheriff," Stella answered.

Stella walked toward Charlie. He had heard the conversation, but had not joined in it.

"Charlie, I'm so sorry that this has happened. I thought the world of Sally, and you know that. You and Sally have always been my friends."

Charlie never looked up; he just spoke with his head facing down.

"Stella, just go home. I don't want to be responsible for what I may say to you. I know what and who I think is guilty of this, but they say it'll be hard to prove. So they'll probably never catch the son of a bitch. So just go on now."

Stella turned numbly to walk away, thinking, "Why do bad things happen to good people?" As she slowly walked home, the anguish, the horror, and sadness filled her eyes with tears. It took all of her strength just to walk while the uncontrollable tears came and came and came.

Rita had come back in the room to check on Stella. She was awake, and spoke ever so softly.

"Come over here, child." Stella reached for her hand and held it ever so tightly.

"Pray that I am forgiven." Then Stella closed her eyes.

Rita stared into her dead face for what seemed to be a very long time, but yet felt a measure of relief that she had died.

CHAPTER TEN

His Honor, Judge Benjamin Stark, looked down upon the defendant in front of him. Jay Thomas Blanking stood there like he had no cares in the world. But the judge knew otherwise. A lot of defendants had stood in front of him in the last twelve years. He knew false bravado when he saw it. He knew Jay T. Blanking very well. Jay T's name had come up quite often in the last few years. The trouble was no one had ever proved any of the allegations against him.

Most of the people that might have helped to put him in jail were scared of him. One that was not scared of him was John Cane. John had turned Jay T in to the law for running a still in a hidden little valley on his property.

But before he could testify, his barn had caught on fire and burned to the ground. All of the hay for the season was in that barn. But that was not the worst of it. His favorite horse that he loved and had trained since it was a colt, burned up also. When the sheriff questioned Jay T, he just said, "Lucky it wasn't his damn house, I guess." After that, John had nothing to say to any of the law officials.

Another neighbor down the road had his only milk cow's throat cut.

When Sam Hanklin found his cow, he knew that his was no subtle warning. It could have been him or one of his young children or who knew what might have happened to his wife. Sam would never tell his secret even to his wife. He could not and would not tell anyone that he saw Jay T leaving old John's place, laughing and carrying a red gas can. The trouble was Jay T saw him too.

All of these thoughts and suspicions ran through the judge's mind. He didn't know Sam's secret, but that part of these mysterious happenings was not hard to figure out. The judge had another event to consider. Today's sentence would determine if he lived happily ever after or had a miserable life at home. The judge's wife, Emily, would be madder than hell if he did not put this man away for as long as he could.

Emily had come home mad and scared. It seemed that Jay T had followed her around in the drugstore. When she would look up and see him, he would laugh softly and lick his lips in an insinuating way. There was always a row of merchandise between them, but it was easy to tell what he was rubbing with his right hand. It had been humiliating and disgusting for her. As she fled the store and ran to her car, he walked out on the sidewalk and laughed out loud at her.

"Mr. Blanking, you have been found guilty of stealing a car."

"But, Your Honor, I only drove it four blocks,"

Jay T said with a pleading tone.

The gavel banged loudly.

"SILENCE, Mr. Blanking. One more outburst and I will have you gagged. Do you understand me?"

"Yes, Your Honor," he said meekly.

His massive head and pig eyes glowered down at his wimpy small defense lawyer. The little man was so scared he stepped three steps away from Jay T and just stared at the floor even though Jay T's hands and feet had been shackled.

"Mr. Blanking, it is this court's decision that you will be incarcerated in a penitentiary for a term of eight years. There, maybe you will learn your lesson and try to conduct yourself properly when you get out."

The gavel banged loudly again in the empty courtroom. Then the deputies led Jay T out into the hallway.

CHAPTER ELEVEN

When Jay T stepped down off the bus, he was shoved in the line of men headed to the prison hospital for a full strip search and checkup. With both wrists shackled to a chain wrapped around his waist, Jay T proceeded with the other men through several checkpoints.

"Have mercy," Jay T said. complacently, circling his fingers in his hands. Defensively, he blushed as he was told to cough again.

As the guards chuckled at his humiliation, his physical condition was noticed by them. It was one not to be played with, at six foot four, weighing in at three hundred and forty-five pounds. Jay T could not believe how small the cell room was, having to turn his bulky body sideways with the help of the guards pushing him through the cell room door.

Five guards escorted him to the cell. Taking off his shackles, they shoved him in. Hearing the closing of the cell door was a sound like he had never heard. It was a loud and empty sound that echoed for what seemed like a long time.

The cell was so small. The color of the walls was an off-white, all nine-by-four-feet. The furnishings included steel bars in the front, a bunk bed, and a concrete floor. He looked bigger than the space he was in.

There was not even enough room to do push-ups on the floor. The space between the bed and the wall was too narrow. So Jay T had to do all his exercises on the top bunk. There was no table, no chair, no place to sit except the bed. The legs of the bed were bolted to the floor. The bed itself was welded together; there was no way to break anything apart.

Feeling the need to vomit, he began banging his fist on the wall when someone said,

"That won't help, get used to it, that's all you can do."

Jay T looked around the cell, his laugh was a half moan but only he knew the truth, self-evident, one might say "HA! HA! HA!" But Jay T felt good, for he had the last laugh.

The prison had control over everything, even sound.

Not even a radio was allowed to be on except at certain times of the day. But during the day, the sounds of inmates talking from cell to cell was all you heard, all having some kind of conversation at the same time. To be heard, you had to talk louder than anyone else; sometimes, the sound would ring your ears.

The smell was something else, with shit, piss, vomit, and just the body odors alone, all mixed up into one bottle, created a different aroma. Every time you move in here, you prepare yourself to take a chance to die.

There is absolutely no privacy, sitting on the toilet to take a nice shit, with guards and inmates walking by and always looking in. Getting used to this, was no problem for Jay T, for he knew that he would be getting out, and when he did there would be hell to pay. After breakfast, Jay T could go out to the exercise yard. There, he could do just about anything. Exercise, play ball, shower, or just sit around and talk. But it was a very dangerous place to be, and he and everyone there knew the risks involved. Some inmates were permitted to work except for those on death row; they were not allowed to do anything. All other inmates were expected to work. They were penalized if they did not. There were many jobs to chose from—construction, cook, gardener, library, janitor—all of which paid very little money per month. But Jay T had a plan. It was to work, save his money, so when he got out he would not be broke, having a little nest egg to start from. Doing this would be easy for there was not much to spend money on in this place. The job that Jay T had only paid twenty dollars per month.

Books on wheels was good, but sometimes, when the guard didn't feel like escorting an inmate from the library, there would be no books that day.

There was a chapel, a church, a preacher, and in Jay T's warped way of thinking, "My mom ought to be here, she would like that."

Sometimes, Jay T would piss on and rub feces on himself, so no one would come near or bother him. There were times that he felt the walls closing in on him, felt like going crazy. But those feelings would not last long, He would think, "Hey, wait a minute. I'm Jay T. All of this is not supposed to be happening to me." But it was. He felt like he was being trapped like some animal.

There were some that could not live with the pain or go stir-crazy and would find a way to kill themselves. They would be found hanging from their cell.

But Jay T had ways to overcome and not allow this place to destroy him. It only made him stronger. He exercised, lifted weights every hour of the day that he could. The only loneliness that he felt was not having a woman, but he took care of that in the late hours of the night.

The strip searches were the one thing that Jay T had a hard time with, but he would psych himself up for it. Every time he left his cell to go out, he faced a strip search. Every time he came in, it was another strip search. The prison officials said the reason for conducting a strip search was to prevent slipping weapons into the prison which could be a part of an escape plan or used against each other. But Jay T believed it was to demean the men here, to break down confidence, making it easier to handle these people.

"Undress, raise your arms, wiggle your fingers, open your mouth, move your tongue side to side." Guards would run their fingers through his hair, behind his ears. "Lift your dick, move your balls side to side, bend over and take hold of each butt cheek, open it up, let the asshole show. And now, cough out loud!"

Jay T learned to go through the search without emotion. He liked it when he had eaten foods that caused him to have a lot of gas. That gave the guards something more than just looking at his ass. This was just a place made up of too many rules.

On the outside world, rules were made to be broken, but in here, they were made to go by and Jay T did just that.

Sometimes, when the stench would get so bad, men were ordered to shower and not allowed back in until they were clean. If rules were not complied with, the discipline could be severe and they would be sent to the hole. That was not where Jay T wanted to be. He and the inmate that was next to him, got to know each other quite well. It seemed that he had spent four years in the hole, because he was suspected of stealing something. Most men did not make it out of that place, and then it became another body the county had to claim.

Jay T learned the term "cell soldier," and from these boys he learned things of the most corruptible traits. That was a splendid thing for his self-interest. He would be carrying this with him when he got out. Jay T was buying time and enjoying eating bread pudding that tasted like shit, and worse than that, it smelled like castor oil. There was no second helping, but who would want one anyway. He had a lot of time to think, and after two years, he had not been in any trouble or bothered anyone, so now he was on the list for the road gang. That meant that he could go outside these walls and work, see the sun, and feel the wind against his face without looking through the prison fence. Even though the road gang was heavily guarded, it was a chance to get out of here five days a week.

It was Sunday while he sat out in the yard on a bench when he got the news that he would start on Monday.

He sat perfectly still, his face not reacting to what was being said.

He stood up. "That will be fine," his voice deep and plain but dry.

Looking around, he continued, "I'm sure not going to miss this yard. And I sure ain't going to miss seeing those towers with the guards holding those rifles. That ol' boy just loves Big Bertha and he doesn't mind firing her down in the yard when a fight breaks out."

Jay T was more concerned about getting out of prison than getting in fights over the race of other inmates. Sometimes, even the guards would create a conflict that would ignite an all-out racial war. And seeing the smaller men who were made to do some things, terrible things, was a common occurrence. Mostly, they were just flunkies. But that was the way to survive if you were small. The young first-time men were forced to serve the sexual needs of the older and tougher men. Held down by as many as four to six men, it was more frightening than your worst horrific nightmare. Most of these men would end up killing themselves.

Jay T couldn't wait for Monday; a day away would be like a day of play even if it was hard work.

CHAPTER TWELVE

Jay T looked over his shoulder at all the men wearing striped shirts and pants. There was normally about twenty men wearing these prison issued clothes, but today there was only sixteen. Two of these men would not be coming back to the road crew for a while; Jay T had made sure of that. He trudged on up the hill, carrying his sack of dynamite. He was on the blasting crew today.

The contractor's people ran the dozers and drills and any other heavy equipment. The prison crew used only shovels, picks, sledge hammers. and occasionally had to use hand drills for some of the bigger rocks that the dozers and drills could not get to. Jay T, for once in his mostly lazy life, did not mind the hard work. It had caused his huge arms to get even bigger, while his waist had gotten smaller. It had toughened him up to peak physical condition. He had even lifted some of the heavier objects two or three times, like a weight lifter would. He had a good reason. He was going to have to fight. At first it was not his idea. But then, something happened and he decided he wanted to fight. Most importantly, Jay T did not intend on losing.

The guard had escorted Jay T up to the warden's office. When they walked in, the warden continued some paperwork, making Jay T stand and wait. Jay T knew the drill. Finally, the warden looked up and said,

"Please, sit down, Jay T." The guard remained at attention.

"Jay T, the prison parole review board meets in two months. You had a clean nose when you got here. And you've kept it clean. If you can keep it that way, you may get an early parole. Well, do you think you can do it?"

"Yes, I mean, yes, sir, I can," Jay T responded. He hated saying the word "sir." It reminded him of another time and place. Using that word was like kissing someone's ass. Jay T thought to himself, "I'm a big man and I Ain't kissing no ass, except, well maybe, today I'd better let it slide."

"If you get in a fight, cause any trouble for anybody, I will not let you speak to the board. Do I make myself clear?"

"Yes, sir, I understand," Jay T replied.

"Good," said the warden,

"Guard, take Mr. Blanking back to his cell. Tomorrow's another work day and it does start early."

Less than an hour after the warden's talk, everyone knew what had transpired. Most of the inmates, or at least the few that ever spoke to him, said, "Good luck, hang in there," or at least some form of encouragement. Jay T was feeling pretty good and proud of himself. He knew that he could stay clean. Then, the very guard that had escorted him to the warden's office walked up to him and said, "Come with me. I want you to meet a new friend." But something in his manner told Jay T this was going to be trouble. When he entered the exercise yard, he saw who the trouble was going to be.

"Mr. Blanking." Then the guard giggled. "This is Hank Gunner and he'd like to have a few words, if you don't mind."

His use of Jay T's proper name told Jay T that he'd been the one that told other inmates what the warden had said. His eyes had shown his evil intentions. He may have been a guard but he was not to be trusted, He laughed again, then turned and walked away.

"Well hell, the now famous Jay T stands before us, boys. He thinks he's gonna be leaving before too long. But we're gonna change that, ain't we, boys?"

Jay T looked at the three men in front of him. Hank Gunner stood just as tall and just as wide as Jay T himself. The other two men were only about half his size. While they eyed each other, Jay

T noticed the points of sharp weapons up the sleeves of the two men standing slightly behind Gunner.

"He thinks he's too good to socialize with anybody in the yard or anywhere else, it seems to me. I think we ought to teach him some manners. What do you say, boys?"

Jay T was set to move when a guard in the tower yelled down.

"Hey, ya'll bust it up."

"Yeah, we'll be doing just that,"

Hank yelled back when he saw the tip of the guard's rifle.

"We'll be seeing you later, Jay T. And maybe when you least expect us, we're gonna bust you up. and you know what? You'd be about right on your knees. Hell, I might even let Mousey and Geezer poke a little. I can tell you'd like that with that pretty mouth of yours."

All three men, Mousey, Geezer and Gunner, turned and walked away, laughing wildly. Jay T knew it would be difficult to avoid them all the time, yet he did not want to ruin his chances of parole. He was not going to fight this time. Nothing was worth fighting three men in here.

Then he saw her! Even from his work area at the top of the hill, he could tell that she was a looker. She was carrying a tray with something on it; it could have been a pitcher of tea or something to drink. She had a light colored summer dress on that did nothing to hide the curves underneath. He watched her walk to one of the trucks and set the tray down. He said, "Man, I wish I was close enough to see if those tits are as big as they look from here." As he continued staring, he saw Gunner stroll casually over and take a glass from her and lean on the beat-up truck's fender. He was talking to her like he was somebody. That could get you put in the hole if you got caught. As Jay T kept looking, he saw the guard watching them, but then he recognized who the guard was. It was Gunner's buddy.

About the same time, a voice from behind him said very gruffly,

"Move it, striper, they ain't a-waiting all day on your ass. You ain't here to view the country side. Now move your ass."

This ole boy with the shotgun behind him was a no-nonsense kind of guy. He was straight up, but he'd shoot you in a second. "At least he's a guard you could trust," he thought as he started on his way.

Jay T's mind was in a whirl. "Now," he decided. "I got something I'll fight for." He was thinking two things now, Gunner's job, which was close to the house by the creek, and the hot little gal that lived in that house. He was going to meet her and see for himself just how good her "tea" really was.

His first chance came two days later when Mousey brought up a new section of drill bit. Jay T's helper had stepped behind a tree to relieve himself. The guard was watching him urinate and not watching Jay T. As Mousey bent over to lay the bit down, Jay T picked up a huge rock and threw it on the other end of the six-foot bit. The other end came up tearing into Mousey's throat and jaw. He shrieked just loud enough for the guard to hear. The guard and the helper came running up.

"What happened?" asked the guard.

"I guess that fucking rock fell on the bit. How the hell should I know?" answered Jay T.

The guard blew his whistle and men came driving up. Mousey was unconscious. Jay T looked at the blood and teeth lying on the rocky ground and laughed to himself. He heard later that Mousey died before they could get him to the hospital. "Well, that's one down and two to go," he laughed.

It took Jay T three days to finish drilling the huge rock. The fourth day, he was loading the holes with dynamite, with the company engineer watching ever move. Someone had to bring up more dynamite and caps. Geezer had volunteered for the job. The first bag delivered, he caught a chance to talk to Jay T without being overheard.

"I'm going to fuck every hole you got, you son of a bitch. I sharpened the edges on my sheave and I'm gonna cut your balls and cock off too. I'm gonna strangle you with your own balls while your own cock is stuck up your ass! Do you hear me, motherfucker? You're gonna pay for what you done to Mousey. He was my friend, and you're gonna pay! Fuck you! You just wait."

"Ahhh, Talk to me, sweetheart," Jay T said patronizingly.

"I'm fucking telling you."

Jay T listened to Geezer's mouth, while he got madder and madder.

"It's all in a day's work, champ," Jay T said.

Jay T still didn't have enough dynamite, so the guard sent Geezer after more. Jay T purposely left three holes unloaded, waiting on Geezer's return.

These holes were in a place that the guard and engineer could not easily see. When Geezer returned, he started cursing Jay T and continued telling him what he was going to do.

Jay T kept his back toward Geezer so he could watch the guard. When Jay T saw the guard talking to the engineer and both were looking away from him, he whirled and punched Geezer in the side of the jaw. He heard the bones in his neck break and watched him fall into a slight depression.

"Every doggie has its day," Jay T whispered.

Jay T hollered at the engineer,

"All loaded up."

The engineer gave the sign and everyone ran to the designated spot. The shot went off and several tons of dirt and rock lifted and then fell. When the dust had settled, Jay T turned around and little by little brushed the dust from his shirt.

As procedure demanded, the engineer first checked the shot to make sure it was okay for all the workers to return. Upon this inspection, he just happened to see one of Geezer's feet. Another horrible accident had taken place, or so the report would say.

CHAPTER THIRTEEN

In the silence of darkness, Suzann was awakened by voices that had become louder and louder. She was unable to go back to sleep. It would have taken a lot of willpower to ignore what was being said, and she did not have a lot of willpower.

Getting up and slipping into her housecoat, she eased to the bedroom door and very quietly opened it. Slowly, she walked down the hall toward the living room. As she got closer there were two visitors there that she did not recognize. The sounds were like an old movie where someone was going to fight.

Standing in the corner of the room was a strange man and woman, people she had never seen before. A middle-aged woman, somewhat attractive, with long brown hair that fell in folds to her shoulders, leaned lazily against the door. Big black eyes with a stern sparkle that were perfectly placed brought out the beauty in her face.

Had her judgment been wrong about Mary and Jim? wondering who this woman was, Suzann stood there listening, not believing the words that she was hearing. The strange woman took delight in making as much noise with her loud voice as she could. Suzann shivered at the thought of what was going on, as she listened to the words that came from these stranger's mouth.

"Kate, Stop it!"

Mary's voice let that sudden edge of anger run through her.

"Yes," Kate said, drawing on her self-control. "You heard me right, I want her to go with me tonight. I want to see what you have done to her, and I might want to make a few changes."

And she wasn't the only one who had some changes in mind. That disturbed Mary at first, and then frightened her.

Mary stood with her face to face. "OK, you have had your say, now let me tell you the way I see it. I'll tell you one thing. I never expected this, not even from you, not from my own daughter. But thinking back on the past, I shouldn't be surprised. Why have you returned? Why are you here?"

The words from Mary's mouth were saddened with a stern coldness, as if she had been heartbroken.

Suzann had never heard her mother raise her voice like this before.

"I think you know the answer to that, don't you, Mother dear."

"Mother? Who is this woman?" Suzann wondered in silence.

Mary was furious. "You're so damned uppity. You really do have a chip on your shoulder, don't you? You act as if you have been asked to humble yourself, to put in a little extra work on something that you never took the time to give a name."

Kate's full scornful mouth made a hard line on her face. "I just want what is mine, can't you understand that?" She said more evenly. "I have a husband now, haven't you heard?"

"No, I have not," Mary's voice came in short as she pulled up and peered deep into the man's face.

"Hello, my name is Jay T. You can't stop this, you know." And Jay T laid his big hand on Mary's shoulders as if trying to reassure her that everything would be all right.

But Mary was having none of it. She turned her back and pulled away from Jay T as she spoke. "For eight years, eight long years, you haven't even tried. And a better one than that, you haven't even seen her. You can't possibly love her."

"Who said I had to love her?"

"Yes, oh yes," Mary said, in a voice that she didn't recognize as her own. Fear clutched at her as she tried desperately to block out what they were demanding.

"Get out, get out, and get out of our house."

"Very well," Jay T spoke. "But we will be back. We're in the process of moving back here. I've already landed a job and a place to live."

"Two weeks" Kate said. "We'll be back to pick up what belongs to me. So you tell her or I will. Do you understand?"

Suzann watched as the two strangers left, watching her mother as she stood by the window looking out as they drove off into the night.

Mary was biting at her bottom lip, an expression on her face as if she was trying to scrape away all the thoughts that turned her mind into madness. She swallowed hard, trying to moisten her dry throat. "Now we are forced to tell the truth," she said to herself angrily. It was something that she had known they might have to do sooner or later.

Jim walked over to where Mary was standing, put his hands on her shoulders and held her against him, tightly in his arms. Suzann ran back into her room, not knowing what to think. She was confused as she turned back the covers and got back into bed. She was tired, and the next thing she knew she could smell sausage cooking from the kitchen and that good smell of coffee perking. Then suddenly, she remembered what had happened last night. It could have been a dream, just a bad dream, she decided, as she got dressed and went into the kitchen for breakfast.

As they all sat around the table, everyone was so quiet you could have heard a pin drop. Suzann could sense that something was very wrong. Talking a long deep breath after she had finished eating, she asked to be excused. But Mary said, "No.

There is something that we have to tell you, it can't wait."

"Have I done something wrong? I don't understand."

"No," baby, you have not done anything wrong but you must listen."

"OK." Suzann sat there, ready to listen. Mary looked over at Jim and began to speak slowly.

"I'm sorry, so sorry. I prayed, your dad and I both prayed, that this day would never come." She reached out, taking Suzann hands.

"But our prayers were not answered."

"But Daddy's prayers are always answered,"

"No," Mary said with a half smile on her face. "Now, please listen carefully and try to understand."

Then it hit her, immediately, Suzann knew that last night was not a dream.

"Please do not say a word until we are finished because this is the hardest thing that I or your father have ever done. You know that we are your mother and father and will always be our little girl, and it has been that way since your birth. But my dear baby . . ." Then Mary could not find the words to say as tears now ran down her face. Looking down into her heart, it was breaking apart. As she regrouped, she said, "We are not your real parents. Your mother is our daughter, and that makes you our grandchild. Eight years ago, you were born here in this very house. When you were two weeks old, your mother left. Please understand that your mother was very young, perhaps too young to understand the ways of the world or how to raise a child. So your dad and I raised you. We didn't know if she would ever return. Oh, we thought about telling you many times, but we just couldn't bring ourselves to do that. We were so afraid of hurting you. But we've hurt you now." Tears were running down her face, and her voice began to tremble. She held Suzann's hands so very tightly. "Please understand that we never wanted to hurt you. Do you understand what I am telling you?"

Suzann responded softly as she tried to absorb the bad news through her head and accept it with the calm sense that she was far from feeling, sitting very quietly, with her head looking down. She could not believe that they hadn't even bothered to tell her. A feeling of coldness shot thought her small body.

"I can't believe this. Tell me this is not true," Suzann stated.

"You have no idea how this hurts us to tell you these things. We could just kick ourselves for being so . . . but we never thought she'd come back and do something like this!"

Suzann felt like her body was going to melt into the floor, like everything from within her had drained to her feet. Feeling that this was not all, that there was more, but she was afraid to ask. Mary went on. "Your real mother is moving back into town. She has a new home and a new husband. You'll have three new sisters to play with. You will have someone to spend time with and not be alone like you are here. She wants to take you home with her. They will be able to give you things that we never could. You won't be that far way, and we will come and see you all the time. You will always be our little girl."

Her voice broke as she turned Suzann's hands loose. The emotional strain had taken its toll on Mary. Not being able to handle anymore, she ran into her bedroom.

Jim eyes were stricken with pain as he let his voice trail into thin air, not knowing what to say.

The feeling inside Suzann was hard to describe. She could not even begin to understand why this had to happen. Sitting there, not believing what she had just heard, she looked up at Jim. "Are you my dad?"

Suzann had never seen him cry before, but tears that threatened his eyes were very visible. She wanted desperately to move, run, or do anything but sit here and have to listen to what she had just heard. She ran into her dad's arms. He held her so tightly and so close. For that moment, she felt safe, like nothing could get to her. All she knew was that she did not want to go and live with that woman or anyone else for that matter. What she wanted was to stay here, for this is where she belonged, this was *home*!

Looking up at her dad, with no words coming from either of them, terror was slowly taking control. Climbing down from his lap, she slowly walked to her bedroom. She felt numb as she eased herself up on her bed. Burying her face into the pillow so no one could hear her sobs, she cried and cried and cried, feeling like her life was ended.

"Why? Oh god, why? Why is this happening?" She curled up in a fetal position the rest of the day. Several times, she heard her mom and dad come to her room to check on her. "Guess they thought that it was better to let me have some time alone and maybe sort some things out," she thought. But even time alone didn't seem to help.

Then there was a knock at her bedroom door.

"Suzann," Mary called. "Supper is ready."

"What time is it?" she asked.

"Time? Oh, it's about six o'clock," Mary whispered.

Suzann tried to smile, but she felt that there was nothing to smile about right now. After supper they went to the living room and sat down. Suzann sat between them on the sofa. The room was quiet, with very little being said. Looking up at Jim, she asked, "Do I have to go and live with them? Do I have to? Is there something you can do?" His words were slow, as he planted a kiss on her forehead. "No, I'm afraid that there is nothing we can do about this right now. Things like this can get nasty, and I know that this is hard for you to understand. But it means lawyers, judges, courts, and money. Try to understand that she is our daughter, no matter what she has done. We love her but we will never agree with this. Anyway, a case like this would be impossible to win, I think, for the law would be on her side because she is your biological mother. You just remember that we love you very much and would like nothing better than to keep you right here with us, but we will have to wait and see."

Answering her question about this situation affected every nerve within his body. A suffocating tension suddenly filled the room, revealing only the breathless silence that had fallen upon them.

"I'm so sorry. I wish it would not have happened like this."

Hearing what he had just said, holding on to his hand, and looking into his face, Suzann knew this was the way it had to be. Not being sure that she understood, but it obviously did not matter.

"Listen, it's not going to be the end of the world. You can come and visit on weekends, I'll come and get you myself if I have to. And when school is out, maybe you can come and stay all summer. And if you ever need anything, all you have to do is just let me know. Baby, I'm so sorry . . ." He smiled as he wiped the tears from the corners of her eyes. "She is your mother. If it hadn't been for her, you would not be here right now. So we have to thank her for that. I know that it doesn't seem very comforting now, but you have your whole life ahead of you. You are a very smart and intelligent young lady, so do me a great favor, don't ever give up. You will be of age before you know it, and when that time comes, you can decide the way of your own life. You can have whatever you want in life, if you want it bad enough. So if it ever gets hard, remember that. Whatever happens, it is meant to be. And it happens for a reason, even if it doesn't seem like a good one at the time. Hang in there; I know you can do it. I know that this is hard to accept, and it must seem like the end of the world for you, but it's not. There will be something good come out of this, just give it a chance. All you have to do is be yourself. Everything will work out, you'll see."

Suzann felt somewhat better, she thought, but she still was not sure. Deep down inside was a pain that made her feel sick all over. She did not think that they knew how this was tearing out her heart. Her whole insides felt knotted. She had listened to what they had said, knowing that she had no choice, but to accept things as they were.

That night came long, as she tried desperately to sleep, but sleep was not going to come easily. Thinking about everything that been said, things that they had done together, was it going to be over? What was her new home going to be like? What would they expect of her? How was she supposed to act? What would she say to them?

"Oh god, how I dread that day." But she knew that it would be coming soon, and a lot sooner than she wanted it to.

The next morning when Suzann had awakened, she found breakfast was served, and realized that a picnic lunch had been packed. She knew that something was up, hearing Jim as he was getting ready. When she entered the room, he snorted. "I think me and you should try our luck at catching that fish that I missed the other day." His voice was stronger as he reached out his hand to her. "What would you want to do that for?" Suzann asked. It was easy to see that Jim was being big and bold. She really had her doubts that they would catch that particular fish, but it was going to be fun trying. After a moment's pause, he pushed his feet against the floor, sliding the chair away from the table.

Suzann felt a smile come across her face. There was something about this man, her dad, that always seemed to make the worst times of life feel better, even now. After she had dressed, they were off for the day. The sparkle in her green eyes grew misty with the memory of her life and what was about to take place. The memories rolled on and on in her mind. A tremor shook her body when she tried to speak, but found that the effort was of no useful results.

Spending the day on the river seemed to lighten the dark cloud above them. Their luck was good, catching more catfish than they could eat in a week. They couldn't wait to get home and show off their catch to Mary. When they arrived, Mary was standing in the front door with all smiles as she went out to meet them.

"Glad you're home. It's been a long day." Her voice was low.

"Well, wait till you see what we caught, you'll love it. Look." Suzann's eyes were flashing and her face showed excitement along with a healthy dose of sunshine.

"My goodness, would you look at this. Ain't that something. Maybe I should stay home more often," she commented with a smile.

Only Jim had noticed that the smile, though very real and sincere, did not show her normal amount of enthusiasm.

Jim took the long string of fish and they all went to the backyard; it was time for cleaning fish. Suzann was helping, or mostly in the way, but whichever, they got the job done.

It was beginning to get dark as they all went inside when Mary suggested that Jim and Suzann should take a bath before supper since they both smelled somewhat fishy. When they had cleaned up and returned to the kitchen, they found the table set with the looks that was fit for a king.

The red checkered oilcloth covered the round oak table, with dishes in place that were rarely used. A set of china that had been handed down from generation to generation was going to be used tonight.

"Well, to make a long story short," Mary advised. "I had a visitor today." It had been Kate again, leaving with her a message that she would return in two weeks to pick Suzann up. It was easy to see that her visit had tried to spoil her day,

Suzann's heart seemed as if it was going to stop, "I should think that would be clear," Jim said as he tried to make things better like he always did.

"Well," he said. "We've got two weeks, that's a lot of fishing." Every day of the next two weeks they went somewhere or did something. Mary and Jim tried to make Suzann as happy as they could, and that they did. It was as if they were trying to cram a lifetime in two weeks. But there was always that empty feeling there that would not go away no matter what.

When the two weeks were over and the time had come, Suzann was packed and ready to go. With the clock ticking minutes, Suzann was praying that something would happen to them and they would never show up. A minute, an hour, an age, or until death would be a good delay. As everyone sat waiting for Kate and Jay T to arrive, the feeling was terrible. Every car that passed, it was as if Suzann's heart would stop. But her dream and her prayers ended. It wasn't long until a car was pulling into the driveway. It was them. The solemn trio watched from the window as the passengers got out of the car. When they approached the front door, Suzann felt a state of weakness engulf her body.

"It's going to be all right," Jim said. But his words did not help this time as it had before.

They were standing in front of the fireplace when Kate and Jay T entered the room. They just stood there looking. Suzann could not move. It was as if her feet were frozen to the floor, and no one was saying a word.

When Mary walked to the center of the room, her voice was shaky,

"Kate, this is Suzann. Suzann, this is Kate, your real mother."

The worst thing was, Suzann had already decided that they would never take the place of her mom and dad and she would never call them her mom or dad. And she already had a plan. As soon as these two monsters went to sleep, she would slip away and come back home.

"Suzann."

Mary interrupted her thoughts.

"This is Jay T who will be your new father,"

"Kate, we have told her about the situation, but it might take her a while to adjust. We love her very much and hope you will love and care for her as much as we have. She is beautiful and very smart. And you won't have to worry about school because she is far ahead of her class."

"So I can see," came the cold and bitter voice of Kate. Then everything was silent.

Kate paused for a moment, looking down at the floor. "Well, you'll love your new home, you'll see." Her voice had changed; it was now smooth, even the expression on her face had changed.

"Are you ready to go?"

"Yes, ma'am. My clothes are in my room."

"Jay T, would you get her clothes, please?"

As Jim turned Suzann's hand loose, he asked, "Won't ya'll stay for supper?"

As he paced the floor, wringing his hands, his nervousness was very easy to see.

"Oh no," Kate said.

"We have to be getting back, it's a long drive and we have a lot to do when we get there. Besides, we've got to get Suzann settled in so she can get used to her new home. But we will take a rain check, won't we, Suzann?"

"Most definitely," Suzann replied quietly, looking down at the floor.

Her voice had begun to tremble and everyone had noticed. Jay T entered the room with one eyebrow raised. "Everything is in the car," he said as he looked at Kate. "Are you ready?"

There was no answer, everything was quiet.

"I say again, are you ready?"

"Are you in hot pursuit? And why can't we stay for supper?" Suzann asked.

"Well, well, aren't you sassy. You welcome us with a mouth full of meanness," Jay T said. "This girl is a real piece of work."

"Whatever do you mean?" Suzann asked.

"Whatever do you think I mean?" he snapped back.

Jay T slapped his forehead with the palm of his huge hand, the biggest hand that Suzann had ever seen.

Feeling unwanted, Jay T folded his arms across his chest and tried to speak easy with a friendly smile on his face.

They all walked out of the door to the car. Jim picked up Suzann and hugged her neck, but Suzann couldn't let go. The tears were running down her face along with a lump in her throat that was so big it hurt.

Jim and Mary both cried as they drove out of sight.

Suzann looked back through the back glass until she could no longer see anyone, with both her hands on the back window, reaching for them.

She sat there in the seat crying, with no one saying a word.

Jay T finally looked back at her.

"You're a mess."

He then reached into his pocket and gave her a handkerchief.

"Here," he said. His words were stern, like he had no heart in his chest and absolutely no pity.

But she didn't want his pity. She didn't want anything they had, all she wanted was to go back home. As hard as she tried, the tears wouldn't stop.

It was not long before they turned off the main road onto a road which barely had room for two cars to meet. They must have driven for miles. There was nothing but pasture and fields on both sides of the road. There were no houses. Some of the fields were a beautiful green. They looked as if they were a painting. As they drove, it wasn't long until they turned off this road onto another dirt road that was even narrower. They crossed a bridge, a kind of which Suzann had never seen before. She asked about the bridge and found out that it was called a cattle bridge. It wasn't long until she could see why. There were cattle everywhere, every color and every size. Cattle could not cross this style of bridge.

As Jay T drove on. It seemed like the road would never end. Suzann was amazed to see so many animals and such a big place. Yet fear clutched at her heart. Watching from the car window and seeing all the tall round buildings, then there was another and another.

"Jay T, what is that? I mean those buildings."

He laughed, like a kid with a new toy.

"That's where they store feed for the cattle in the winter." An answer in that tone of voice, no more words or questions were necessary as they finished their long journey home.

Suzann grabbed her pillows and stretched out in the back of the car, it seemed as though she had only closed her eyes when she heard Jay T hollering.

"Wake up, sleepy head, we're here. And this time, *you* will be unloading your stuff out of the car, not me."

He bent his arm at his elbow, letting the palm of his hand cradle his head.

Suzann sat up in time to see some man go by on horseback. Never before had she seen anything as beautiful. Then they went through a gate that went up a drive that made a circle, and in that circle there were eight houses. They were homes for all the hands that worked at this farm. The house that Kate and Jay T lived at was the third one, built from rock. When the car stopped, Suzann got out, still amazed at everything new to her eyes.

CHAPTER FOURTEEN

"Your mom will show you where your room is and then—"

"SHE IS NOT MY MOM!" Suzann interrupted.

"Get your clothes and things out of the car and put them up. When you are finished, then you can eat supper."

When Suzann entered the door, she stopped and stared. The place gave her the creeps, along with the strange smells that filled the air. Her face was reddening with hurt, and suspicion clouded her voice as she jerked her head up looking at Jay T as if he had lost his mind.

"Are you serious? Those bags are heavy."

"What is all this?" Jay T said as he grabbed her face with his large hand and squeezed her checks together.

He continued to hold her cheeks for a while without speaking; pulling his shades down over his eyes so she could not see in. The look that he was giving, she would not have understood anyway.

Her eyes widened, but she was still somewhat dazed from the short nap that she had taken.

"There is one very important thing you need to learn starting right now." His laugh was short, mean, and sarcastic.

She wanted to tell him that he was hurting her, but she was afraid to speak.

"Your days of being a spoiled brat are over. And don't you ever talk back to me again, DO I MAKE MYSELF CLEAR?"

Suzann didn't say a word.

"Answer me, girl."

"Yes."

"Yes what?"

"Yes, sir."

She got all her clothes and bags and carried them up to her room. As she was putting up her clothes, the feeling of sadness engulfed her once again, filling her with such emptiness. She hated it but it would not go away. It left her with the feeling of being so alone.

"Maybe Kate and Jay T are being kind, maybe it's just me." But she didn't think so. "Their words and actions were so mean. And the way they looked at me! Especially Kate. It was as if she hated everything about me, my looks, my size, everything."

Suzann walked over and sat on the bed, trying desperately to re-orientate her thoughts, when the call came out for supper.

She sat perfectly still at the supper table, listening to the conversation being spilled out between Kate and Jay T. The food they were eating was far from being good home cooking. When everyone was finished eating, Jay T said, "Make sure you clean up this kitchen before you go to bed."

Then they left the room. For a moment, Suzann sat there enjoying the pleasant sound of thunder that rumbled far off in the distance. Listening closely at how quiet the house had become, she could hear the night sounds outside. As the wind picked up, the leaves started their own symphony of sound with a soft mellow, lonesome musical tune. As the wind would almost stop, the crickets would seem to chime in, adding to this wonderful display of Mother Nature's musical abilities. Somehow, this made Suzann almost forget the terrible pain and suffering that she had endured that day.

By the time she had finished cleaning up from supper, she was quite ready for sleep. She pulled back the single quilt and crawled into bed, falling into an exhausted tormented sleep.

CHAPTER FIFTEEN

The next morning, Suzann was awakened by the noise of kids playing in the house—three of them, all little girls. They were so pretty but so dirty. The house was dim, with half opened windows, and the wind was blowing the curtains over the table then sucking them back out. One baby was lying on the floor, screaming and crying.

"Shut the hell up," screamed Kate. It was a madhouse.

Suzann walked over and picked up the baby, walking it round and round in circles, trying to get it to be quiet. She took it into the bathroom and gave it a good bath. It smelled so much better now, and putting a clean diaper on seemed to do the trick. After doing that, Suzann looked around to see the other children standing at the doorway, watching. When Suzann was finished, she asked,

"Would you like for me to give you a bath too?" They were all for that. When she was finished, their hair was combed and put up in little pony tails, they looked like two different kids.

By the time school had started again, the chores—if you wanted to call them chores—around the house that she had been given were unreal. It was more like manual labor. As the days went by, more and more things to do were added to the list. The worst thing of all was so many things had to be done before school time or she wasn't allowed to go to school. Suzann loved school so much, so she would get up early enough to get things done. Then, after school, there were even more things that she had to do before she was allowed to go to bed. There was never time allowed for her studies unless she hid from Kate and Jay T to do her homework. Suzann was beginning to feel like a slave, except slaves were treated better.

If she didn't finish her work on time or forgot to do any part of her chores, she would be punished.

The punishment that was inflicted upon her left a sound physical and emotional draining that left bruises which took days, sometimes even weeks, to heal; not to mention the mental stress which would never be healed. Weighing heavily on Suzann's mind and heart was Jim's promise that everything would be all right. But it was not all right. Suzann knew that the worst punishment would come if she told anyone about what was going on, about the bruises or how she had received them.

Often, the beatings would take place in front of Kate. Jay T was so strong that when he would backhand her, it sent her all the way across the room and into the wall. When he had finished and gone, Suzann would lower her trembling body onto the floor in front of Kate, dropping her head into the palms of her hands, sometimes gasping for breath from the burning sensation that coursed through her body. "God, it hurts, Kate. How can you allow him to do this terrible thing? Look at me, I beg you. There is no way I can cover up all these bruises. And what hurts inside, nothing can fix. My heart hurts, Kate. I have to lie and tell people that I fell again. All my friends in school think that I am accident prone."

But Kate was, as always, being her usual bitchy self. After seeing Suzann at near total collapse and the aftereffects, the only thing that Suzann got from Kate was betrayal. Kate would go and tell Jay T everything that Suzann would say to her, and sometimes adding things that had not been said, getting Suzann in even more trouble.

Suddenly, Suzann knew what she had to do, and that was to never say anything to Kate anymore about anything, no matter what. There will never be another whipping on that account, *never*. One way or another, Jay T and Kate had managed to destroy or get rid of any and everything that was important to Suzann. Even the things that Jim and Mary had brought her had been torn to shreds. Once, Jim had brought her a new notebook with paper for school and Jim also knew that she liked to write poetry. But when Kate had found it, she gave it to Jay T. Her laughter had turned into insane shrieks while she watched Jay T tear the notebook into pieces. But what she had enjoyed the most was seeing the hurt on Suzann's face along with the tears running down her cheeks. That was just part of Jay T and Kate's way of trying to control her.

Every evening when Suzann got off the bus, she checked the mailbox to see if she had any mail from her mother and dad, for she had found some letters in the garbage that had been torn up and thrown away that was from them. Sometimes, Kate would keep the letter until Suzann got home and show her what had come in the mail. It would be a letter from Mom and Dad but Kate would not let her have it. Instead, she would hold it over a cigarette lighter and make Suzann watch as it burned up. In doing this, there was no feeling of guilt working inside of Kate. Most of the time, after Kate would do something like this, there would be there would be a moment of silence, her brows gathered into a frown, then she would laugh and make fun of Suzann if she cried.

"Cry me a handful," she would say, followed by, "Shut the hell up."

There was nothing that she could do but take it. Suzann could never do anything right, she could never do enough, there was always wrong found in everything. There was no way of pleasing them.

CHAPTER SIXTEEN

It was in the fall of the year, when the leaves were turning into nature's most beautiful colors, on an early morning, when Suzann was suddenly aware that it was already time for the bus. Being already exhausted, she continued to get dressed and try to make it before the bus run. But as luck would have it, the bus had already gone.

Suzann slowly began the long walk back to the house, nervously approaching the house, shaking her head as if to clear it. When she went inside, there was Miss June, who was their next door neighbor. She was there visiting Kate.

They both knew what had happened as soon as Suzann entered the room. After closing the door behind her, June suggested that Kate let Suzann go home with her and spend the day.

Kate shook her head unsympathetically; a mask of indifference had slipped over her face.

"Jay T will never have to know," June reassured Kate.

"You know what will happen if he finds out she missed the bus."

"If you think that I don't know the way he treats her, you're wrong, because I do."

"Well, all right." Kate finally agreed to let her go with June. But it could have been written on the wall; Kate would not have let Suzann go if it had not been for June's persistence.

Suzann pulled her shell-shocked body together and took hold of Miss June's hand and they made their way out the door, knowing that it did not matter whether or not she stayed or went with June. Jay T would know about it because Kate would tell him. Suzann was scared for she knew that when he found out he would be furious. It would be another chance for him to inflict his sadistic punishment upon her. The act itself was painful enough, but what scared her even more was the look in his eyes. Even at her young age, she had sensed a thinly veiled tension in his angry eyes when he was punishing her. Something evil, something dirty lurked behind his bulging eyes during these episodes. Aside from the bruises and pain, Suzann always felt the need to wash herself afterwards, although she never understood why.

"June," Suzann said. "This is insane. I shouldn't . . . We shouldn't . . ."

"I know," June groaned. "We shouldn't stand here talking about it, just go. I hope that I have not disappointed you."

But it didn't matter. Call it what you like, but tonight would be soon enough to question any temporary loss of sanity. It was too late now to stop as they were walking swiftly across the yard to June's house.

June's basement had been finished off and fixed into a playroom. The kind of thing that Jim had talked about doing but never quite got around to it. The thought came with a little pinch of sadness for Suzann. The walls looked like logs with huge speakers embedded in them. There was no ceiling, just rafters. On one side of the wall was a long bookshelf filled with books and puzzles and games of all types, such as Suzann had never seen before. There were posters all over the walls, even president Kennedy's poster hung high with a big grin on his face. The mirrors embedded in the logs gave it a touch of class.

"Just make yourself at home. And if there is anything you need or want, just let me know. I'll be glad to get it for you," June coached.

Suzann walked over to the couch and set down; straight in front of her was a fireplace built in white stone. "I am glad now that I came," she thought. Her dark mood seemed to lift somewhat. "I'll just be upstairs if you need me," June said. "I'll bring your dinner down later. Oh, the bathroom is to your left, you won't have any problems finding it, it's only one room down here."

"God, this is the most different, but beautiful place I have ever seen," Suzann said aloud. Already, she felt like she could stay here forever. She was going to enjoy this day and worry about what was going to follow later.

The day went so quickly. It was over way too soon.

Miss June leaned over and kissed her on the forehead. "It's time for you to go now. If you make it home without him seeing you, everything should be all right."

"No," Suzann said fiercely. "I want to stay here. Can you understand that?"

"Of course I do," Miss June's chin tilted as she spoke. "Come on," she said, calmly. "You can spend another day with me if we can arrange it."

They walked out in the direction of the house. Suzann set off, zipping up her light jacket all the way to her chin. She was slowly approaching the house, looking for some indication that Jay T was home, praying that he wasn't.

Sometimes, he would pull his boots off at the door if they were really muddy or had cow manure all over them.

There were no boots sitting at the door, so maybe that meant that he was not home. Opening the door, she entered and walked past the living room. There he sat.

Carrying her books, she went to her bedroom to put them up. Suzann felt at first that everything was going to be all right, when she felt his hands as he took hold of her hair, pulling her head around. She felt his grip become tighter as he pulled her head backwards. He stood there for a moment staring at her and then he slammed the door shut.

Trembling and clenching her teeth and holding her breath, Suzann was so frightened but the tears, this time, would not come.

"You silly little bitch," he spoke, and at the same time, a horrible shaking anger swept through him, making him want to strike out and just beat the living hell out of her.

She stood there looking at him, noticing that he still had on the same clothes that he had had on since the beginning of the week.

"Where in the hell have you been? And you better not lie to me either, do you understand?"

Then he just stood there, waiting, as if he were letting her make her own decision in her own time. He enjoyed the fear on her face and knew that she was trying to find the right answer, but he and she both knew that there would be no right answer.

"Honesty is the best policy," she remembered hearing somewhere.

"I missed the b-bu-bus . . ." but before she could finish, she felt a burning pain across her face.

"But I can explain!"

"Shut up," he said. "Just shut up."

He sounded so brutal.

She did as he said. He gave her one final shake and then turned her loose. He slammed the door when he left the room. She fell across the bed, almost wishing that she was dead. For a moment, she thought, "If he would just stop long enough to listen he would understand." Yet in the same instant, she knew it was not about understanding. It was just another chance to put his cruel hands on her.

Suzann could hear words being passed back and forth in the kitchen. Kate wasn't even telling him the truth, she was lying to him, telling him that she thought that Suzann had been in school today, that she had no idea that she wasn't. Suzann couldn't believe what she was hearing.

"Jay T, if she wasn't in school, then where was she?"

"I don't know," answered Jay T. "Why don't you tell me where she was because she didn't get on the bus this morning, for I was working in the field next to where the bus runs and she was not there. So I made it a point to be there this evening when the bus ran to let the other kids off."

There was a period of silence. The only sound in the room was the ticking of an old grandfather clock.

As she lay across the bed, Suzann very quietly prayed, "Please, Lord, show me what I have done wrong for I don't know. Have you meant for me to see something that I have missed? I have done no wrong that I know of, oh God, please hear me." She knew better than to get caught praying. The last time had gotten her a beating and then she had been forced to listen to a string of profanity from Jay T while Kate laughed hysterically. Jay T had then told her, "All you need to know about the Bible is right here." Then he reached behind the door and pulled out a razor strap. It was a four-inch wide, almost four-foot long, thick leather belt. He used it to sharpen his razor although he rarely shaved. Then he had said,

"Hey, Kate, we don't just live in the Bible Belt, we own one. What do you think of that?" Then he had looked at Suzann and said,

"The next time you feel the need to pray or you get any questions about God, I'll give you all your answers, little girl. Hell, I've got all the answers. They're right here in my Bible Belt. Now, I tell you what, you hang this here belt back up and then you get the FUCK out of my face!" Oh yes, Suzann would always remember that episode.

Suzann raised her head and looked around the room in a kind of stupor. Bitter tears began to fall down her face as she got up slowly to her feet and walked to the window and looked out at the sunset which was so beautiful. As she went to her closet and got out a blue cotton nightgown, she began to unbutton her blouse and let her jeans fall to the floor. She didn't even want to take a bath. No one else seemed to care about cleanliness, why should she? Pulling the cotton nightgown over her head, she noticed that blood had fallen onto her dress. Her momentary panic caused her heart to jump in her chest. Then she saw that it was only a nosebleed, but that had never happened before. Cleaning up the blood and settling back in the bed, she lay there letting her thoughts run away, looking out the window at an old crow that had lit onto an electric wire on the far side of the road. At that distance, he almost looked like a small black bird. Tangled in her thoughts, Suzann slowly drifted into sleep.

Then there were two doors that opened slowly. It was dark inside, with pinholes in the walls that let the rays of light shining through from the sunlight outside. It was a concrete floor, with only one way in and one way out. It was place to not get caught in, yet a good place to hide for some but not for others. "A Devil's breeding ground" was the thought that came to mind.

Suzann awoke with a start, realizing that it had been just a dream. But it had left her with an eerie feeling, almost like a warning. "That's it," she thought. "Something is trying to warn me." She lay back down and started thinking about the farm and the many new things that she had seen. There were places such as this all around the farm, dark and haunting and yet interesting, with things that would stir your curiosity. Some of the biggest barns that you could imagine—hay barns, cattle barns, calf barns, barns for equipment, milk barns—were scattered about. There was a barn for everything. Silage pits, feed stands, corn stands, feed troughs, hay lofts, and then there was the office with a desk, a bed, a coffee pot. It sat off by itself. But it housed a man that had returned from the war that could not shake the aftermath of images that he had seen and had to live with them. He was struggling just to live in a place where he was now forgotten. Even though he was haunted by his past, he seemed to have heart but no name. He was just called "the handyman," and that was his job on the farm. He was very kind and very quiet. There were those on the farm that called him the "gentle giant."

Most of the workers there did not have anything to do with him; the wives were scared of him and none of the children were allowed to be near him. Maybe it was his size or maybe it was the way he looked, but none of that bothered Suzann. He had become her friend, and she called him Handy. Suzann was not allowed to be around him like all others, but she would always find a way to visit him and talk to him. He was the only one that made her smile. Handy knew that she was not to be near him, so he tried to make sure she was not seen when she was there. Suzann wondered how anyone could even have the thought that Handy would hurt someone. She thought that he put up this front and used the war so no one would bother him. He really did like being alone, but with her, his feelings were different. She had won his heart. He took his hot showers in the cattle barn. He sucked in his slight belly and pushed his shoulders back when she was around, not to impress her, but because she had a way of making him feel alive and that he was somebody. He had known that feeling sometime in his past, but he wasn't sure when or where. She felt at ease around him, and at least he was clean, and that's a lot more than you could say about most of the workers that lived here.

Handy had seen the bruises on Suzann before and had listened to her stories about falling down, but Handy knew better than that. He knew she was being beaten but he let her believe that he believed the stories she told were the truth. He hated it and hated the man that was doing it to her worse. He saw the bruises that could be seen from the outside and wondered what was hidden under her clothing that could not be seen. A slow burning anger was starting to build inside of him. He was careful to not let it show to anyone and especially not to Suzann.

As Handy sipped from his cup of coffee, he knew that killing a man would be easy to do for he had done plenty, but then he had not had a choice; it had been his life or take a life. That was war, but this was different. He knew that Jay T was not worth the oxygen that he breathed, but taking him out . . . what would that do to Suzann? He would never let her know his feelings.

Handy was not a praying man but he now prayed to God to give her strength and protection. For this man had to be the son of the devil to attack the heart and mind of a child. He is evil, he is the real enemy.

CHAPTER SEVENTEEN

After breakfast the next morning, everyone except Suzann was going out of town to visit Jay T's family and to see his mother's grave. He couldn't care less, but to please Kate, he would take her to where he had been raised. They would be gone all day.

Suzann had been curious about the cliffs behind the dairy barn, and it would give her a chance to have a long visit with Handy—When she got things done that Jay T had told her to do and have done before he got back. He had fixed two tires for the car and she was to pump them up using a hand pump. She hated doing that, it was hard to get the pressure to where he wanted it. But after that, the rest of the day was hers. She wanted to climb down the cliffs to where the river ran. She had heard Jay T say that there were trails and paths that led to the bottom, and she wanted to do a little exploring. If for no other reason, she just wanted to be alone by herself.

After they left, she got herself ready and went out to get the tires aired up so she could leave. While she was pumping the tire—pull up, push down, she had a rhythm going—she heard someone say, "What are you doing?" As she turned around, she saw that it was Handy.

"I got to air up these tires."

"Hey, let me help."

"No, I have to do it or Jay T will be mad."

"OK, tell you what. You let me do it and you don't have to tell him that I helped."

"You won't tell him?"

"Of course not. What he doesn't know won't hurt him," he laughed.

He pulled his work truck up and pulled out a hose, attached it to the tube, and in ten seconds he was done.

"There you go, all finished. Now you can do something besides work.

"I'm going to the cliffs that lead down to the water."

"NO," Handy said." I mean, you should not go there. It is very dangerous. I'm afraid you might get hurt,

OK. Don't go. Promise?

"All right then."

"You never saw me today, right?"

"Right," Suzann answered.

When Handy got back home, the horror he faced was back again. Miss June was standing in his room when he walked in. She closed the door behind him. Pulling her dress up, showing just a little leg that had nothing on them, He was surely certain that things higher up had nothing on them either. He should not think that. But he did. She walked over and sat down on the bed, raising her dress a little higher, letting her eyes look at him in the midsection, right below his belt. She was so enticing with those long brown legs showing and they shone like silk. She reached out and placed her hand on his belt and pulled him over in front of her. Then she reached for his hand and placed it on her breast, squeezing his fingers tightly on her nipple. His mouth was dry and his head was spinning. He had not been with a woman in a long time, but this was not his kind of woman. She was just trouble, and he knew that. Taking her by the arm and pulling her up, he said,

"Get out!" He spoke loud and rough.

He opened the door for her and pushed her out the door.

When Handy had left, it got the best of Suzann; she just had to go. So she left for her little journey. When she got there, looking over, it was a long way down but she could see the river. She began to climb down, following the trail and rocky path, which was not so easy. About halfway down the cliff that rose high above her, she heard a noise from the top, and glancing over her shoulder, she saw rocks falling. Then there were more and more rocks falling; and then suddenly, she was falling. Her hands scraped at the rocks on the cliff, and then somehow she grabbed hold of some wild vines that hung up and down the cliff. The vines held her for only a short moment and then tore away. She cried out, but there was no one to hear her. For a moment, she thought death awaited her, but then some trees growing from the water's edge caught her. Looking down beneath her feet and seeing the fast-flowing water from the rains, she was afraid to move. But she had to get back to the top. With hands shaking, she slowly began to crawl upward and over the sharp pebbles and rocks, finding her way back to the top. Hours had passed, and now she was worried about getting back before anyone else got home.

When she got home, she saw that she was safe because no one was there. She was furious when she saw the marks on her face and hands from the fall. This time, she would really be telling the truth when she said that falling down had left these marks.

All she had to do now was get supper on and have it ready to eat when they got home.

Suzann was in the kitchen when she heard them pull up. As they entered the house, Jay T was called to the barn to work because something had broken down. But supper was ready; good thing, because everyone was starving. Since Suzann did not get to eat last night, hunger pains tugged at her. She filled her plate and ate quietly in her bedroom, thankful that she was spared the humiliation of having to face Jay T; she could eat in peace.

That night, after everyone had eaten, Suzann was cleaning up the mess when she overheard Jay T telling Kate that the boss was going to downsize the dairy and let Jay T run it for him, there would only be two hands left to work. Suzann hoped as she listened that Handy would be the other worker that got to stay, but Jay T never mentioned any names. She walked to the doorway and said,

"I could hear what you said about the farm. "Is Handy going to stay?"

"Girl, what is it to you if he stays or not?"

"I just wondered."

"You just mind your own business. This don't concern you. And you stay away from that handyman!"

"So that means he is going to stay?"

Jay T raised his finger and pointed it at her. "Get your ass back in that kitchen. He eats little girls like you for lunch."

"I AIN'T A LITTLE GIRL!" She answered.

"Oh, is that right? Then maybe I should start treating you like a woman."

Suzann went back in to the kitchen, thinking, "I got to find Handy. I got to find out. I don't want him to leave. He's my only friend."

Mr. Butter who owned the farm thought that Jay T was the best man for the job. Suzann could not believe it, but that was the way it was.

Things had surely changed in the last three months. Now, there were only fifty head of milking cows left and all of the houses had been sold off of the farm. It felt so empty and deserted now. The only people left were Suzann, Jay T, Kate, the three babies, and another one on the way. Mr. Handy was still working there but was not seen a lot, for Jay T kept him in the fields somewhere on the tractor.

CHAPTER EIGHTEEN

Another year had come and gone and a new class had started. Suzann's grades were still good but she was no longer ahead of her class like she had always been. There just too much work and no time for study at home. Even if there were time, it was not approved of. Jay T said that education meant nothing. He could not read or write, not even his name. And Kate could barely write her name. But Suzann would slip off to the big hay barn to a place Handy had shown her; he had fixed her a place where she could hide and study. He had even run her a light so she would not have to read in the dark.

But a lot of times while she was hiding to study, her studies would turn into daydreams of her mom and dad. She wished she could still be with them. If only they knew! And so many times she had thought about telling them, but she was too afraid to tell them what had been going on for she had been warned when Jay T told her that if she ever breathed a word she would never see them again. Suzann knew that he had meant what he said. Her thoughts would even scan deeper as she wondered how Jay T could possibly get away with this. When he was around other people, he was a totally changed person. When he was in the presence of outsiders, he was the nicest person you could ever want to meet. Everyone thought he was great except Handy, he hated Jay T.

It had been a splendid afternoon when Suzann got in from school and she had plans to get her work done as quickly as possible, then maybe she could spend some time at her hideaway. But when she got home, she found that Jay T had brought in two loads of wood. With a message from Kate for her to stack all of it up beside the fence row, she knew it would have to be done neatly. It was long after dark when she finished. Suzann entered the house through the kitchen where everyone was already eating supper. She was washing her hands when Jay T informed her that no one had called her for supper.

"When we are finished, you will clean up the kitchen and do the rest of you chores," demanded Jay T.

"But it is dark!"

But the look in his eyes was a warning to say no more. Suzann looked over at Kate as if expecting her to intervene, but Kate was too busy feeding her face.

Suzann went to her room and sat down on her bed for a minute when Jay T opened her bedroom door and ordered her to get started. As he started out the door, he turned and stated, "Don't forget to slop the hogs either!"

Suzann passed him as she started down the hall when she felt his large hand against the small of her back. He shoved her halfway down the hallway.

"Give these babies a bath and get them into the bed."

When she approached the kitchen, she discovered that they had raked out all the food that was left from supper into the slop bucket. The only things they left were the dirty dishes, pots, and pans. After giving the babies a bath and getting them into bed, she got the five gallon bucket that was half filled with slop and went out to feed the hogs. It was a long way from the house and it was pitch-dark. There was an eerie feeling inside her. She noticed the shadows that had gathered in the hollows and heard crickets that were beginning to sing for the night. When she had finished, even though the hunger pains haunted her, she was relieved to know that at last she could sit down and rest. She had just sat down on the couch to relax when Jay T opened his mouth.

Suzann knew even before the words escaped his tongue that he had thought of something else for her to do.

"Pull off my boots and socks and get a pan of water and wash my feet." Sitting there, he scratched his head, causing flakes of white to scatter down the front of his shirt.

Suzann swore under her breath, never before had she had to do anything such as this. Looking him in the eye, the words came from her mouth to her surprise.

"Are you serious?"

But there was that look to let her know that he was very serious. She had no other alternative except to do what he said. She got down on the floor, sitting still for a minute as she watched a roach wiggle across the floor and go underneath the couch.

His boots were sloppy, dirty with mud and cow manure all over them from working at the barn. Even after unlacing them, they were so hard to get off. His socks were wet and the smell from his feet would gag a maggot. Watching her gag as she pulled his boots off, he sat back on the couch, taking it in and enjoying every bit of it.

Suzann went into the kitchen to fix a pan of water and she got the soap and a rag. She had to roll up his pants leg where she saw scars around both of his ankles. She sensed a terrible strangeness. She had an unusual feeling about doing this. This isn't right, she thought. But she did not dare ask where the scars had come from.

After she had finished, she hung his socks in front of the fire to dry, knowing that he would put them back on in the morning and wear them again. As she cleaned up the mess, Jay T sat there looking at her with his eyes cold and full of wickedness. The wickedness was easy to see. She poured out the water and dried the pan and put it away. When she turned around, she ran right into Jay T. He leaned over and took hold of her face, with his hands so big and rough, calloused, and cracked from the hard work.

"You're hurting me!" she muttered.

"Is that right? Someday I'll show you what hurt really is." Pushing her backwards, he let her go. She went around him and then ran to her room.

The night was long and she must have cried for most of it for the next morning her eyes were swollen almost shut. Getting up early was at three in the morning in order to get everything done before time for the bus. This morning she had hoped that her eyes would look better before school time.

That evening, when Suzann had gotten off the bus from school, the baby was crying as she entered the house. Kate was lying on the floor unconscious. Suzann ran from the house to the barn, looking everywhere for Jay T. He was nowhere to be found. As she went running out of the barn door, she saw a pick-up truck all beat up and rattling, turning in front of where she was standing. She waved, attracting attention. It was Handy driving the truck. As always, he was proud to see her. For a moment, he listened. His face and hands were dirty from working. But he always had that welcome look in his eyes when he saw her.

"Please, you have got to find Jay T. It's Kate, something is wrong. She's sick." Handy knew that it was time for the baby to be born.

"OK, OK, you go back to the house and I will go and find Jay T." Suzann had barely gotten into the house when Jay T's truck pulled up into the yard.

When Jay T came out of the house carrying Kate, he glanced over his shoulder, advising Suzann to take care of everything until they got back. The tone in his voice was as if she hadn't been doing it anyway.

Suzann walked down the porch steps and watched them as they left, wondering what could be wrong with Kate. Her eyes flashed open as it hit her, "It's time for the baby." She moved to the big oak tree that was standing in the side yard where Handy had hung a tire from the tree line, making a swing. Crawling into the tire, she swung for a little while, enjoying the peaceful atmosphere as long as she could. Then she knew it was time to get things done. So she got supper finished and put it in the oven. She gave all the babies their baths and was working on cleaning the house when she heard a knock at the door. She wondered who it could be as she opened the door.

"Miss June, come in." Suzann hugged her neck, showing her happiness to see her. "Sit down. Can I get you something? A glass of tea, perhaps?"

"No, but thanks anyway.

I saw Kate and Jay T down the road. And I wanted to come over and talk to you with them not present." Placing her hand to the side of Suzann's face, stroking her hair, she said, "You don't deserve this. You should not even be here." Her words seemed to be from her heart.

"No, I should not. And as soon as I get old enough, I'm out of here. I am going to leave the day I turn eighteen. But it feels like that day is never gonna get here."

"I've something to tell you. But first, you must not repeat anything that I say. I know that you are young, and you have had to grow up way to fast. But that time will be here before you know it."

Miss June cleared her throat as she kept right on talking in a voice smooth as silk.

"I know you don't call her mother. And I know the reason why, and you have good reason. I met Kate several years ago in another state. We become very close friends at that time. It was . . . she needed someone, and I felt sorry for her. I was engaged at the time but she had no one. Outwardly, Kate would put on a brave front, but inside she was very unstable. We lived in the country and drove into town every day for work. It was a long drive but I hated the idea of living in town. Kate did not seem to mind where she lived. She moved in with me until I was to be married. She planned to keep the apartment when I moved out. That was when she met Jay T. He saturated her mind and messed with her head. Then one afternoon, a knock at the door caught her attention. Kate thought the door was locked but when she walked into the living room

Jay T had let himself in. Somewhat frowning, she glided across the room, wondering how he got there. Jay T told Kate that he had only a few months left to go, but he could not stand it any longer. She had no choice but to let him stay. That's what putting up a front will get you in most cases. There had been only one man in Kate's life that she really loved, but something went wrong, leaving her bitter. Jay T's urge and need for Kate at that time was desperate. His hands were everywhere, forcing himself on her. He used his fingers to open her, but when he reached his limit, he ripped the clothes from her and slid her down on the bed. Raising her hips, he forcefully penetrated her, going deeper and deeper until he was embedded like a cocoon. Kate could not resist him anymore, and together they moved as a unit. Then it was all over but for the crying. Jay T left with the promise that when he got out he would take up where he left off and also telling her that she had the best tea. Kate did not tell me this until about two months after it had happened. When she told me, I could tell that she was lying, but she swore that it was her fault and that she had led him on. That I don't doubt, but even if she had, it was no reason for him to force himself on her, leaving her pregnant, which was going to change everything. On the road where we lived, there was a very steep hill; I mean, it went straight up. I hated to drive up that incline. But anyway, the State sent out the road gang to work on the road and that was where she met Jay T. I doubt if you know the meaning of the word *road gang*, that is a group of men who are serving time in prison for crimes they have committed. It is where they are punished for the wrong that they have done. We tried to talk to Kate when she started to talk about marriage to him, but it did no good. He had only a few months of his sentence left. She wrote him, went to visit him, every day for the rest of the time he had left. When he was released, they went straight to the courthouse and were married. They lived there in the apartment for a little while, and then their first troubles began. Jay T could not get work. No one would hire him because of his record, and having no education didn't help. He cannot even write his name. That is why he makes an X and someone else signs his name.

"Why was he in prison?" Suzann asked.

"I don't know," June answered. "Kate and I always told each other our thoughts, but she never told me why. It was never talked about. That is why he is here, this is the only place he can get a job.

When the four of us moved here, we were still very close friends, but that has changed now. You must be careful, for Jay T is a very cruel man. Our friendship has been destroyed because I no longer could tolerate or accept Jay T, because of things that have happened and things that he has done in the past. But the past is not important, only the future is. I know that he mistreats you, and the only thing I can tell you is to do what he says to prevent him from hurting you. I know that you have been told by Kate that I'm just a nosy neighbor, and I guess that you could say that I am. But I just could not give up on Kate until now. I know that she will never leave him, and from what I have seen, she is becoming more like him every day. I am not going to hang around to see what is going to happen. And I don't want to know how it's going to end.

We're leaving this weekend. We're going back home. If Kate should ask you, tell her that I came over to see her but she was gone.

I have told you these things because I know that Kate never will. I hope this will somehow be helpful, but if not, you will at least know the truth about Jay T. Don't let Jay T or Kate know that I have told you anything. Well, I must go now. I guess I've talked enough. I love you, and I wish you the best. Goodbye and good luck."

Miss June left as Suzann sat there thinking about what all she had said, wondering if she was ever going to stop talking. But for some reason, what she had said came as no surprise.

Chapter Nineteen

It wasn't long until a car pulled up into the driveway. Suzann looked out the window only to see that it was Jay T and Kate. As Suzann opened the door, Jay T was helping Kate to the house. Kate appeared to be a little weak.

"What did the doctor say?" she asked.

"The doctor said that the only thing that was wrong with your mother was that she is pregnant."

"She's not my mother!"

Jay T sat down in the chair, looking at Suzann as he spoke, ignoring what she said. Pointing his finger at her and ordered her to sit down.

"SIT . . . DOWN!" he shouted.

"You will stay home from school from now until the baby is born and help Kate. That means that you will do all the housework and take care of the kids. I don't want Kate doing anything. That means you will continue to do all your other jobs, and there will be no time for school."

"I can do all the housework and still go to school."

"You heard what I said, and I will not repeat myself."

But what Suzann said was true; the only time Kate did anything was only if Jay T was around.

"I feel like I could sleep around the clock," Kate said.

She was holding on to his arm to steady herself as she rested her head against his arm.

"Please help me to the bed."

Suzann went into the kitchen and washed her face with cold water. Across the room, the drapes had been pulled shut, leaving the house with a darker feeling than it already had.

Suzann's mind had learned to be open and intelligent, so she would ride it out with Jay T. She knew that it was going to be a long hard ride, but it could not last forever. Someday, there would be a way out. She then decided to go outside for a breath of fresh air. She had already had things done in the house for the day.

Overhead, the man behind the roaming clouds looked like a picture you would see in an art gallery. Suzann stood there, admiring the beauty, thinking of what Jay T had just ordered her to do. Her thoughts were greeted with silence when she felt a lump rise in her throat.

What he had ordered her to do changed nothing because she had been doing Kate's work all along. Jay T did not know that Kate's days of work consisted of sitting on the couch watching TV and feeding her face. She sat there all day, waiting for Suzann to get home to do all her work because it would not get done during the day. The babies' diapers normally had not been changed since the morning, so Suzann had to change them. The babies' butts stayed raw from being wet all day.

Nausea filled her throat and she tried desperately to swallow against it. A chill shook through her entire body from the thought of Jay T pulling her in one direction and Kate pulling her in another, leaving her with no avenue of escape. There was no reason for her to stay home and she knew that she was missing too much school already. Her grades were dropping but no one cared or had time to notice that. That was not important to them. Jay T and Kate only thought of themselves. Pain filled her eyes as she closed them, remembering, recalling all the thoughts over again.

The following night, Jay T came home, being very quiet. He wasn't shouting orders like he normally did. Suzann was in the kitchen finishing supper after a long day of work.

Kate was taking advantage of being waited on hand and foot. She would not even get her own glass of water. She pretended to be so sick. It was just an excuse, and she was using it very well.

Suzann stood to one side of the stove with her head lowered as she thrust her hands into her blue jean pocket. She felt like a prize ring that had just been won at the county fair. She could hear them talking when she called them for supper, but no one came. When she went to see why, she was told by Jay T to fix their plates and bring them into the living room. His voice trailed off when Suzann stepped back into the kitchen to avoid looking at their fat dirty bodies that covered the surface of the couch where they sat.

Her mind struggled and she had to bite her tongue to prevent speaking her mind, knowing that they had no cause to be that tired. Ultimately having to do what he said, mainly because of being terrified not to, she carried their plates to them along with their tea. Suzann stood at the entrance of the doorway with her back to them, listening to them as they guzzled down their food as two hogs would eat slop. She sat down at the table to eat alone, and just as she finished, she heard Jay T as he called out to her once again. The echo in his words sounded more like a drill sergeant as it rang through her ears. Afraid to even wonder what he could want now, she entered the room. He ordered her to sit down; he was so dry and harsh.

"I will be leaving for a couple of weeks."

"Why?" she cut him off, as if she really cared.

"If you would just shut up and listen until I finish, I will tell you why.

We're changing the way we milk cows at the milk barn. We are getting new milkers in and I have to go out of town to learn how all these things work. Then I have got to go and pick them up, and then I have got to go to the warehouse to be shown how to install them so they will work in this barn. I will be back in a couple of weeks. I want you to stay here with Kate and do what you have been doing. I will be leaving tomorrow and Kate will tell you when the baby is coming and you will go and tell Handy and he will bring someone here to help her. I have all the arrangements made."

Suzann studied his face, craggy with scars, as he exhaled his orders across to her.

The next morning, Jay T and Kate were up early, getting ready for him to leave. Kate moved about the house as though she had never been sick in her life. It was hard to believe that she had been so sick the day before. Frustration was starting to fill Suzann to the top, for she knew that Kate had been pretending to be ill all along.

Kate was taking him to meet up with Mr. Butler whom Jay T was going with. And then they were on their way.

All the kids were asleep when Suzann decided to go back to bed; it felt so good to sleep in for a change. Her sleep was deep and long. When she woke up, it was two o'clock in the afternoon. She could hear her heart pound against her chest as fright overcame her. She was scared to move as she let her feet rest on the floor. She walked softly into the living room, being careful not to make any noise. When she reached the living room she found all the kids watching TV and being so quiet. It was like they knew that she needed the rest. That was something that she didn't get much of.

Then it hit her. "Oh man, Jay T is gone." She had slept so hard that she had forgotten. The tension was gone. She felt relaxed and a smile curved the planes of her face.

Suzann then put on a pot of pinto beans and then raced through the house with an effort to pick up and put everything away. When she had finished, she and all the kids piled into the tub and took a good old bubble bath and had so much fun, splashing and laughing, playing around; something they could not do when the grownups were around. It was such a good thing; even the kids had so much fun.

They spent most of their time hiding because Kate and Jay T kept them scared half to death.

After the nice bath, they all climbed up on the bed and Suzann read to them from a book that she had got from the library.

The oldest said something that just about broke Suzann's heart.

She said, "Will you be our new mommy? Cause Mom never does things with us like you do. She never reads to us like you. And you always say that you love us. Mom has never said that to me."

"I know, but your mommy loves you, all of you. She just doesn't know how to say it."

Hearing this and watching them, there was a feeling of uneasiness as a shiver ran through her, and she suddenly felt sorry for them. Trying to be supportive

Then the eldest, Dwan, asked, "When we get big like you, will we be treated like they treat you?"

"NO, I won't let that happen. I will keep you safe."

"You promise?" she asked.

"Yes, I promise."

Then they heard Kate pull into the driveway. "Well, break is over," Suzann thought. "Time to get back on my head."

"What have y'all been doing all day?" Kate asked inquisitively.

Then she shook her head. "You know," as she glanced over the room, her voice was low with concern. "What we are going to do with Jay T gone?"

"BETTER!" Suzann said. "It would be better if he would stay gone!"

Kate could hear the anger building in her voice.

"Don't you raise your voice at me that way!"

"WHY? You talk to me that way, and as a matter of fact, that's the only way that you ever talk to me. You're not my mother. You will never be my mother. You're not even a mother to these babies, and now you're bringing another one in this house of hell. Why? You won't love it. You don't love anything, and you don't even love yourself. You treat me like shit. The only reason you came and got me was so that you and Jay T would have a slave to work for you. Well, I hope you enjoy hurting people and causing so much pain to others. 'Cause that is all you do. One day, all of this will stop. It will be over, and you will never hurt these babies. I will make sure of that one way or another! Oh, I know that you will run and tell Jay T what I have said. And I know that I will get a beating with his Bible Belt again, but this time it will be worth it. BUT I WILL NEVER BE LIKE YOU. You can hate me. You can beat me or have Jay T to do it for you. You can kill me, but you can't eat me. Someday, you will pay for what you have done."

Unable to look at Suzann in the eyes, Kate just dropped her head. After saying all of this, Suzann had a feeling of relief. She had wanted to say this for a long time but she had kept it bottled up inside of her. Now, at least Kate knew how she felt and where she stood.

Kate ran off to her bedroom and closed the door.

Suzann face was tense and unsmiling. She could feel the heat in her cheeks as she took a long deep breath. Then she forced a smile so the babies would know her anger was not directed towards them. Then she felt a horrific hurt in her heart. Kate was contemptuous of Suzann and everyone around that lived in this home. But outside of these walls, she was a sweetheart. Suzann knew that what she had said would not change a thing.

Anyone could recognize that Kate was a lot older, but in actions and feelings, Suzann was the older of the two. Any other person in Suzann's shoes, and being used to having things and a certain way of life, would find it was not a natural thing to have to change and adapt to a hard new world that was turned upside down with cruel indifference and selfishness.

Later that night, there was a knock on the door; Kate was still in her room with the door closed. Suzann went to the door and opened it; standing there were three ladies from the church down the road.

"Hello, I'm Miss Hall from the South Baptist Church. Your family's name was turned in to the Church for need of clothes. We have a lot of things in the car.

Is it OK that we bring them in?"

"Yes, ma'am," Suzann answered.

They just kept bringing boxes of clothes in.

"If there is anything that can't be used, don't worry about it. Just throw it away or give it to someone that you know that might be able to use it."

"Yes, ma'am," again, Suzann answered.

"It was so nice to meet you, but we have to go. We have more stops to make."

"Thank you so much, this was so nice of you. Please tell everyone thanks from this family."

"You are so welcome."

The ladies walked back to their car and pulled away into the night.

All the kids were having a ball, trying on the clothes. There were shoes, sweaters, coats; all kinds of clothes. There were even diapers and bottles, even vitamins. They may have been hand-me-downs but they were new to them. Then Kate walked in. "What in the world is going on in here?"

"Look, Mom, look at all these clothes."

"Where did they come from?" Kate asked as she raised her arms and lowered them again.

"Can we keep them?" Dawn asked. Suzann explained where the clothes had come from and who had brought them.

"Is there anything there for me?" Kate asked.

"Yes," Dwan answered. "Look, here are five dresses, Mom. And look, here are some shirts and tops for you."

"Oh, that's nice. Oh, I like this."

"And look, here are some shorts for Suzann and they are blue jean shorts."

"Now, Suzann, you know that Jay T will not let you wear shorts."

"But these are as long as my dresses," Suzann said. "They come down to my knees."

"Well, you better ask Jay T first."

Suzann had enough clothes to last for a long time, and now she couldn't wait to go back to school wearing her new clothes, knowing that now she would look as good as all the other kids. Now, they would not have any reason to laugh at her or make fun of what she was wearing. Maybe now she could make a friend. Suzann knew that friends should not be made by what you wear. But in school, she discovered that this is not the way it works.

She had been dressed in faded, ragged clothes that had tears and rips when she made friends with Handy. He didn't care about the clothes that she wore and he was her best friend, her only friend.

After hanging everything up and putting all the clothes away, it was way past time for bed. When sliding underneath the covers, there was that feeling that tugged at her heart, being alone. Her thoughts wandered as she said her nightly prayer under her breath so no one could hear. "God, how I wished that I was still with my mom and dad. I love them so much and miss them more every day." But there was not a day that went by that she didn't wish that.

When she dreamed, most of them had been bad dreams. She always felt like she was there, a part of them. She could feel the pain, the warmth of blood that runs down her body; her dreams were always in color. It was always bad. She was always running but she never knew if she was running to something or away from something. But it was as if she knew when it was a dream because she could most of the time wake herself up from them.

This night was different. Suzann could hear the moans of someone in pain and she could hear heavy breathing. And it went on and on and on. Then there would be silence; then it would start again. She tried to push the sounds out of her head but there was something about this dream that was wrong. A huge scream with the sound of rage and terror interrupted the night. After that, there was a haunting quietness that added to the eeriness of the early morning. Then, she heard a sound like the one a newborn baby makes as the doctor slaps it on the butt to welcome it into its new world.

A moment later, there were sounds in the house that forced her to wake up. She propped herself up on one elbow, listening to drawers being opened and water running, along with the high winds that seemed to howl warnings of forthcoming disaster.

Suzann stuck her head through the door and saw Kate with something wrapped up in a bag. She could hear sounds coming from it. Her thoughts were unable to contain what was going on. She questioned herself, should she check it out to see what was happening? But she didn't. Reflecting on her own advice, she stood there frozen. Suzann looked at the clock on the wall from the shadows. From the light in the other room she could see the time. It was a little past two in the morning.

The front door shut. Suzann rushed to put some clothes on and slipped out to see where Kate was going. Slipping around, very cautiously following her but staying where Kate could not see her. With the wind like it was, it would be hard for Kate to hear anything but the sounds of the rough winds.

Kate's actions looked like she was half-reluctant to so what she was about to do. When Kate opened the toolshed door, Suzann watched as she laid the bag down on the ground and got a shovel, walked back out, and picked up the bag. Her movements were not very frisky; she was moving slowly like she was feeling sick.

This was not a good sign. Kate looked around several times to make sure that no one was there. Suzann was only a few feet from her, but Kate never noticed. There was evil excitement in her face when she passed through where the night light was. Suzann could see her very well. Kate was mysteriously hiding something as she turned to walk down behind the big hay barn where there was a row of pine trees about two hundred feet behind the barn. There, she laid down the bag again on the ground. Then she took the shovel and began to dig.

Suzann became impatient with herself. A lot would ride on her decision. "Just what the hell should I do?" she asked herself over and over. She couldn't prove that anything was wrong, but yet a strange and scary feeling had completely overtaken her. And then there was Kate, acting like something out of a horror movie. One minute she was digging and talking to herself, then she would start laughing, getting louder and louder until it would turn into a screaming shriek. At one point, she threw the shovel down, raised her hands toward the sky, and then started muttering low and evil sounding sounds. Then she continued digging for a few minutes until she was out of breath.

Suzann placed her hands over her mouth when she recognized that Kate was burying something. Suzann's first impulse was to shout at her. This was not Kate's normal or standard shit. Suzann thought about going to wake up Handy, but what would the consequences of that be. She could not take any chances on losing the visits that she got when she could spend the weekend with her mom and dad. And she knew that if she pushed too hard that was exactly what would happen. That had already happened several times when she had done something or had said something that Jay T didn't like. Then Jay T would tell them that she was grounded, so she couldn't go home with them.

Then she grasped her thoughts and watched Kate as she was still digging. "How deep she is going to dig that hole?" Suzann wondered. Suzann studied her as both of her feet would come off the ground with each downward stroke, using all of her body weight. "What would she want to do this for?" Suzann concentrated on this night and what was happening as she watched Kate struggle to fill her lungs. Then she shoved a lock of hair over her shoulder. Her broad face was lined with concern for what she was doing.

She stopped digging, laid down the shovel, and picked up the bag and threw it in the hole. This time, there was no hesitation. Suzann saw that this act was done with a deep burning rage. There was no pity or compassion. Suddenly, the wind momentarily died

down. Suzann heard a few words that Kate was saying. "Fuckin'
boy! I ain't having you! I hate all you dick wagging sons of
bitches. You deserve . . ." Then all at once the wind picked back
up. Suddenly, Kate whirled around in a half crouch and stared
into the darkness, checking to see if there had been any prying
eyes or ears. Satisfied that no one was around, she began to put
the dirt back in its place. She would step on it, trying to pack
it down. When she had it covered up, she dragged a limb over
it so no one would know that the ground had been disturbed.
Taking one last look, Suzann saw Kate spread her feet to brace
herself. Suzann lowered her eyebrows and took a final hard
stare, still wondering what had just taken place. She was very
confused about this night and her feelings. For some reason,
fear was causing her heart to pound. But why fear? For whom?
For what?

Suzann got a grip on herself and went back to the house so Kate
would never know that she had been there.

She slid back into the bed as if she had never been out of it,
with nothing but thoughts sliding in and out of her head about
this night and reliving the scenes of what she had seen and heard.
The shadows in her room had changed, shocked and shaken, as
she tried to shut out everything, even the sound of the wind, and
closed her eyes for a little sleep.

Suzann had gotten up this morning at first light after a sleepless
night. There was no one stirring up yet. Very quietly, she opened
Kate's bedroom door to look in on her; Kate was still fast asleep.
Standing there looking at her, Suzann was thinking that this woman
needed some help because she is definitely sick in the head. With
the stern light that was creeping through the windows from the
bright sun, there was something in the floor that caught her eye.
She walked forward with clenched fists at her sides, trying not wake
Kate as she tippy toed across the room.

There lay in a pile were clothes that had blood all over them.
Looking at this, there was a fiery grin on her face as she shook her

head and eased back out of the room. Getting caught in Kate's bedroom would not be a good thing because no one was allowed in there.

Suzann got the kids up and cleaned them, fixed their breakfast, and while they were eating, she left the house and went to the barn.

Handy was there doing the milking while Jay T was gone. When Handy saw Suzann, he thought that she was there to let him know that it was time for the baby, so he ran to her.

"Is it time?"

"No."

"What's wrong, Suzann?" He lowered his voice. "Come over here and talk to me." The cool morning air carried the scent of the cows in the lot for milking. Suzann saw their noses as they stuck them through the gap between the boards, with snot streaming to the ground.

"Now what's wrong with my girl?"

Pulling her hands up into the sleeves of her shirt, her words were toneless.

"Handy, will you help me get away from here, away from Jay T and Kate? You are the only one that I can trust. I feel like something bad is going to happen."

"Have they threatened you? Have they hurt you?"

There was no answer from her, she only hung her head down and looked at the ground.

"You don't have to answer that, I know more than you think I do.

Suzann, look at me. I would never hurt you. Anything that you tell me will go no further. I promise. I'm sure that there are some things going on that I don't know, but you know where I'm at. And any time you need me, you come and get me.

Now, has Jay T put his hands on you in a way that made you feel uncomfortable?"

"No."

"Do you know what I'm talking about?"

"Yes," she answered.

"Are you sure?"

"Yes. I hear them doing it all the time. I hear the bed hitting the wall and dirty talk. I know what they are doing. And Miss June told me a little about the birds and bees."

"Well, you had a teacher that should know what she was talking about."

"Do you know her?"

"Yes, I know her."

"Was she your girlfriend?"

"NO!

Suzann, you are spreading into womanhood, and there are a lot of crazies out there. If I could, I would take you as far away from them as I could, but we would always be on the run and that would not be a life that you deserve. Oh lord, girl. What are we going to do?"

Handy took her in his arms to give her some comfort as he took her hair in his hands. "You have the most beautiful hair, and don't you ever cut it. It is so long."

"I know, I sit on it when I sit down and the boy that sits behind me in class is always playing with my hair."

Handy turned half around, and looked at her in the eyes. After exchanging some of Suzann's silent secrets, they just looked at each other for a moment. Each one of them had thoughts on their minds that would not be shared to one another.

Suzann was sorry that she had involved Handy in her problems. But he was the only one that she could turn to. She threw her arms around him and hugged his neck, thanked him for his time.

"I've got to get back," she said.

When she got back to the house, Kate was sitting on the couch. And when she rose to her trembling legs, she asked,

"Where have you been?"

"I had to go and feed the calves like I do every morning.

Are you all right? I have got to go back and finish feeding. I had to come and use the bathroom."

Kate made her way back to the bedroom and closed the door. She looked weak, and her face looked pale. Suzann went into the kitchen and saw that Kate had eaten while she was up.

CHAPTER TWENTY

After returning to school, Suzann found that someone had prepaid her lunches for the rest of the year. Though the school officials would not give her information of whom, she knew that it had to be Handy because he'd seen that she wasn't eating enough and he knew that she wasn't eating at school because Jay T would not pay for her lunches,

Suzann had noticed that Kate was looking a lot smaller and there was no baby yet. When Suzann asked her about the baby, Kate had to wet her lips and the only thing that Kate would tell her was that there would be no baby, things had gone wrong.

Suzann felt weak as she caught her breath; then she felt a rage of guilt run through her. In her heart, she just knew that this baby lay meaninglessly in a shallow grave behind the hay barn.

"What happened to her?" Suzann asked.

"IT WAS A BOY!"

Kate's anger was creeping upon her. "I MEANT TO SAY THAT IT WAS BORN DEAD," she shouted and immediately regretted it, then folded her arms against her breast, letting herself have some time to think.

"OK, you don't have to scream at me."

Suzann knew that what she had said was a lie, she just knew. But there was no proof of what Suzann was thinking, and the dead can't talk. She shook her head in confusion. "What have I done? Why didn't I stop her? I know that I wanted to, but something would not let me. That will be a night that I will never forget." She could still hear the wind and smell the pine needles. Suzann lifted her face and pushed her long hair back that fell down to her butt.

"What have you done?" Suzann asked.

"There will be another baby. We got to have another girl, and we are working on that now."

"Great, that's just great! That is just what you need to do."

Chapter Twenty-one

Winter had passed and spring was upon us and another birthday—that was the slowest thing of all. The spring colors were beginning to sprout through, spreading their beauty gently across the countryside. But that wasn't the only thing spreading, so was Kate's belly.

And there were other things that were filling out in all the right places, Suzann thought as she looked into the mirror at her long blonde hair and her dark skin, along with those big green eyes that had their own sparkle. But the windows of her soul were deep and held a lot of pain.

In the middle to late spring was when all the newborn calves came one after another. There were calves everywhere. Once all of them were born, they had to be gathered up and taken away from their mothers. Suzann always hated that because the mothers would cry for days, looking for their babies. Then they were put in the calf barn, which was a long barn with stalls on both sides; there were fifty stalls on each side. There was only one calf per stall. And of course, these little critters had to be fed twice a day. Hanging on the front of each stall would be a bucket with a nipple for the calf to suck. It was Suzann's job to give the calves their milk every day and to keep all the stalls clean. She enjoyed the babies. They would let her pet and play with them, and they would suck anything—her hands, fingers, shirt tail—anything that they could get in their mouth. All new mothers had to be hand milked for about five days before they could be put back in with the milk cows for normal milking where the milk went into a large milk tank. This milk was picked up and went to the factory where it was processed, then delivered to the stores. When the cow has a newborn, her milk is bad for five days. Suzann had learned a lot, but she couldn't wait to forget it.

With all the work, it kept Suzann so busy that most of her days went pretty fast, and the only times that she saw Jay T were in the mornings and at night. Three o'clock had become the regular time to get up. It gave her time to get all of her work done before school.

Suzann had to get up and dress, put on the coffee, build fire at the house if it was cold. She had to go and gather up all the cows, put them in the milk lot, wet down the entire milk barn. Start the first four cows milking. Then she would go to the house and fix breakfast for everyone, change the babies, then get ready for school. Every morning was the same thing. Once Jay T had his coffee and breakfast, he would go to the barn and finish the milking.

Even though Handy lived there, he did not know that Suzann was doing all of this work in the mornings. His day did not start until about eight o'clock, by then Suzann had already left for school. So he never saw her until the evenings when she came to the barn to feed the calves. He knew that she was doing that; sometimes, he would even help her if he didn't have to do something else. But Jay T made sure he worked a ten- to twelve-hour day, seven days a week.

When it was time to get the hay in, Suzann's job was to drive the tractor pulling the wagon. Jay T and Handy would throw the hay and stack it, sometimes there would be some schoolboys from the football team that would help just to help them get in shape for football. But on this job, Suzann had the best job, unless she messed up, like running over a terse the wrong way and dumping the load of hay. That would be a bad day for her.

Jay T would never whip her in front of anyone; he always would wait until he got her home. That made for a bad day when something went wrong and she knew that she would get a beating with his Bible belt; she would have all day to think about how bad he was going to hit her.

Since Suzann was doing so much work at and around the barn, Jay T was more careful not to leave any bruises on her where they could be seen. But they could be seen on her back most of the time. If he left marks on her legs, she would have to be sure to wear long pants until they healed. Everyone had to work and steady to keep the dairy farm going.

CHAPTER TWENTY-TWO

"So here you are," Mary said as she placed her fingertips on Suzann's face. "I've missed you so much."

"I've missed you too." And Suzann looked into her eyes with the urge to cry when she felt her heart being torn from her chest again. Mary stood staring down at her, with only the two of them in the room. Suzann registered the feeling, then ignored it. She wanted to tell Mary that things were far from being good here, like she and Dad had said they would be.

Suzann sent a strange and frightening look through her eyes to Mary as she picked up a glass of Coke and ice, taking a sip then handing it to Mary.

"Is something wrong?" Mary asked as she drank without hesitation from the glass.

Suzann answered her, "No," knowing that she had to because she couldn't tell Mary the truth about anything that was going on in her life.

"You're growing up so fast, too fast." Mary took hold of Suzann's hair, slinging it back behind her.

Suzann then looked back around the house where there was no one around but Mary and her, retracing some old footsteps, some of which were very unpleasant. Suzann felt the tension in the room from her own self with a threatening need to just spill the beans about Jay T. But she surrendered to her own self-will and stopped the ambition that she felt, because it would be a high expense to lose her mom and dad.

Suzann walked out to the back on the porch, dipping her hands into a pan of water that she had set out there earlier that morning.

Jay T came around the corner of the house, seeing Suzann standing there, where he stopped and stared. Suzann saw the way that he looked at her, with that look that maybe she had done something wrong, or was it that he was worried that she might be telling Mary something she should not have.

"Mount up. There's work to be done," he said in a friendly gesture.

Suzann hurried on so she could get things done. Coming around the calf barn, straining, she was loaded down so she wouldn't have to make so many trips.

A cry of laughter rang out. "I think you've got a load. Let me help you," Jim said as he gave her a hand along with a smile that rippled across his face.

Suzann was feeding the calves; when she looked up, Jim had disappeared. A couple of hours later when she finished, she went back to the house where she found that Mary was in her bedroom hanging new curtains that she had made and brought for her, along with that smell of fresh wood from the oak desk and chair that Jim had made and brought. Moving the big four-poster bed that now sat in the center of the room brought a welcome change in looks.

Suzann opened the window, letting the cool air of the night breeze in. It had been a long day. She groaned as she started getting ready for bed.

The next morning after Suzann left the barn, she was to go to the house and help Kate with the housework. Actually, what Suzann had to do was everything that Kate ordered her to do while Kate sat on her fat ass and dished out orders. Kate had driven Suzann to disapprove of everything that she stood for. When Kate spoke, her words were flat and cold, filled with hatred, with the sound to inflict punishment on Suzann.

This morning when Suzann walked into the house, she heard one of the babies as she tried to yell but she sounded like she was choking. When Suzann got to her, she found that Kate had rammed a rag into her mouth. The baby was gagging on the rag, trying to cry but could not, choking on her own vomit.

Suzann ran and pushed Kate back as hard as she could, seeing and hearing her cursing anger. She shook her head and pointed her condemning finger at Kate.

"WHAT ARE YOU DOING? Are you crazy?"

It tore Suzann apart to see what she had. "This is wrong!

I will not let you hurt these babies. Even God will only tolerate so much. He hates evil, and you are an evil woman. You and Jay T deserve each other."

Suzann grabbed the baby and took her to the bathroom and cleaned her up, then finally got her to stop crying. When she had finished, she called out for Dawn, "Take her and y'all go outside and play, and don't come back in until Kate is feeling better."

CHAPTER TWENTY-THREE

The handful of people that lived in this small town thought that Jay T and Kate were fine people, that they were only poor. Jay T made twenty-five dollars a week, for his work. Suzann got nothing for all the work that she did. All the milk was free, the utilities were free, and there was always money to buy bootleg whiskey or to get what it took to make or run off a batch of home brew.

If Suzann did the least little thing that did not suit them, she was not allowed to go to school. They used that against her only because they knew how much she loved it. She worked as hard as she could and did everything so that they would not keep her home. Going to school was her only sense of freedom from this place, and she loved it so much.

In school, Suzann was somewhat different from the others. She sometimes prayed that the evening would never come, while everyone else couldn't wait until they got home.

Suzann understood that many people lost the fear of God and let him become small while they let themselves get bigger. One of the scriptures that she had heard Jim discuss with someone was, 'To fear him is to hate evil.' he would quote from the book of Proverbs.

But Jay T and Kate appeared to fear nothing, not even the devil himself.

Apparently stunned by Suzann's taking control of what just happened, Kate grabbed her bag and walked out the door. "I'm going to the store," she screamed.

Knowing that Jay T was in the field and Kate was gone, gave Suzann the perfect opportunity to do something that she had wanted to do for a long time. In Kate's bedroom, an old scrapbook that she kept stored away, hidden or so she thought, contained pictures of her when she was young and very beautiful. There was one picture that stood out from all the rest, where she wore a black silk dress trimmed in lace with a shawl around her shoulders. Jewelry laced around her neck and wrist, with rings on every finger. She was standing in a pair of six-inch heels that gleamed below the hem of her dress. All of the pictures would have gotten a stare from any man. Her face was golden brown, with her hair hanging long, brushing against her shoulders. Her eyes reflected the gentleness of good breeding and her lips shone with the desire for expensive brandy.

"I wonder what ever happened to her. She looks nothing like this now. Her hair is all chopped off, she never takes the time to fix it. No makeup on, and she does not care how she looks. Another thing, she never smiles. Of course, if I smelled like that, I guess that I would never smile either. She just sits in the house, thinking up how she can hurt someone or do something mean. She keeps the room dark, watching game shows and soaps on TV. I wonder how she can live like this." This was every day. Sometimes Suzann felt sorry for her, but she would never let Kate know that.

The hate in Suzann's heart returned more often every day, in spite of all she done to prevent it, because she knew it was wrong to hate. She remembered what her dad had said to her, "Everything happens for a reason." She could still hear his voice echo in her ears from the last weekend that she had visited with them.

Suzann was a prisoner in what should have been a home, like Miss June had said. Being punished for something done wrong is one thing, but Suzann, most of the time, never knew what she had done wrong. Suzann was hardly ever allowed to spend any weekends with her mom and dad anymore. Jay T's excuse was that there was always something to be done. Kate was fixing to drop another one; she was as big as a cow. If you put Kate in the pasture with the cows, it would be hard to distinguish which one to milk.

Things were changing every day, but not for the better. Suzann was being tugged back and forth between them, with each demand being harder and requiring more work. She wondered what it would be like to have normal parents like all other children. Neither Kate nor Jay T could write their names. When Suzann needed help with homework, she could forget it at home. She would have to get it from school. For a long time, her feelings would be hurt when she would bring her report card home and they refused to sign it. But now she knew why. Suzann would have to sign Kate's name on it and lie to the teacher by saying that was Kate's signature on it. Suzann finally figured out that they did not have enough education to write their own names. Instead of telling her the truth, they would get upset, giving her the impression that they were refusing to sign out of pure meanness. Suzann had to forge their names on anything that she had to bring home to be signed. This caused bitterness and she was frightened and afraid that her teachers would recognize her handwriting and think that she was not showing anything to them from school. But if they did, they never confronted Suzann or said anything about it.

On the first of the week, during the middle of class, Suzann was told by her teacher to report to the principal's office. Scared at first, she walked down the long hallway to the office, there she saw her dad standing outside the office area, in the hall, waiting on her. Suzann's pace turned into a run as her feet carried her quickly to meet him. Neither Suzann nor Jim took the time to speak as she threw herself into his arms. He picked her up off the floor, slinging her round and round, and then he stopped and held her very close and tight. The love that he felt for her was much greater than all the shame and sorrow in the world. Jim's voice was ragged with emotion and he was still troubled with guilt for letting her go so easily. It had been a few years since that day, but pain, guilt, and shame are like love, they are not easily forgotten. Suzann had almost forgotten what it was like to have someone to show her that they loved and cared for her so much.

"Would you come outside with me? I have a surprise for you."

"But my classes!

"Don't worry about your classes. I already have permission for you to be excused for a few minutes."

As they walked outside, curiosity hit. "Where is Mom?"

"She is at the doctor's office getting something for a cold. But she sends her love. You know your mom, she would not have it any other way. She was afraid if we waited until she got out from seeing the doctor it would be too late to see you at all." Suzann welcomed his outstretched arms, once again making her feel so secure.

Reaching the truck, Jim placed his hands about her shoulders. "Let me look at you." Suzann was embarrassed for the clothes she was wearing were hand-me-downs. They were nice, but the shoes . . . well, they didn't look like anything you would see in J.C Penney's catalog.

"Suzann, what is going on? Please tell me. I feel that something is wrong, but I don't know what. They won't let you come home with us hardly at all, and I know that you don't get to go to church unless you are with us."

Suzann let her thoughts drift, thinking that this might be her chance; maybe even a chance to go back home and live with Jim and Mary. She thought, "No, no, I can't tell him! If they really cared and loved me, they would not have let them take me from my home to start with." She knew that this was not the truth, it was just a way to strike out. Rules and laws would hold in this case, but Suzann was starting to think that rules and laws were made to be broken.

Holding Jim's hand, she could feel her grip relax with the feeling like she was sinking into a deep slumber. Her words came slow and were spoken quietly, with a lot of deep hurt.

"Look, I never expected or asked for any of this to happen. Maybe I should apologize for having been brought into this world since I have obviously caused so much trouble to everyone, but I had nothing to do with it. I am the result of one night of pleasure, and at my expense. I feel like I am the one having to pay the price." There was no advance warning of this abrupt answer from her. At first, Jim didn't understand, and then he realized her meaning. A sick feeling settled in his stomach for he could surely understand where she was coming from.

Suzann dropped her head for she never expected such words to explode from her tongue, especially to Jim. And she knew that she didn't tell him what he wanted to hear, which was the truth.

"I'm sorry that you feel that way, but you were brought into this world for a reason," Jim replied.

"Oh, I'm sorry. Really, I am. I'm not happy there at all, but everything is fine, really."

Jim got the feeling that she was not telling him the whole truth, but he didn't press the issue any further. Changing the thickness in the air, he asked, "Can Jay T not at least buy you a decent pair of shoes to wear to school?"

"I don't know for sure how much money Jay T makes. I know that when they buy groceries they say that there is never any money left.

I do know that all the other expenses are paid through his job."

"What you mean to say is after he pays for groceries and gets his whiskey there is no money left."

"How did you know about the whiskey?" Suzann asked.

"Handy told me that Jay T drank a lot."

"Handy?"

"Yes,"

"Is that all he told you?"

"Why, yes.

Is there something else that he should have told me?"

"Oh no, I mean . . . I guess not, I mean . . . I don't know."

Then they both laughed,

"Tell you what, tomorrow I will meet you at your bus before you get on it and I'll have you some new shoes.

Suzann, do you want me to talk to Jay T?"

"No, no, please, Dad, don't do that!"

"But why?"

"Please, for me, please. Don't say anything to Jay T about anything."

Jim was surprised at her reaction but he would grant her wishes.

"Well, all right. I won't say anything, but only because you don't want me to. Here, I have something for you. Your mother got this for you and she said that you would like it."

It was a new purse.

"Oh my god, it's beautiful. I love it, and I needed this so bad."

Suzann could feel the smile that stretched from ear to ear with excitement and happiness flowing, and then suddenly everything stopped.

"But how I will tell Jay T where I got it?"

"Tell him the truth. Tell him that I brought it to you at school."

"OK, OK I will."

Brushing her tears from her eyes, she watched Jim drive away while she held her new purse to her chest. It was the first new purse that Suzann had ever had and she would treasure it forever.

Suzann knew that when she got home that afternoon that she would have to tell them about the purse, being scared to at the same time. Getting off the bus, there was no one there except for Kate. Suzann put up her books and went to get her work done.

That night at supper everyone was so quiet. Jay T was drinking again but tonight he was charming and telling jokes and being quite funny. This was different. "Maybe he should drink more often if it changes him into this kind of person," Suzann thought to herself. Most of the time when he was drinking, he was mean. But tonight, everything went so well. As she finished cleaning the kitchen, she wished that all nights would go this well. When she was done and had gone to her room, everyone was already in bed. Suzann was standing in front of her mirror while undressing; she noticed a change to her body. Really surprised at the size of her breasts, she gently massaged their swells, making her nipples hard. Her thin face stood out from beneath her long hair that hung below her slender waist, with a natural silky texture and was golden brown. Thinking philosophically that only the good endured, she slipped into her gown, turned out the lights, and then snuggled deep into bed. She knew that this had been a good day and she hoped for many more like this one. Enjoying the warmth, she noticed odd feelings in her stomach, not realizing that they were just growing pains.

Chapter Twenty-four

It was the next morning, as she was getting ready to go to the barn, she heard someone up and discovered that it was Jay T. Not having to bother with waking him was a total surprise.

After rounding up the cows, Suzann was starting the morning milking when she realized the feed was getting low. She went to the feed room which was adjacent to the front of where the cows were being milked. There was a step down into the feed room of about two feet. The room held nothing but pellets that were only used for feed during the milking. She was shoveling up enough feed for that morning when she felt the presence of someone being there. Looking up, she found that it was Jay T. He was just standing there, watching her every move.

His eyes held something that she had never seen before. Suzann stood there, feeling her heart as it fell to her feet. He was scaring her. She had never seen him look at her like this before. Moving in her direction, he stepped down into the feed room where she was standing. An inch at a time, she began to slowly step backwards without any conscious direction in mind.

"Jay T, what is it? What is wrong with you?" Suzann queried.

"What is it? What's wrong? Oh, nothing is wrong. At least, nothing that you can't take care of in time."

"What do you mean? What are you talking about?" Suzann asked.

Taking his hand and putting it on her face, he pushed her against the wall.

"One of these days," he said. "One of these days." Turning her loose, he looked in her direction as he walked away until he was out the door.

Suzann felt her heart pounding so fast that she could almost see the movement through her thin shirt. Looking out from the room, she wondered where he was at. Not being able to see him, she hauled herself upward and forward from the feed room. She began to run wildly, and as she cut the corner, not quite sure how she managed it, her feet slid on the wet surface, causing her to fall painfully hard. Her body lay flat on the wet, slippery floor. She lay there, feeling pain in her forearms and elbows. But her main concern was that she wasn't sure if she could even move. She heaved herself upward. As she did, she expected at any minute to feel the grip of Jay T, pulling her back into the barn.

Slowly but steadily she walked out of the barn and then began to run towards the house. She discovered when she was getting ready for school that she had blood all over her face from where she had busted the inside of her lower lip, unaware at the time that she had done it. She tried to relax and shake off the case of nerves, and stop her hands from shaking. The only thing that she knew to do was to put this whole incident out of her mind and go to school. But Suzann's fear of Jay T had changed. Now, she had become terrified of him. In her mind, she could see his narrow eyes that seemed to be examining and drawing a line around her. And there was that uneasy feeling that Jay T was up to something that could only induce pain. That was the thing that he was best at.

The weather was cold and the snow lay heavy upon the ground. And at three o'clock in the morning in the month of December, the chill could be breathtaking. In weather like this the cows were kept in a smaller pasture, about ten acres, that was directly behind the house. The only shoes that she had to wear were her school shoes. She couldn't wear them, and so with no shoes to wear to gather up the cows, she put on three pair of socks. When the cows were awakened and headed for the barn, Suzann stood in their still warm beds, absorbing the warmth on her cold feet. When she reached the barn, Jay T was there. He even had a fire going for the first time that she knew of. Not having much feeling in her feet, she staggered as she walked. Jay T was mad because she had no shoes to wear in the mud and snow.

"I will find some rubber knee-high boots for you to wear. They will be too big, but they will serve the purpose. Now go on to the house." She shivered as she warmed her feet by the fire. Most of the shivering was from being cold but some of it was from the surprise and fear of Jay T's unexpected presence in the barn. Agonizing pain masked her face as the coldness escaped and the heat was drawn within.

Two weeks later, it was Christmas, and Jim and Mary had come to spend the holidays with them because Jay T and Kate would not let Suzann spend the holidays with Jim and Mary. But being with them was all that mattered. There were apples, oranges, and nuts and Suzann's favorite homemade fruitcake that Mary had made. They had never had food like this in this house. Most of the food, Mary had cooked and brought and the rest she cooked after they arrived. Before supper on Christmas Eve, two parishioners from the two churches of the neighborhood came over and brought bags of food and clothes and shoes. There was even a pair of boots that would fit Suzann for working in. One of the ladies that handed her the boots said,

"I was told to make sure you got these, they were for you special."

"Thank you so much!" Suzann answered.

After the ladies left, Jim went out to his truck and brought in gifts from him and Mary. Suzann eyes flashed as she opened her package to find a new notebook with everything that she could possibly need for school. This was the best Christmas that Suzann could ever have hoped for.

"Dad, would you go with me? I want to take Handy a plate for Christmas. He is all alone."

"Why yes!" Jim got a bag and put apples and oranges and nuts, and cut him every kind of cake and pie that was there. Suzann fixed him a plate that needed side boards on it to hold all the food.

They knocked on his door and Handy invited them in from the cold.

"What in the world . . ." he said. As he looked at Suzann with so much love, he recoiled a little, and then his face lit up

"Well, if you are not the sunlight of my life tonight," he said.

"Merry Christmas," answered Suzann.

He opened the plate and looked, breaking off a piece of ham, blowing on it as he put it in his mouth. "You shouldn't have. I been living here for years and you are the only one that remembered me at Christmas time." His eyes watered although he tried not to show that. But it was easy to see that he was touched. Suzann had a bag in her hand.

"This is for you. t looked like something you might wear, it was in with the clothes that the Church brought over tonight and no one there would wear it." It was a green pullover sweater. "The next time you go out on a hot date, this might impress her."

"I don't know so much about that," Handy laughed.

"But it was a good thought, and perhaps rightly so," he said as he lowered his head.

"But I'm happy just having friends like you."

Handy felt something that night; it was as if a new light had been turned on in his world. Thinking that Suzann had enough to take care of without have to take care of him too, but she always found the time in her busy schedule to check on him and leave him with a smile.

Handy put his hand over hers. "You are in my prayers," he said with a smile.

Chapter Twenty-Five

Suzann had to mix instant milk in a bucket with warm water to replace mother's milk. When this transition was done, they always got the running scours. The young calf had to be taken away from their mothers so the milk supply for the farm would not be interrupted. This change nearly always calls the calf to have diarrhea better known as the scours. It brought a special aroma of its own. But that afternoon, the interest in the calves helped to take her mind away from the storm that was sounding rapidly worse. The dirt road weaved through the fields, and the dirt was being picked up and twisted in the air like a red twisting cloud. A booming roar of thunder made her clench her teeth. The house was usually easy to see from the calf barn, but it had now disappeared behind the rushed curtains of rain, leaving a scary feeling as the barn darkened. Feeling very uncomfortable, she listened to the rain and winds that were blowing so hard. At the very back of the barn, it opened up into a big storage area where hay was stored for the calves. Thunder boomed and lightning flickered in the sky. The flashes of lightning helped Suzann find her way to the back of the barn. There she remained, silent and snuggled up in the hay. At that moment, that was the best that she could do. Her muscles tightened at the frightening sound of limbs and debris blowing about in the air, slapping the sides and the top of the barn. She listened to the howling wind as it whistled around the buildings and it sounded like something she might have heard on a TV show. Thinking that she heard someone, she raised her head in attention and looked around. It had sounded like someone calling out her name.

It had to be Jay T, her insides wrenched violently. What could he want and why was he looking for her? Even more disturbing, she did not want to be caught in this barn in this storm alone with him. That would be more frightening than the storm itself. It didn't seem like the storm could possibly get any worse. Then she saw Jay T as he entered the other end of the barn, walking toward where she was, taking one step at a time. And then closer, and then he stopped. His eyes were dark and narrow with a frown between his thick eyebrows. "Shi-it," he cursed. He crammed his hands into the pockets of his pants, standing there looking at Suzann, making her feel quite unnerved. She got up and looked past him towards the front end of the barn, and then started to run towards it instinctively. Unexpectedly, Jay T's hands grabbed her shoulders and pushed her roughly back down into the hay. Then a sudden flash of lightning zigzagged down in front of the barn.

"What are you thinking? ?You can't walk in that wind. It is too strong and it would blow your ass over the damn river." All of a sudden, several pieces of tin blew from the roof, and not being able to hold it back, Suzann's scream of terror echoed through the barn. Her hands were shaking, she could not stop them. Then she felt Jay T's grip closing around her waist. His movement gave her a sort of comfort. Her terror of him was outweighed by the ferocity of the storm, and it was not letting up!

"We've got to get out of here," he yelled against the wind.

Holding on to Suzann's waist, he guided her towards the opening at the front of the barn. The rain was so hard and heavy it was hard to see where they would be going. As they stepped out into it, trying to get ready to make the run for the storm shelter, a sudden a gust of wind blew rain all over them, soaking them instantly and completely with gallons of cold, freezing water, causing Suzann to gasp.

Jay T yelled out at her, "We've got to get to safety."

Suzann clamped her jaws tightly together as they tried to make a run for it. They had only moved a few feet when something hit the fence and fell across the ground in front of them, startling them both. Suzann looked in the direction and saw a huge tree that had fallen and crushed the pasture fence that ran alongside the barn. As they were looking to try and see where they were going, they could see the air above them was filled with flying debris from everywhere. Holding tightly to Jay T's hand, Suzann walked forward with him, trying to get to the storm shelter where the rest of the family was. The wind was so strong that when they would take one step forward, it seemed like they would lose two steps backward. Suddenly, something hit them in their faces, lifting them up in the air, taking them off of their feet, and slinging both of them on the ground, knocking the breath out of Suzann. Jay T had been knocked out cold but still maintained his grip on Suzann. Something heavy, whatever it was, had mounted itself over them. In the blackness of the storm, Suzann could not see what held them pinned down on the ground. Jay T was not moving and Suzann was screaming but could not hear herself. Whether it was from lack of breath or the screaming wind, she didn't know.

"Don't you have any better place to be," said a voice she heard.

Once again lightning flashed and she recognized the face looming above her. It was Handy.

"Handy, I think he is dead," Suzann said.

"I hope so!" he answered.

"What did you say?" she asked.

"I said, I don't think so.

"Put your hands over your face, I've got to get this tree off of you."

He struggled almost angrily in an endless effort to move the tree, but it was not moving.

"I'll be right back," he screamed.

"NO, don't leave!"

"I'll be right back."

It wasn't long until she could hear a tractor running. Suzann looked around and saw Handy crawling under the tree to where she and Jay T lay, handing her a flashlight.

"I'm going to try to pull this tree off, but it has got to roll over. If it does not flip over you, turn on the light so I will know to stop. If it starts to drag you, turn on the light, OK?"

"OK."

Their voices had sounded like whispers in the buffeting howling wind even though each of them had been almost screaming at the top of their lungs.

She felt the tree start to move, it was rolling over. Once it had cleared them, she turned on her flashlight. Handy hurriedly ran back to find the tree off of them. He grabbed Suzann. "Are you all right?"

"I think so."

Then there was a groaning sound, it was Jay T.

"What happened?" he asked

"Oh, you ran into a tree head on."

Handy helped him to his feet.

"Can you walk?"

"Yes."

Handy turned around and picked Suzann up and carried her to the storm shelter.

On the way there, Handy was thinking, "Man that could have been a perfect accident, if Suzann had not been there."

Suzann snuggled close beside him when Jay T slammed the door shut behind them.

Standing on the steps with water and blood running from his head and his sight was a little bit fuzzy, but quickly he was back to himself.

"Suzann!" Jay T called out to her. "Get over there with the rest of the babies if you're going to act like one." Then he pushed away from the wall and walked toward her. He rubbed his hands together and looked at her out of the corner of his eyes. She knew this look all too well, so she got up and walked over to the other side and slid down the wall, putting her head down on her knees.

"H-how dare you!" Handy said. "If she had not been with you out there you would have died. She saved your life."

Suzann wanted to close her eyes but could not; she was so embarrassed that Jay T was acting like this in front of Handy.

"You may run this job but you don't run me! And don't even think about running me off this job because that will never happen."

"And why is that?" Jay T asked.

"I tell you what, you try doing something and you will find out real quick why!"

"I'm sorry, man. I don't know what came over me. You are right, and I must have hit my head."

Jay T sat down on the steps, thinking to himself, "You son of a bitch, somebody will find your ass dead under a tractor somewhere. If I can get away with killing so many in the past, I think I can get away with one more. Your days are numbered."

Suzann looked up at Handy with a hurting smile, and her eyes were bloodshot from the rain, or was that tears he saw. Then something slammed against the door and over their heads. Everyone turned to look in that direction, but it was only the wind blowing things around. Suzann sat there cold and shaking, unsure if it was from being cold, or half scared to death. There were loud crashing sounds all around them. The wind was howling and things were breaking above them. It seemed like it lasted forever.

But then everything was quiet. It was dead calm, and an hour later, the sun was trying to come out. Almost immediately everybody started to work, cleaning up the debris scattered by the storm. Mr. Butler hired some extra men to help with the cleanup. Everyone was working as one unit, cutting trees that the wind had blown over, along with all the branches that were scattered about. All of this was cut up for fire wood and stacked along the fence row; there was enough to last for three winters.

The sun peaked out and the temperature rose. The sun beamed down on the exposed ground and what was wet became dry and dusty. And in just a few days, everything was all cleaned up and back to normal.

CHAPTER TWENTY-SIX

It was Saturday, just after the morning feeding was finished, when Jay T told Suzann to go and dig him some grubworms for fishing. Always before when he had told her to dig him some worms, it had always been red worms that he had wanted. But today he had to be different. After the rain he decided that the catfish should be biting. But this time he wanted *grubs*! Suzann was deathly scared of them. She could not do it. She could not handle having one of those things near her, and she was definitely not going to pick one up.

Jay T did not know that she was afraid of them, and she dared not tell him. "Oh god, what am I going to do?" she wondered. She then went on and started doing some other work, pretending that she had forgotten about the worms. It wasn't long until she heard Jay T calling out for her. Knowing what he wanted, she felt her heart as it almost stopped. She paused, clenching her teeth against each other.

"Where are the worms that I told you to dig for me?"

"I haven't got around to digging them yet."

"And just why not?"

"I've been doing all the other things that you told me to do,"

Suzann answered with the psychic feeling that she was going to be forced to do something that she could not bear. Feeling her stomach muscles tighten from the words that Jay T spoke which had been well lubricated with whiskey. He said,

"I told you to dig me some goddamn grubworms and that's exactly what I meant!"

"I can't, not grubs, I'll dig you some red worms, OK?"

130

Suzann felt her lips as they began to tremble along with the rest of her.

"Hell no, it ain't OK and you WILL dig them too." His voice raged with intoxicated anger. He pulled a razor strap down from the barn wall that he used on the cows to make them do what he wanted. Grabbing hold of her arm, he started beating her, leaving a burning stinging pain each time the razor strap raked across her back.

"I can't, Jay T. I can't." Her words were breaking with the tears that flooded her face and ran down her neck.

"You will or else!"

The hostility in his screams echoed above her cries. Then he stopped, taking hold of her shoulders with a strong grip. He began shaking her so hard that her eyes were out of focus.

"Why can't you?" he shouted.

"I'm . . . I'm scared of them."

"YOU'RE WHAT? You're scared of them? I AIN'T NEVER . . . We'll fucking fix that. I'm going to help you not to be scared of them."

Suzann hesitated, not knowing what to say or what he was going to do.

"NO, Jay T. What are you going to do? Jay T, please. I'm begging you."

Pulling her with him to the shed, they went inside, getting a hoe and a can. He started dragging her along with him to the back of the barn. It was all she could do to stay on her feet and keep up with him in this tangled disaster. Jay T began to dig until he uncovered a bed of grubs that lay just beneath the surface of the earth.

"Now," he said. "Pick them up and put them in the can. Pick them up!" He was shouting so hard that there was slobber coming from his mouth.

"They won't hurt you, so pick them up."

"NO, NO, NO," Suzann screamed in fright.

He began to hit her with the front and the back of his hand, leaving clear hand prints with the force of each blow on her face.

"Pick it up," he said, and then he slapped her again. "Pick it up!" And then he hit her again. Over and over. "Pick it up!" When the fury within him had reached its peak, Jay T reached down, picking the razor strap up off the ground. "Pick them up," he shouted.

The strap wrapped around her body, across her arms and legs, leaving no place untouched. He was screaming and cursing, on and on and on. Ripping and ripping with slashes, he continued to beat her. Her breath had become hoarse from the screams that tore through the air like the strap that was tearing into her skin. Her screams stopped as her body went into shock.

The pain was no more, it no longer hurt; the crying had stopped. She just stood there and took it. This might cost her her life, but she had the strength to endure what he was doing. "Pick them up, I said. Pick them up!"

When he stopped, he turned her forward with her back to him and kicked her with his powerful foot to the small of her back, causing her legs to fold up underneath her. He jerked her to her feet by the hair on her head and screamed once again, "Get to the house, go to your room, and don't you even think about coming out for any reason until I tell you that you can. Do you understand?

WELL? Do you hear what I'm saying?"

Suzann could not speak for the agonizing pain that was starting to dominate the senses of her body. She somehow slowly walked back to the house, going through the living room. There was Kate sitting on the couch.

"OH MY GOD," Kate said, in breathless words. The shock she felt was apparent by the grimace on her face. This made Suzann's pain grow even more. Even as the grimace remained, Kate's face began to show a strange sense of enjoyment upon seeing Suzann's pained motions. She continued to just stand there, grinning with malevolent enjoyment, silently waiting as if Suzann needed to give her an explanation.

"Your face," Kate exclaimed. Suzann stared at her through her eyes of broken sprit, filled with self-doubts, trying to fight back but losing in defeat. Suzann just turned and walked away, giving Kate no explanation as she walked into her bedroom and closed the door. Pulling off her shirt only to see what made her heart reach out, begging God to help her. No wonder he had sent her to the house. Her body looked alien. Both eyes were swollen almost shut; blood was running from her nose and one of her ears. Her bottom lip looked like it had been turned inside out. Most of her body was covered with whelps, and there were places where blood was oozing through the breaks in the skin. Her body was stinging and burning so bad. Oh god, how it was now hurting.

Suzann slipped into her house coat and then walked into the bathroom and ran some cool bath water. She sat in the tub, letting the cool water soothe the stinging pain that she was feeling so intensely.

Then there was a knock on the door. She heard her name called out, it was Jay T.

"You don't listen very well, do you?"

"I just . . ."

"I just don't give a damn," he said. "Maybe you would like some more, huh?" OPEN THE DAMN DOOR.

You're gonna start minding me, girl. Now, do like I said and open this door."

Trying to find the strength to do just that, she got out of the tub and dried herself, touching the towel lightly to her skin. Then again she heard his mean voice.

"Come on."

Still standing at the door, he refused to leave.

When she unlocked the door, he stepped in, shutting the door behind him, locking the two of them in the bathroom. Refusing to look at him, Suzann turned her head.

"Come on," he shouted impatiently.

Totally confused, not even knowing what he wanted.

"Turn around, take off your housecoat."

In that moment, Jay T had the look in his eyes, that of a serious one.

Suzann's hands were shaking uncontrollably.

"Well hell, I'll do it."

Reaching out his arms and jerking her housecoat from her, he let it fall to the floor.

The fear that she felt caused her heart to beat frantically. She wanted to burst into tears, searching for any kind of relief. But she held it back and felt the shiver as it went through her bones. As she stood there with nothing on and a broken heart, a tear ran down one side of her face. Jay T was putting his hands on her body, pressing in on the places where the strap had cut into her flesh, letting his eyes fall upon forbidden places. Then he reached down and picked up the housecoat and wrapped it around her. He kept looking at her, licking his lips. Still, she wanted to burst into tears. Guilt and horror filled her. The room started to spin and everything went black as Suzann's limp body hit the floor.

Jay T was looking over his shoulder calling out for Kate to help him. And of course, Kate was in no great hurry, taking her time to get there.

"Open her bedroom door and spread a quilt over the bed."

"What happened?" Kate asked.

"She just passed out."

After laying her down on the bed, the silence magnified the sounds in Suzann's head. She could hear them talking but it sounded so far away, like whispered echoes of words in some deep canyon.

Suzann lay sprawled on her back with one leg hanging over the side of the bed. Looking at her bare body, he picked her leg up and laid it on the bed and then covered her up as if he were trying to hide what he had done. Standing in the shadows of her room, Jay T momentarily enjoyed what he had done, but he had a fear that he had carried it too far this time.

"S-H-I-T," he voiced under his breath. He involuntarily stepped backward out if the room and dropped his stare to the floor. Stumbling over his feet, reluctantly looking at Kate with her darkened, flushed face as she rolled her eyes wildly, he turned and walked away towards the kitchen.

Jay T went to the stove and ladled out some salted bacon grease and rubbed it into his hands and went back into Suzann's room.

Kneeling down beside her bed, he began to rub the grease on her in the places that were cut, thinking that this would minimize the pain and help it heal without scarring.

Then he called out to Kate to come into the room.

"Kate, we have got to keep her locked in this room until this heals. I mean, you will have to take care of her. I want you to bring the food to her and make sure that she does not leave this room. When I get finished here, I will go to the shed and get a hasp and put it on the outside of her door."

"How could you do this? Look at her face, Jay T. You should have never hit her in the face. This will get us caught, you know the plans."

"Right now I don't need you copping an attitude. My resistance weakened, and I lost my temper when she refused to do what I told her. I let my guard drop, I just fucking lost it."

"What if she talks or what if someone sees her?" Kate asked.

"She won't talk and we have to make sure no one sees her. She will recover, she will be fine."

Suzann was trying to wake up and look out of her bloody half closed eyes, there was nothing but a blur. His fingers were open as he continued rubbing the grease all over her body. Her body was throbbing like a toothache. Suzann was awake.

"I know that you are plotting against me, to tell Handy or Jim and Mary. No matter." His eyes narrowed.

"This might interest you and you might want to reconsider before you decide to run and tell." He leaned back, then hesitated for a moment as he rolled up his shirt sleeve. He tried to make it a light joke, but Suzann knew that he meant what he was about to say. "If you tell anyone about this, I'll get revenge and whoever you tell will vanish from this earth."

"You may destroy me, but I will bring you down." She closed her small fist. "I give you my word."

Again, she expected the worst from him because backtalk was not a good thing to do and it always set him off.

"You will not be going to school, and you will not be seeing anyone. And I'm going to lock the door so you can't get out. When you need to go to the bathroom, Kate will be going with you.

"This is all your fault. None of this would have happened if you would have done what I asked."

He was smiling as he opened the door and left. Suzann kept her thoughts to herself. "I hate you. I hate you. I hate your guts, and I wish you were dead." Confined to her room, she knew the nights and days would pass so slowly. It had been a long and trying day. When her pain began to subside, she slowly drifted into a deep sleep.

It was three weeks before Jay T decided to let her go back to school. The bruises that were on the exposed portion of her body were still slightly visible. Jay T told her if anyone asked she would tell them that she had been in a wreck.

During school, everyone pretended to not see the bruises. However Suzann knew that they had. Suzann's fear of Jay T was worse now than ever, and was beginning to affect her dreams. With tears of gratitude she thanked God for letting her live through this and not be scarred.

There was something in hidden silence, something dangerous about Jay T. Her need had been growing, eating holes in her soul, to see her mom and dad.

It was on a weekend when Kate was in the kitchen making cookies, that you could smell the sweet aroma even outside. Suzann went into the house to see what was cooking, complimenting the sweet smell that filled the air.

"Take one, it's made from one of Mother's old recipes that I found. Mmm, they're good. Get you a couple and take Jay T some."

Not having to be told twice, Suzann filled her hands and headed out the door. As she approached Jay T at the barn, she said, "Lunch time," as he took them from her hand. Letting his fingers brush against hers, with a tingle of electricity running through his body, he swore under his breath. He stared at her and shook his head, going into the barn and kicking the barn door shut behind him.

"What did I do?" Suzann wondered. "Just existing is enough," she thought.

That night, Kate went with a neighbor from down the road. She left a message that she would be late coming home, for she had gone with Betty to do some shopping.

After supper and the kids were in bed, Suzann was lying in her bed reading a book by the nightlight when her bedroom door opened. It was Jay T. At first she thought something might be wrong, and then she heard him softly laughing. He then closed the door. Suzann could feel his nearness as he stepped toward her. She braced herself, prepared to scream, to fight if he touched her. Then he took a deep breath, turned, and walked out. After a moment she heard him singing in the bathroom. When had she ever felt so worried? A chill came over her with the various possibilities going over in her mind, wondering what that had been about. Jay T had never come in her room like that before. Then it dawned on her, suddenly thinking that maybe he was drinking again. That's what it was, he was just drinking. Trying to put the thought out of her mind and knowing that three o'clock would come awfully early, she turned off the light. She could still hear him singing in the bathroom and the sound echoed off the walls as he laughed. She lay there thinking that this man is so deranged. Then hearing her stomach as it growled with displeasure, she turned over, hoping sleep would come.

Suzann lay there thinking about all the days when she felt like she could just die, and some of those days, she wished that she had. Then there was nothing in her mind as she slipped into a bothered, sleepy state, observing the stillness and deathly quietness of the night.

Then all of a sudden there was Jay T standing over her, looking down with a halfway smile on his face. When his body came to a stop, he stood there naked with his penis and testicles in his hand.

Suzann couldn't move a muscle. She knew that it was time for Kate, any minute now, to be returning home from shopping. Then he moved closer, his arms seemed forever long, as he reached out and took hold of the covers.

"Shhhhh," he said, "don't be frightened. I'm not going to hurt you this time, I'm going to make you feel good." As he pulled back the covers, Suzann was unable to speak. She was helpless, and her body was paralyzed. He began to unbutton her gown, not moving it out of place. He ran his hands down her legs, they were hard and rough. Then he slowly sat down on the side of the bed, letting his fingers slide underneath her panties, lifting the elastic up and letting it fall against her stomach. He looked like he was foaming at the mouth, with fire in his eyes, from what she could see from the small amount of light in her room. She was terribly afraid as she gripped the sheet and shivered, making a choking sound in her throat. She felt like she was going to throw up.

The alarm clock was going off; it was three o'clock in the morning, time to get up. She woke up on her last nerve, looking about the room to see if anyone was there; the room was empty. It had just been a dream. "Dream, hell," she thought. "It was a nightmare."

She was feeling mad and upset with herself, wondering how she could possibly have such a dream. "Stop it," she commanded her mind desperately as she threw back the covers to get up. As she pushed herself to her feet, she panicked instantly. With mingled feelings of disgust as she stretched out her arms to wake herself, she saw that her gown was unbuttoned and thought that she must have not buttoned it the night before. Fright masked her face as she stood in front of the mirror, getting dressed.

"You are so pretty," Dwan complimented.

"Oh, you scared me. What are you doing up this time of morning?"

"I was getting a drink of water. Well, goodnight again; I'm going back to bed."

Suzann could feel the verge of failure, wondering if she should throw in the towel or try to keep hanging on. She felt the need to have a long talk with Handy which would be a relief if only she could do that. With the most powerful impulse and her innermost feelings, she hated Jay T so much. Knowing that she was supposed to love not hate, but she loved hating him.

He had her under his control and now she was trying to do anything to keep him from beating her. But it was so hard to please him. She didn't know what to do until she was old enough to get away. She would have to keep a strong will and be determined to get through this.

She hated to imagine what he would do if she told someone and he found out about it. This was a tremendous burden, living every day in fear for her life and the lives of others that she loved. She had to stay strong, she thought to herself without much enthusiasm. But first and foremost, she had to protect her mom and dad and Handy.

Suzann was down at the barn doing his jobs while he lay his fat ass up in bed. She was uncomfortable and defensive even when he wasn't around. She had become paranoid, but she had learned to never utter a complaint to Jay T, not a word. She knew she wasn't wanted or loved by them, she was just needed there to do their work for them. In spite of her determination to survive this ordeal, she would retreat behind a wall of self-pity on occasion. These moments didn't last very long. In her mind she could always see his eyes. They seemed to reflect something that was deep and dangerous.

Suzann sensed the danger every time that she was around him; nevertheless, there was nothing she could do about it at this time. She was tossing and turning with the dawning of the new day. After getting breakfast done, she had to gather the cows up and get the milking started. She went into the feed room and shoveled up enough feed to last for the morning. After using the shovel for a while, with the fire going in the barn and closed doors keeping out the cold, it began to get very warm. She pulled off her coat and threw it over in the corner of the room where it fell to the floor. Suddenly, Jay T appeared in the doorway.

"There is no denying it; you should not be so good-looking," he said. Suzann raised her eyes only to find that Jay T was standing at the door, watching her with his eyes centered on her slender body, staring at the shirt that was tucked in at the low waistband of her jeans, making her painfully aware of his nearness. She felt that distance was the best and most effective weapon to counteract this looming threat. He stepped down into the feed room, slamming the door shut behind him,

"Stay put," he ordered.

Suzann eased the shovel down onto the floor, knowing that something was up from reading the message in the smoldering darkness of his eyes. She instantly forgot all and any thoughts she might have had and centered her attention on him.

"What's wrong?" she nervously asked.

"Oh damn," he muttered, looking at her as he moved from the door towards where she was standing. His presence dominated the room along with his perspiration, mixed with the rest of his body odors from what smelled like two weeks ago that was still clinging to him. The stench drifted in her direction while he was licking his bloodless lips. Biting her own lower lip, she turned and rolled her eyes upward throwing her hands outward.

"There's just no place I can go," she declared.

"You're right about that," Jay T responded.

She cocked her head to one side with a doubtful expression covering her face.

"Oh, Jay T, no. You can't allow yourself to do this."

"Why not? I'm perfectly capable of . . ."

"What about me?" she asked.

"You? It's your fault. All them nights looking at yourself in the mirror. Playing with yourself, running you hands over and around your tits and playing with your little cunt. You're always wearing these . . . these tight-ass pants, showing every curve in your ass. Prissing your ass around here and letting me unbutton your gown and feel you while you lay there enjoying it."

"That's a lie."

"Why, you little bitch."

Once again she felt the burning sting across her face from his open hand.

"Please, just leave me alone. I do everything that you tell me." Her voice was low and breaking. His eyes hooded over her again,

"That's the whole problem," he muttered in a strange tone.

"You get your way too damn much."

"That's not true and you know it."

Not listening to a thing she said, his fingers cupped her face and lifted it up and forced her to look into his eyes where she saw the melting roughness of his face. She swallowed hard as panic and the need to escape once again overtook her mind. Instead, she just stood there, afraid of what he would do if she tried to get away and afraid of what he would do if she didn't. Her composure snapped

"You're disgusting," she screamed, fighting back the deluge of tears that was lodged in her throat.

"What the hell is wrong with you?" Her words were interrupted by his half amused and half impatient laughter.

Tearing her eyes away from him, she breathed deeply in an effort to calm her ragged nerves.

"I've got to go," she said, knowing that if she didn't get to the house and get the rest of her work done she would not be allowed to go to school, and she could not stand the thought of being here all day.

"You'll go when I say you can and I have not said that you can go yet."

"But the cows out there are almost finished milking."

"What you need to do is not worry about those goddamn cows." He nodded briefly. "OK?"

Through her trembling lips, Suzann managed to whisper an answer.

"Yes, I understand. Just don't hurt me anymore."

"Well, stand your ass still then and stop fighting me."

He guided his rough hands that roamed her breasts leisurely, until he started to unfasten the hook that freed them to his touch. With no bra on for a deterrent, they spilled freely into his seeking rough hands.

"God, Suzann," he moaned. "Your tits are just right, growing like they have been. In another year they will be too big for both my hands."

With a starving urgency in his voice, the knotting hardness of his muscle was a dead giveaway. He took hold of her hair, pulling her head backwards, plunging down on her lips with bruising force from the desperate pressure that he forced upon her, hunching at her bones like a vicious dog. Yet he didn't venture any father.

Suzann gave in completely to the new experience, she didn't know anything else to do at this moment. As the tears spilled over and ran down her face, she could feel her heart beating through her chest wall. Not knowing what to expect next, she knew that she had no choice but to stand there and take it, letting him do as he pleased. She knew that her purity, her virginity, was somehow of importance to him. But now, he was taking every advantage of her that he could. It was like she was in training to do as he wanted. But his method of punishment to make her do as he pleased was not understood.

Continuing to let his hands roam, he slid them down the front of her pants to unsnap them. Suzann was trying to pull his hands away but it was like trying to pick up a truck—absolutely no use.

"Don't worry about school this morning," he said.

"If Kate should say anything to you, just tell her that I kept you here to help me and that I said to let you go on to school."

Pleading with him to leave her alone was like talking to a brick wall.

"If you ever tell anyone about this, I'll kill you. This is between you and me. We will call it our secret. No one else is to know, you do understand?"

She looked at him helplessly, knowing that she had no other choice, feeling shame and disgust from being manipulated by him for all the wrong reasons.

"I want to hear you say it!" She shook her head violently at him with her answer. "Yes."

Tears threatened her once again as she opened her mouth to tell him, quietly and firmly, once and for all what he wanted to hear.

"I'm not going to tell a soul."

That night, with sleep far from her eyes, she paced the floor, now blaming herself. Her feelings were coming unraveled, and her thoughts rose suddenly with an unexpected idea that gave her goose bumps. Trying to close her eyes, thinking there's always tomorrow.

Drying the tears from her eyes in the stillness of her bedroom, she lay across her bed unable to find peace within her heavy heart. Her nerves exploded as she began to pound the pillow and feel the tears once again spill over onto her checks as she lay there staring at the ceiling. Recollections of past horrors nagged at her and made her wonder what tomorrow might bring. With the want and need to be in one place and being forced to live at another, she spent most of her days trying to be happy but feeling the sadness beneath her smile. Her heart ached for Jim and Mary and was sometimes unable to analyze her own feelings, or could it be that she was refusing to face the facts. And when she looked deep within herself, she got a choking feeling. With nothing to live for but tomorrow and a prayer that it would be better than all yesterdays, she continued on.

Suzann was now fighting another feeling of hate for Jay T and having a thought that was hard to accept, thinking of ways to get rid of this sadistic man. In her heart and mind, she was saturated with the evilness of his doing to the point that she could hardly bear it. She wondered if maybe he was Satan himself.

Outwardly to the public and people that she knew, she always put on a brave front even though she sometimes felt that she was mentally and physically falling apart. She made sure that no one could see her suffering and grief. She fed off of the good memories of her mom and dad and having a friend like Handy. But she knew that she was being engulfed with hate for Jay T, and she felt assured that a trigger would only be too easy to pull. But there was no gun in the house and no access to one that she knew of. She knew that Jay T hated guns and would not allow one in the house.

"Now I know why," she thought to herself. "I might be smaller than he is but a gun would make me as big as he is. Could I pull the trigger?" she asked herself, knowing all along that she could and would at this point in her life.

Suzann would not dare to speak a word of this to anyone. She felt cold and sticky all over as if she had just made a bargain with the devil. Reconstructing all the events that had happened, this dark evil movie now went racing through her mind and it would not go away. Hearing his inhuman laugh and hearing the echoes of her own cries was creating a dark empty place inside of her. She could feel a stab of fear when she realized the things that she was thinking. But still there was a touch of rational hope left.

Then she remembered something that Jay T had said. "Either shit or get off of the pot," meaning, don't think about it, just do it. Maybe she'd do just that. One thing was for sure, Jay T wouldn't like the results. The thought made her smile.

CHAPTER TWENTY-SEVEN

There were now so many skeletons in Suzann's closet that it was unsafe to open the door for fear of getting buried underneath them. She was stuck between a rock and a hard place, with no way out. Her feelings grated on her like sand on raw flesh. Her need to talk to Handy was swelling in her heart and mind, knowing that she was hanging by a thread if she got caught and that she would be putting Handy in harm's way. She knew that she could confide in him and trust that it would go no further. The timing could not be better than now because Jay T was in a meeting with the boss man today, and usually that was an all-day affair. Fighting the impulse that ran through her, she decided to play her hand and pay him a visit.

Handy appeared stunned when he saw her standing at the end of the gravel drive where he was working. Then she walked down the drive and slipped through the gate. As she drew closer, Handy guessed that something was wrong by the look he saw on her face.

He paused briefly, wondering what to say to her, and it was easy to see that she was struggling to find the strength to force the words from her lips. She was weeping.

"Oh my god, Suzann, what's wrong? Come on, come with me and let's go somewhere where we can talk, where it will be safe."

They walked to the big hay barn where Suzann's hideaway was, that Handy had fixed for her to do her studies. Handy spoke in a comforting voice. "Talk to me, baby girl. I'm here and no one is going to hurt you while you are with me."

146

"Suzann looked up at Handy with tears in her eyes and again struggled to speak.

"Handy, things are really bad. There is so much that you don't know, nobody really knows." Handy was alarmed by her actions. Suzann proceeded to tell him about the beating and being out of school for three weeks to give her time to heal and being locked in her room with no way out. Handy's face turned red all over, the air had a soft warm feeling to it, but now it was filled with anger and it was all from Handy. There was no problem to see that he was very upset. "Why haven't you already told me about this?"

Suzann dropped her head, and softly spoke. "Handy, he told me that if I breathed a word to you or my mom or dad that he would kill you and them and me for telling."

Handy thought resentfully and wondered to himself what kind of world this was and why would God let such things happen to someone like her. "Listen, I want you to promise me that from now on you will tell me everything that he is doing when it comes to you. You don't even worry about me, I can take care of myself. But I don't think you should tell your mom or dad. And I am going to keep a closer watch on you."

"Handy, I just remembered that you do a lot of hunting and I wondered if you would show me how to use a gun."

Handy lifted his head, and with a stern voice he said, "What are you saying? What are you thinking? I would be glad to show you how to use a gun but not for the thought that you have in mind. You forget what you are thinking; you put that out of your mind. I will take care of things. You just keep in touch with me. Any time you can't find me, you leave me a note. I will leave my window raised enough so you can stick it in my room, and I'll make sure no one sees it."

She looked away and he grabbed her tightly and held her, trying to give her comfort. What he had seen had only been a part of the picture but now he knew more of the truth. But Handy still didn't know everything. Suzann could not believe that she had told him this much but she just could not bring herself to tell him the rest. She felt so ashamed and embarrassed to tell him that Jay T put his hands on her.

Suzann stood there awkwardly, not knowing what to do or say now.

"Suzann, you do realize that I'll do anything that you asked of me. Do you hear me?"

She unfolded her arms and hugged him.

"I don't want you to do anything to him. He doesn't treat the others like this, just me. Maybe he will change because I think that they were really worried that I was going to be scarred but . . . I don't know. I don't know. I would demand his execution but everyone that knows him would defend him, they would think that I would be telling a lie just to try to get back home to Mom and Dad. No one would believe me. Jay T has already told me that. And I believe him." There was a little sob as she tilted her head up to look at Handy, seeing him wring his hands together in front of him. Suzann was trying to control her feelings but was having little luck. What she had told Handy now had him badly frightened for her sake, for her to have been brought into this hellish nightmare and having to live in the same house with the likes of Jay T, facing one great hurdle after another. It had to be stopped.

Handy, in his own wilderness of experience, had learned inexplicable truths about life but this was one way of life that he never thought he would experience.

Satan himself had too much credit, like Jay T. Satan is fallen, so is Jay T. Satan's time is limited and now so is Jay T's. And Satan will someday find his second death, and the day is coming that Jay T will find his first. Jay T is one of our bigger enemies and he has to be stopped.

Handy walked out and stood on his front porch steps after Suzann left to go back home. He looked on both sides where the grass was cut fresh and green and full of rich life. His thoughts were cold, stiff, and cunning; she left him somehow feeling responsible for her life. He felt like she could not make it without his help, and he recognized pain when he saw it. His exasperation had taken form and recalled senseless sights from the war that he had hidden deep within himself. Kill them all and let God sort them out, that was what he heard and the children were the ones to suffer. His thoughts unfurled as he remembered the last engagement where he saw women and children put to death by their own people. He was ordered not to interfere, not to engage. He and others had to stay hidden in the bush. All they could do was watch. After that, he made himself a promise that he would not do that again, that he would never stand by and watch another child be hurt or killed.

His thoughts held danger and he knew it. His soldiering days had taken away any qualms he had about killing as long as the right people were getting killed. Handy thought to himself, he could not afford to fuck up. He would have to set up and plan things right in this delicate situation for Suzann. He found himself changing somehow, going back to the other side where he felt alone, living in a section of hell called war. He knew that it could not be a dastardly plan, or could it be? Deep down, he felt an exhilarating thrill with the thought of standing face to face with Jay T. Combat was simple, one winner and one loser. In his mind, the fact that he was standing here thinking was testament enough of his abilities as a fighter. This is something he could do, he would defend her. He knew that an element of surprise would work to his advantage, he would keep his mouth shut, his eyes open.

Jay T was riding a broomstick and flying by the seat of his pants and he had no idea of the vengeful plans being put in place or who opted to remove him from the ground that he soiled as he walked on it.

CHAPTER TWENTY-EIGHT

Homemade biscuits and blackberry jelly were hot on the stove with a big bowl of scrambled eggs,\ waiting to be eaten. Suzann started to leave for her usual morning work when Jay T stepped out in the hall and into her path. It was an accident for the two of them almost ran over each other. Suzann hesitated to open the door as she stood there receiving the astounded look that Jay T was giving her. Speechless for a moment, his voice had softened when he said,

"Good morning."

Implicitly reading his eyes, she reached for the door and proceeded out with no desire or intention whatsoever of speaking to him. With hostility clouding her mind, she wondered if this morning would be good and if she had induced any sleepless nights of regret on him, like the sleepless nights of horror he had brought upon her. As she walked down the stone steps and off the front porch, a question was running through her mind, what would be his expectations of her today.

In this early morning, the shadows from the moon were long and eerie as she walked quietly through the field, rounding up the cows. Most of them were like trained dogs. When they saw you coming they automatically knew to get up and where to go. Following the path to the barn on the right side of it, she could see the fog rising from the ponds, giving it a ghostly atmosphere with the flickering light from the moon.

Walking down along this path was always spooky and it gave her a feeling of not wanting to go any farther. But even with the restraining feeling, she knew that she had to continue.

Suzann wanted to laugh as her mind somehow compared this dark trail to the darkness that she was facing every day. The trouble was that nothing was funny about either one, and these days, the essence of a smile or laugh was hard for her to find.

Living with her mom and dad with kindness and gentleness and now living here was a 180-degree turn around, and having that flash through her mind only reminded her of Jay T's violence and his torment. It was becoming a rage that burned within her with no exit out. Without a pause in her ethics there would no compromise. He would not stop taking until she was completely broken and or dead. She needed someone to hear her out. But more than that she needed a savior, a white knight to champion her cause and lift her from this fecal mire that she was being forced to live in. "Yes," she thought. "I shovel shit in the morning, I walk in shit all afternoon, and I have to put up with Kate and Jay T's shit all day and all night. I would definitely call it fecal mire." The thought brought only a sarcastic smile. Maybe only a fool would listen. Jay T and Kate could put up quite a believable front. Maybe she would be the fool for telling because Jay T had promised cruel retribution for the telling of her tales to anyone. Each step upon the old cow trail took her a step through her dark memories. In judging, she wanted to think of herself as one of a kind. Her individuality and independent spirit had been nurtured and allowed to grow with Jim and Mary. Here, it had been and was squashed and stomped on like some kind of unwanted insect. As her thoughts cascaded through her mind, she found those that would never be known by anyone but her. These private keepsakes were like dark ominous rolling and twisting thunderclouds, full of deafening thunder with jagged lightning. The earlier teachings from her mom and dad of love and kindness were like the lighter wispy little clouds that floated daintily above the evil chaos. They were still there but hardly ever seen.

But she was trying to escape this storm by calling on Handy who gladly acknowledged the hell and wrongdoings to the innocent by

Jay T. He welcomed the chance to right this wrong even more than Suzann knew. She believed in her intuitions. She had unknowingly sensed the strength that Handy normally kept hidden.

Handy understood himself and knew that he was better off away from people. Suzann had invaded that privacy and he had welcomed it. This invasion had brought back a part of himself that he had stored away a long time ago.

On the opposite side of that, she somehow knew but did not understand the evil natures of Kate and Jay T. Her young mind constantly questioned why they acted as they did. Was it a sickness or was it Satan running the show? "It is evil," she decided.

What she did not know was that evil has a way of creeping into a person unknown to them. Even if she survived this ordeal, she would not come out unscathed. Her soul, like her body, would always carry the scars from this nightmarish hell.

"Justice," she decided. "Would be served with the death of Jay T and probably Kate." Her decision came not only for the things that they had done to her; it also came from their cruelties toward the younger children. These acts had been seen and noticed by her. She felt that there were probably as bad or worse happenings buried in each of their pasts.

It would be just another soul the county would have to claim, one more identity in the dirt. "That would be the first time he could not open his mouth." Suzann was thinking out loud to herself. What she could only tell would be the story, and even then, she would repeat it for good measure as she heard the gasps of the crowd and saw the anticipation of the listeners for the words to come. There would be no reason for her not to reveal the truth; if for nothing else, to prevent this kind of pain and help someone else in life. To stop anyone from taking advantage of those who could not protect themselves from someone who might be guilty of doing what Jay T had done. Regardless of the consequences, you make your own bed and you sleep in it. No matter who you might be.

She wondered how many cruel and senseless acts he would take to the grave with him; uncalled for, but forced upon others by him. A chill coursed through her as she tried to pull her thoughts back to what she was doing. It was not from the early morning coolness. She dreaded to see Jay T when he arrived, but she was now waiting for him. She waited and waited but there was no Jay T.

Suzann started for the holding room where the milk was stored into a large tank and kept cool while waiting for pickup. Passing the window, she saw the top of Jay T's head. Trying to swallow the lump that had risen in her throat, she stood in the shadows watching something that she knew she should not be watching. Her eyes grew larger as she crossed her hands over her mouth, watching.

His hands were extended a short distance in front of his body and then they would disappear. With a grabbing, swiping, and encircling motion, he groaned for a second, jerking. Then he seemed to slump with the appearance of relaxing every muscle in his body. Suzann could not believe what she had just witnessed. Her heart pulsed with the thought of how to escape without attracting his attention.

"God help me," she thought as she stepped slowly back into the part of the barn she had just left, praying that he had not seen her. She felt somewhat sick to her stomach. Her numbness had just worn off when Jay T entered the barn where she was. With no words passed, Suzann headed to the house with another image painted in her head. She wanted to run and just keep on running, but like always, on tiptoe. She trailed up the steps and directly into the house. Being grateful to just get away unnoticed, she quickly changed her clothes and ran the distance to where she would be getting on the school bus. Only after she was seated and the bus had taken off did her heart begin to slow down.

CHAPTER TWENTY-NINE

Suzann was becoming quite a writer in her hideaway. If the opportunity arose, she would slip out to the hay barn and climb to the loft where she could be alone to study. Curled up in the hay, she was cooled by the draft spiraling up from the hall of the lower part of the barn. She loved to write poetry. She could not and would not let Jay T or Kate know, because she knew that they would burn it like they did all things that were close to her. Things that she wrote would be related to her life or what she was studying in school. That would sometimes get her extra grades to help make up for the many days that she had missed.

There was one poem that she wrote, when the class was studying the Bible, that the teacher liked very much. She was impressed to the point that she had it published in the school paper. When Suzann's teacher approached her and asked for permission to publish the poem, it was one of the best days of Suzann's life. For once, she felt that she had accomplished something, done something right, that someone was proud of her. Even if she was only Suzann's teacher, she cared.

Excitedly, Suzann waited for the next issue of the paper to be published so she would be able to read her poem in print. She could hardly wait to show her mom and dad, for she knew that they would be proud.

Finally, Wednesday came. It was the day that she had been longing for. Today was the day that the school paper came out. There it was. She could hardly believe her own eyes as she slowly read.

I KNOW I KNOW THE ANSWER

I know I know the answer
God lives on earth today
He gave his son for you and me
So that our souls may be saved

They made him drag that rugged cross
Upon Calvary's hill
And if they had not taken it down
It stands there still

They drove the nails in his hands and feet
And on his head there sat a crown
With blood dripping from the thorns
Running to the ground

He stayed on the cross,
And finally gave away
And then there came a special moment
Of that special day

They took him down, took off the crown
And threw it miles away
And then they put him in that tomb
On that special day

He stayed in that tomb, with time slowly counting down
Until the darkness filled the air
And rocks moved upon the ground
Then he arose and entered the sky
And why we say that the Lord never did die.

Written by
Suzann

Suzann loved the last part the best, the part that showed who wrote it. It was her name in print. Then after reading it, she felt somewhat downhearted. Her tears lay very near the surface but she tried hard not to show it. The reading of it had made her feel so homesick that she could hardly endure the happiness of it. She was angry with herself for her own weakness, but nevertheless, she could not control the tears that were shed.

As her teacher approached Suzann, she leaned down and planted a kiss on Suzann's forehead.

"Stop looking on the dark side. You're young, strong, and you have your health; and that in itself is a lot more than some will ever have. I just hope that you keep on with your writing. True, I know that it is hard for you. But whatever you do, don't quit school."

The sound of her voice and the words that she said got Suzann's attention and she vowed to her that she would never do anything to jeopardize her education.

There was a long silent and worried look that fell over Suzann. Jay T and Kate had no idea of what had happened for she had kept it a secret. Only Handy knew. But Suzann knew that it would only be a short time before they found out about the paper. Jay T and Kate could burn this one if they wanted to, but there were other copies. They could not destroy all of them. What has been done is done and she was not going to worry about it now.

That night after supper, Suzann found herself staring at Kate who seemed to be smoldering over something. All puffed up like a big frog with one big roll of fat from her double chin that sagged down to her shoulders.

"Suzann," Jay T spoke. "Dwan showed me the school paper this afternoon when she got home. What have you got to say about it?"

Suzann suddenly drew up and became very still, feeling her heart sink. Not being able to look at him, she dropped her eyes towards her plate. "I did it to get extra work in school to help pick up my grades. Did you like it?"

"Dwan read it to me. I can't say that I did. What you wrote about I think you should leave alone."

Suzann answered him, "I wrote about God, what's wrong with that?"

"What God? You sound like my mother. Now she's dead."

"My teacher liked it and had it put in the paper, and I got the extra grade that I needed for the days you kept me home from school."

"I reckon you could have come and asked me," Jay T growled.

"I didn't know," Suzann explained.

Jay T was rolling a cigarette from a bag of smoking tobacco that he always kept in the bib of his overalls or in his shirt pocket along with a pack of rolling paper. Suzann rearranged the food on her plate as she watched his yellow stained fingers that positioned the tobacco carefully in place.

Then there was a deep peel of thunder that went rolling, tumbling down from the heavens and lost itself in the distance. Nothing moved except the curtains stirring in a sluggish breeze that whispered through the open window. The wind passed, rustling the branches on the trees outside. Then large rain drops began to slap the roof of the house like acorns that had broken away from their stems, while everyone sat silently and still.

"In the future, I hope you will be more careful and not let this happen again." His voice was precise and to the point.

Suzann cleared her throat nervously as she poured the second cup of coffee into his cup, watching him as he dipped the sugar and cream, losing herself in the swirls of the tan coffee moving around in his cup. She answered the question to his satisfaction so Jay T got up mumbling to himself as he moved away from the table with his fresh cup of coffee in hand. There it was again, that useless emptiness and not being able to please anyone, that feeling that she so often encountered.

After everyone had left the table and was getting ready for bed, Suzann hesitated but only for a moment. Rolling up her sleeves, she began to rake out the dishes. Standing over the sink, looking out the window, she watched the rain fall to the ground. She felt terribly disillusioned about everyone here. After she had finished, she filled the tub with water, as hot as she could stand it. A long relaxing bath was what she needed. She splashed the water over her, letting it run over her skin, soothing her aching muscles, ones that she didn't even know existed. Drying herself with a towel, she slipped into her nightgown. "Wonderful," she said under her breath as she entered her bedroom and closed the door behind her. That night, when she finally went to sleep, it was with her school paper snuggled tightly to her chest. But she had read it over again and again until sleep closed the words for her. No matter what Jay T and Kate thought, she was proud of what had happened.

The first thing that Suzann heard early the next morning was the roosters' crowing. It sounded like they were trying out for a duet. And in Suzann's uncalled-for opinion, it sounded so much better than Jay T's screaming voice. The moon always had a friendly face when gleaming down, like a spotlight on a stage for the waking birds.

Then she heard a tone with an icy chill. "Get off your ass and on your feet." It was the one and only Jay T.

She quickly swung her feet to the floor and hurriedly put her clothes on. Then she walked into the kitchen.

"Well, if it ain't our little poet and don't I know it," he said with rueful look on his face. Suzann was curious why he was already up and in the kitchen putting his own coffee on. She watched him hesitantly measure the amount that he was to use. But she was ignoring his imperfection and his early morning amusement with himself. Usually, these sarcastic moods that he got in were followed by a drink and then accompanied with something bad.

"What's wrong with Mom, is she sick?" Dwan asked.

"Yes, your mother is sick."

Suzann was becoming more involved in the bad events, and each time she would ask herself, "What is happening? Everything is so hush-hush, and having to play dumb so much, I am starting to feel dumb."

Then Kate prissed her ass in front of Suzann and started to say something, but Suzann stopped her before she had time to get out the first word.

"Spare me your crap," Suzann said, cutting Kate off short with a fast and irritated movement, moving away from her, for Kate had touched a raw nerve with Suzann. Then she looked in to Kate's face but there was no sign of a guilty conscience to be seen.

CHAPTER THIRTY

Suzann hurried down the long shiny hallway running late for her class with her heels clicking, the sound echoed like she was stepping on small firecrackers. She was hoping that the classroom door would be open so she could slip in without so much notice, but that did not happen.

"Please join us," Miss Wiggly said with heavy sarcasm in her voice. "Take a seat; we were discussing how to obey the golden rule and forward thinking. You know, like, reading, writing and arithmetic."

Miss Wiggly was solidly built with a touch of gray at her temples, a small frame and suspicious eyes. She most certainly would have had to have some rugby experience on her resumé. Suzann felt particularly stupid as she searched her brain for the right response.

"I'm sorry for being late but I had an unavoidable delay," she said.

It had been a long and interesting day at school. Suzann got off the bus to find Handy sitting on the front porch steps. His smile told her that there was nothing wrong even though it was unusual for him to be there. "Jay T had to take Kate to the hospital. She'll probably have the baby today or tonight. The young ones are napping so maybe you'll be able to do your homework or at least enjoy some quiet time before you have to do your chores. I've got to go finish a couple of things before my day is through. Do you need anything?"

She smiled back at him and said, "No, I think I can handle it from here, but thank you for watching the kids. I'm surprised that they even thought about it."

He laughed at her comment and replied, "I know what you mean. Well, if you need anything, just holler at me. I'll see you later."

Hours passed and it was later in the evening when Jay T came in.

"It's a boy," he said, as he walked in the house.

"Kate is fine, but the baby . . . well, I don't know."

"What is wrong with the baby?" Suzann asked.

"The doctor said that it may not survive. But even if it does, it would have to stay in the hospital several weeks even after Kate comes home. I can't remember the words that he used, let alone know what they mean. It was something about a water head and it coming a little before it was time. It looked almost inhuman, with all the tubes going into its body, and its head looked almost as long as the rest of its body."

If Suzann didn't know better, she thought for a second she saw a tear in his eye but again she was wrong. Jay T placed his hand on her shoulder. "The doctor said that if the baby did make it, it would have to get special attention for a good while. Until Kate gets home, I need you to stay home from school and take care of the kids and the house; it should only be for a couple of days. And then it will be the weekend so you should be back in school on Monday." His voice was deep and worried, and somehow he seemed a different person. That was a person that Suzann would like to see more of. She gazed at him with sympathy blanketing her features, not for him but for the baby. That night she silently prayed. The next morning Jay T was up and getting ready to leave for the hospital when he informed Suzann that Handy was taking care of everything at the barn this morning.

Jay T stood out in the hall of the nursery looking at the baby through the window. The baby was slid back behind the panels for viewing. The nurses moved around what looked like a little monster admiringly, checking and testing the complex gnarl of plastic tubes with a series of expert palpations that almost looked like small caresses.

"Hello, Jay T," Dr. Somers spoke.

"What chance does he have to live?" Jay T asked in a shaky voice.

"Jay T, I'll be as honest with you as I know how. He has about a fifty-fifty chance right now. All of his vitals are stable but he has other problems, which is an enlargement of the cranium or head caused by an abnormal accumulation of cerebrospinal fluid within the cerebral ventricular system. And all that means is he has water on the brain. Now don't get all bent out of shape. This is something that can occur in what you would think to be a normal adult. But it is usually associated with a congenital defect in infants. Four out of one thousand infants from birth to three months of age develop hydrocephalus. Now listen, I know that this is hard for you to understand, but it is the only way I know to tell you. Now, there are two types of hydrocephalus. Number one is whether there is abnormal absorption of the cerebrospinal fluid or an obstruction to its flow. The first one that I mentioned is communicating hydrocephalus where there are some abnormalities in the capacity to absorb fluid from the subarachnoid space. There is no obstruction to the fluid between the ventricles. Now, in non-communicating hydrocephalus there is an obstruction at some point in the ventricular system. An infection can cause a ventricular hemorrhage, and can be a frequent problem in premature infants, and is what we have here. Medical treatment has had only limited success in controlling the secretion of cerebrospinal fluid and relieving hydrocephalus. Now, in my opinion the baby's chances are slim to none if we were to go in that route. The most effective treatment would be surgical correction in this case. This child will require frequent changing of position of the head as well as the rest of the body. If this is not done, decubitus ulcers will take over the head, that means sores will form due to its lying on its head. This is a constant threat because of the weight and size of the head and the child's inability to move it. It has to be picked up frequently, especially during feeding periods. You've got to be careful and support the head well when it's being held. Now all these things have to be done when you take him home, be careful with the head, because it will be weak, and it will take a while for its strength to regain. Now when we get through all this, the major complications to be avoided are obtrusion and infection. So it's very important that he gets the right care at home. Now there's some paperwork to be signed by you so we can get started. If you have any questions, let me know. Don't be afraid to ask. Oh, Kate is fine and she can go home in a couple of days. I'll let you know when the baby can go but it will be a while."

The next couple of days passed quickly and then Kate was home. She didn't seem to care one way or another what happened to the baby.

Suzann didn't know what the solution to Kate's problem was, but Suzann felt like an outsider trapped in the inside of a place that was filled with cruelty. She was mortified. It takes two to make a bargain and it takes two to uphold it. But Kate and Jay T didn't even know what the words meant. But there are those who do.

It had been seven weeks now and they were finally going to let the baby come home. Suzann was so shocked that Kate had only gone to see him one time while he was in the hospital. Jay T went to the hospital every other night. Suzann was glad of the nights that he was gone because it gave her a chance to get caught up on her schoolwork.

The afternoon that the baby was to be brought home, everything was all ready for him. The wind had a freshened sent to it as everyone stood outside waiting for the new arrival

"Does it come with an instruction book on how to take care of a newborn?" Dwan asked.

"No, it is not a toy that you put together, it has already been assembled." Suzann shook her head and giggled as she answered. Suzann admired Dwan's face even as she looked very confused.

"You are so not right," Suzann said.

"What does that mean?" Dwan asked.

"That means . . . look, here they come."

Concentrating now on nothing but seeing this new baby, they watched the car pull into the drive and Jay T get out of the car.

You would think that Kate would have shown a happy face but it was not there. It was quite the opposite. But like everything else, things come to surface when least expected. After all the ooohs and ahhs, Suzann and Dwan decided to go walking to the old cemetery that was only a few feet across the pasture but they went around the road. Suzann had seen this cemetery all the time but had never been in it. Today seemed to be the perfect day to go. It was a good two-mile walk. There was an old house that sat next to it and no one had lived there for years because it was said to be haunted and that was a good reason not to go there. But today, even though it was getting late, their curiosity got the better of them. When they got there, there was a steel rod fence that went all the way around; like it was trying to keep something in or maybe it was to keep something out. In the front, there were double gates that swung open to the left and to the right and met in the middle when it was closed. It had at one time been the color of black. It had once been black but was not quite rusty. The years had taken its toll on it and even the rails were now bent in some places. The gates were not hard to open; they just made a squeaking sound that would make anyone grit their teeth, plus send a chill down their spine. After they had entered the gates and walked a few dozen steps, they looked behind them and the gates were closing on their own. The eerie sound of the closing gates and the heavy stillness of the graveyard left conflicting feelings in their bodies. It was everything but comfortable, even in the daylight hours. The trees there stood tall and big around and must have been there for over a hundred years. There were limbs and brush lying all over the graveyard. As they walked hand in hand, they could feel the dampened breeze as the wind pressed against their face. It was hard to make out the faint letters on some of the stones from age and moss. Nature was doing its best to erase the fact that any person, living or dead, had ever been there, while the long dead and the stones lay there in peace. Some of the bigger limbs had given their life to the earth as they lay there in decay. The leaves lay over the cemetery like a carpet laid by the majestic winds of time. There was little grass, for the leaves and limbs had smothered it out. They were looking for two graves which were supposed to be of the people who had lived in the house across the fence. Even their names were creepy, Mr. and Mrs. Lucifer. But there were so many, it was like searching for a needle in a haystack. The tombstones were so weathered by wind, rain, snow, and ice from the many years past to the point that some of them seemed ancient, even primitive. Some of the inscriptions were impossible to read but some were easily deciphered. Of the legible tombstones there were a few that were marked with strange significant biblical words that seemed to magnify the mysterious feeling of a supernatural presence. They found a couple of stones that had strange symbols engraved in them that made Suzann wonder if the writings were indeed heavenly or demonic. The chill that she had felt earlier seemed to grow and tighten its grip on her. The farther back into the cemetery they went, the darker it got. But of course it was getting late as the day was slowly giving way to the darkness. There were graves that sat on top of the ground like boxes with concrete lids that sat on top of them where all you would have to do is move it and find the corpse looking back at you. But it would take some awfully big men to move one of those.

Dwan asked in a whispering voice, "Are you ready to go?"

Suzann answered in a joking manner, "Wonder how many of those poisonous tales are true that people tell and say about this place which they call evil. We live in a house of evil; it is safer here than there."

"Will you hush and come on," Dwan said in a serious tone. Then they noticed how quiet it was except for the twigs snapping under their feet and some rustling of branches among the trees. But the earth was soft under the underbrush. They came upon a couple of graves towards the back, next to the fence, which had sunk to the point that they looked as if nature or something had uncovered them for a reason. It looked like if you were to move the leaves, they could have seen what was preserved there. But they respected the dead and their reserved rights and began to find their way out. Then, like a magnet, something stopped Suzann as she turned around to see if there was a readable inscription on the tomb. To her surprise the writing was very clear, and it read:

Mr. and Mrs. Lucifer

They live Wife and Husband

As Suzann knelt down beside the tombstone and brushed way some of the dirt that had embedded in some of the leaders, there she found written in fine print:

We cometh forth like a flower

And are cut down . . . yeah,

Man giveth up the ghost

"Well, that does it," Suzann said, the dampness soaked into her and it was chilling to the bone.

"Let's get out of here."

"Amen to that," Dwan whispered.

"It's funny that you would say that," Suzann giggled.

"There's nothing funny about this place. I can't believe that I let you talk me into coming with you," Dwan answered

In their rush to leave the cemetery, they ran into each other head-on, laughing as they made their way slowly to the gates. It seemed the further they walked the farther the gate was.

Suddenly, a rotten stench wafted in the air, making them nauseous. It was easy to follow their noses to the end of the graveyard where there was a carcass that appeared to have been at one time a large dog-like animal. The scene was gory. From out of the dog's nostrils came a yellowish-whitish thick runny mucus that had spilled out onto the ground.

The silence hung between them, with their hearts pounding and both feeling a little sick to their stomach. The dog's eyeballs were now completely gone from its perfect skull and had been replaced by little fat creatures that were working in a rhythm to no end. The hair and skin that once were attached to this muscular frame were now in a stage of gastric distention waiting to erupt so that it could finish its cook off and decay. Dwan placed her hand on Suzann's shoulder, trying very hard to speak, a sharp expression contorting her face. "What is that?" Dwan asked.

Stepping backward, Suzann tripped over a limb that was lying behind her and she landed on her butt so hard that she thought her tailbone had been driven into her stomach. Dwan rushed towards her, reaching out her hand in an attempt to pull her up. Taking hold of Suzann's hand, Dwan stepped backward, forgetting about their smelly friend that now lay behind her as she placed her foot down into the feculent matter that was scrambled with blood and full of foul odors. Suddenly the dark heavy feeling was broken as Suzann laughingly and loudly said, "Now that was funny!" It must have been for they were laughing and crying, holding their hands over their noses and puking all at the same time. After all that, they finally got to the gate. After they got out on the road, Suzann felt a touch of irrational hope again. The events of the last few minutes and the wonderful fresh smell of clean air made their long walk worthwhile. They continued walking for a while and then slowly picked up their pace until they were running as hard as they could, feeling that something was going to grab them at any time. By the time they got home, the both of them were so out of breath that neither of them could talk. Both of them were sitting on the steps with red faces, letting their adrenalin slow back down to normal.

"I ain't never going back to that place again," Dwan said.

"I think that I will pass on going back for a while too," Suzann mumbled. "What time is it?" Dwan asked. "Time? Well, who's counting?"

"Not me." She smiled, contented. Then they both laughed it off.

CHAPTER THIRTY-ONE

"Suzann," Jay T called and as usual she figured he wanted her to pull off his boots or wash his feet like he did most every night.

"I want you to meet someone."

As she entered the room where Jay T was, getting up from the chair was a tall frame at least six four in height. He swung around quickly and stared into the most beautiful eyes which were so perfectly placed. One of the few times in his life had he seen such beauty.

"Steven, this is my little girl Suzann.

Suzann, this is my little brother Steven."

There was a lengthy pause for Suzann could not believe what she had just heard. And as far as Steven was concerned, she didn't know what his problem was. Even though Suzann wasn't dressed in a tailored suit, her jeans and shirt fit her long, well tucked-in look from head to toe. She looked so desirable and dangerous but so very young. It was hard to tear his eyes away as he boldly stared at her curvy body from top to bottom. His first impression of Suzann was that she represented the most pure natural beauty he had ever seen in his life. But his upbringing had taught him something of manners and he made his eyes meet hers. Knowing that she had been aware of his impoliteness, he took a deep breath and then he spoke, "Yes, I am the baby of the family."

Ignoring his rudeness, she smiled pleasantly at the total stranger, thinking to herself the whole time that he was probably just another copy of Jay T.

"Steven will be staying with us for a few weeks while he is on break from summer college. He will be helping with all the planting in all the fields."

Wanting to be anywhere else, Suzann said, "Well, we can sure use the help and it was nice meeting you." Then she quickly left. Her quick thinking had gotten her out of the room and away from Jay T. "Score one for me," she thought and then she almost giggled; almost, but then she remembered what Jay T had said. The memory brought on a dark raging anger that was hard to control.

"'My little girl,' you bastard. I'll never be your little girl no matter what you do to me, you son of a bitch! One day," she thought. "I'll be able to say that to your face, you dirty, nasty motherfucker!" The use of profanity was something that Suzann hated. The fact that she had put those words in her thoughts both shocked and amazed her. She felt her anger ease up just a little. Then from nowhere, she remembered the trip to the graveyard. In her mind's eye she could see Jay T's body lying in that shallow grave with corruption flowing from it. The scene not only brought satisfaction but also planted the seeds of deeper, darker sinister thoughts.

Suzann was still thinking. "Before you embark on a journey of revenge, dig two graves." What did this mean to her? In her mind she was thinking of one grave. Back in her room, she could almost feel how good it would feel to reach up and knock that false smile off Jay T's face; she could not believe what he had said. It made her sick to her stomach. And why in the world did Mr. Butler hire a brother of Jay T's. That is just what we need around here, another Jay T.

That night at supper, Suzann set another plate for Steven, but when she called, "Supper's ready," everyone was there but Steven,

"Where is Steven?" Suzann asked. "I set him a plate."

"Oh, he'll be along," Jay T said. "If he's not here by the time we finish, just put a plate for him in the oven."

They had just started to ea, when Steven stepped in.

"Well, better late than never, I always say." Suzann didn't know if she got Steven's attention but she certainly got Jay T's. She could see the look that Jay T was giving through his long and bushy eyebrows, and if looks could kill . . .

"Hey, come on. Let's eat," Jay T said. "It ain't much but it will fix the empty."

This was not the welcome that Steven had envisioned but he had just met her so he really didn't know what to expect from Suzann. He tipped his chin and shot her a glance with his baby blues and swallowed hard, and he then started to eat his supper. Looking around the table at all of the people and thinking of the events to come, he knew that he would be involved and wanted to learn as much as he could about farm life. "Steven, don't be an ass! Get a hold of yourself," he thought to himself. Hearing the tremor in Suzann's voice brought him back to reality.

"Do . . . do you live around here?" she asked. She was waiting for his answer with a gentle smile on her lips. He was overlooking the sadness hidden deep beneath the beauty he saw on her face. Steven rested his feet on the faded linoleum that Suzann kept so spotless as he sat there indecisive for while, but he gave no answer. He sniffed and wiped his mouth with a clean handkerchief. Then put it back in his back pocket. Steven was apparently stunned and did not give an answer to her question. Everyone else in the room noticed his unwillingness to respond and wondered what the deal was. Little did they know the question had caught him off guard even though he had asked himself the same question many times. In his mind that question meant, "Do you have family living here? Do you have friends and acquaintances that you have known for years?" The answer that had haunted him for years was, "No." His life had consisted of living in or around the schools that he attended.

That night after all the kids were tucked in bed, Jay T and Steven sat around the table exchanging war stories from when they were very small. As Suzann listened, there were a lot of years left out that were not talked about. It seemed that Steven's mother had sent him away to a school to get an education. She wanted one of her boys to finish school and Jay T was not having any part of that, he had his mind set on bigger and better game.

Suzann enjoyed hearing Steven talk about his school and how much he loved it. Now he was in college; he had one more year to go. To hear him talk, it sounded like he could go to school for ever. Then he repeated a story that his mother had told him about Jay T and some predicament that he had gotten into when he had been a toddler. They both laughed. Suzann was cleaning up the kitchen when Steven got up and started helping her. "Well, this is a surprise, certainly something different," she thought to herself. Jay T interrupted her thoughts by telling Steven that she did not need any help but Steven ignored what he said with an answer. "This is the least I could do for such a fine supper." He helped put up each and every little thing until the kitchen was in proper order.

The next morning he helped her feed the hogs with very few words said between them. He followed Suzann's directions to the letter without comment. All these years that she had been doing this work, he had been the first to offer a hand. His eager efforts and willingness to work had caused her apprehension to lessen. "Maybe he's not so much like his brother," she thought to herself. Even though the morning had been very pleasant, Suzann was still nagged with worry.

Suzann was scared to death that Jay T was going to be furious with her for the help that Steven had given, but he hadn't said a word; at least, not yet. She refused to look at Steven, afraid that he might see the fear in her eyes. But even if he did, he would not have a clue as to the reason why she feared Jay T.

Supper that evening came and went without incident. Stepping out of the kitchen and turning out the lights, Steven went into the living room where Jay T was sitting, and Suzann went into her bedroom and closed the door. Setting her tired self down on the bed, she began to look again at her school paper and again read the poem she had written. She was thinking that it would be great to be a writer and a singer. There was nothing wrong with being able to do two things at the same time. She was about to turn on her radio when she heard the sound of a guitar playing. The sound was coming from outside. It was funny that she had just been thinking about music and now she was hearing some. It sounded like it was coming from the woodpile out behind the hedges. The tunes carried from the distance in the night were so beautiful. She sat there and listened and was beside herself. It had been a long time since she had heard someone play, and she sat there for as long as she could but the curiosity was killing her, and then it got the best of her. She jumped up from her bed, knocking off the loose-leaf scrapbook that had been lying on the bedside table. Falling to the floor, the open book revealed pages that were filled with clippings. Her eyes were drawn to the open scrapbook because it had opened to her most favorite part which was the school paper, but even that did not hold her interest except for a short glance because of the music that she could hear. She walked out of her room and into the hall with no sound in the house. Everyone was outside watching and listening to Steven play and sing. He was great, very talented; she could have sat and listened to him play all night.

The wind had fallen to a whisper and the smell of spring was gone. There were hedges all around the house, just like all the hedges that were around the haunted house by the graveyard. There were so many hedges that you could hardly see anything else.

Steven saw Suzann as she rose from where she was sitting to go back into the house, but he continued to play and sing in the warm darkness of the night.

Steven would not be living in the same house with his brother. Jay T had made arrangements so that he could stay in one of the shacks on the farm.

Sitting in the strange green colored room, Steven liked to get up early in the mornings and enjoy all the hours of the day. This morning he was unpacking and getting settled in. He was going to start a job that he was unfamiliar with and he was excited to learn something new about the ways on a farm. As he worked, he reviewed the events of the previous night. This strange young lady was still weighing on his mind. There was something about her that he could not read. But it was something that he would like to get to know. For that kind of beauty, he could wait a lifetime for her to become of age, to be a woman. He didn't know how old she was but she acted and talked like she was twenty-five; but he suspected that she was a lot younger. While he was brushing his teeth, his thoughts were interrupted when he heard strange noises behind the barn.

Suzann was bringing in the cows and she was surprised to find Steven standing at the gate. As the cows were entering the holding pen, Steven hesitated in the shadow of the gate where he paused and then lifted a hand to help her close the heavy gate. He Looked surprised to see that it was Suzann in her overalls with a few patches here and there and her face lazy from lack of sleep.

"I'm glad I am an early riser," he said cautiously. "Where is Jay T?"

"Where he always is this time of morning, still in his cozy little bed!" She blurted out.

"I'm surprised that you are not still there, in the bed, I mean."

"Why?" Steven asked in a nice tone.

"You're his brother, aren't you? Doesn't it run in the family?"

"You think you got me all figured out, don't you? Well, I hate to burst your little bubble but you are dead wrong. I'll only be here for a few weeks, and in that time I will try really hard to stay out of your way." His words ripped through the quiet morning like pellets from the end of a shotgun.

Suzann stared at the ground as she said, "I'm sorry." And then she looked him straight in the eyes and said, with her voice gaining strength, "Believe me, it would be safer for me if you did just that."

Her heart sank with the words that she was saying because she really would love to have had his help or just someone to talk to would be nice. Handy was the only one she could do that with, but even then she had to slip around and hide. With a puzzled look on his face, he turned and walked away. But Suzann knew that she was right and that if he were to continue to help like he had last night it would cost her the skin off her back. She knew that Jay T would not approve for her to have a friend. Suzann was working and thinking to herself.

"Sure do wish I had a big brother. Someone to take care of me when I needed it, to protect me, to be there to talk to, to love, to be able to say I love you to without getting into trouble. Someone to pray with and not have to pray in silence so no one could hear me."

Suzann knew that Steven was just trying to help and to be friendly, and she had just run him off. The last thing she needed was more enemies. Finishing her work, she wanted to apologize but didn't know how, didn't know if she should, afraid that he would tell Jay T what she had said about him this morning. Even though it was true, she knew she shouldn't have said it. Then it hit her. She had decided to go by his room when Jay T came to the barn. Think of the devil. He walked through the door. As she started to leave, Jay T called out to her.

"You stay away from Steven, do I make myself clear?"

"I have not been around him."

"You heard what I said!" His voice was mean and his action was angry and impatient.

'OK," she said, pulling her hair back up in a ponytail. Jay T dragged his eyes away and went back to work. A lot of different thoughts slipped through her mind now. If she went to Steven's room and Jay T saw her after telling her to stay away, she knew that would be trouble.

"Damn him. He's so disgusting. I'm not allowed to have any friends, not allowed to go anywhere, not allowed to talk to anyone.

No one is allowed to come home with me, not allowed to wear shorts, not allowed to speak at the house unless I've been spoken to, not allowed to pray, not allowed to tell the truth. He goes through my things all the time and makes me sit and watch. If he finds something that he doesn't want me to have he tears it up or burns it. He has burned everything that my mother and dad had given me." A tear welled up in her eye as she remembered seeing her purse burning, that one her mom and dad had given her at school. She remembered a couple of pairs of cutoff jeans that she had on when he had come in early in as many afternoons and she wasn't expecting him. Even though they came all the way to her knees, he had said they were still shorts and then he tore them off of her. He would not even let her change. He had ripped them off with animal force, leaving her half naked. He had pulled everything out of her drawers and closets to see if he could find any more, not believing her when she said that there were no more. And then he had made her watch as he burned them. These memories were flooding her mind when she noticed her own voice and actions. "I hate you, Jay T. I hate every bone in your body, and if I had the power I would take the oxygen out of the air that you breathe." She was stunned by the way that she had been mocking him, flapping her arms helplessly in the air then slapping them on the sides of her legs. As the realization of what she had been saying out loud and her actions hit home, she momentarily wondered about her sanity. "I can only imagine what someone would think if they were to see me talking to myself and carrying on like that." The thought made her look around to see if anyone might have been watching. She didn't see anyone and said to herself, "Thank God for that." All in the same instant she decided, "Jay T has got to die." She was tormented by the hem of her life as she looked up and saw the halo that encircled the flaming face of the sun as it too was starting to wake up to face a new day.

Suzann swallowed hard as the panicky need to escape once again invaded her limbs, but instead she just stopped, stood there, looking at Steven's door with her heart caught up in a ridiculous feeling of not knowing what to do.

"Ehem," Steven coughed. "Am I interrupting something?" he said with half amusement in his voice. A sick feeling settled in his gut as if he had been cut with a knife through the heart. He had seen and heard everything, unknown by her.

"Listen, I overheard what Jay T said to you this morning, about you staying away from me, and I understand why. I would probably be the same way, I would not want you around strange men either. So I want to apologize to you. I thought you were being mean at first, but now I understand what you meant by what you said." Then he took the opportunity to step away and not stand so close to her and it seemed to help the both of them breathe easier. Suzann stood still as she looked Steven in the eyes. There was a lengthy pause and then she said, lamely, "I'm headed to the house." "A cup of coffee sounds great to me," he said.

"I'll make some fresh." And they walked back to the house in silence. Suzann struggled desperately to reorient her thoughts, praying that Steven wasn't anything like Jay T. When they got to the house, she put on some fresh coffee. Steven sat at the bar, watching every move that she made.

"You move around in the kitchen like you have been doing it for years. And I don't mean to stare at you but I have never seen any living thing as beautiful as you are. Girl, you could be a movie star. This don't make any sense. I didn't mean to fight with you this morning but every since I got here you have treated me as if I were some kind of monster or had something contagious and you don't want to be near me." Steven shook his head sympathetically,

"I wish I knew what was going through your mind, what your thoughts were. And I only want to be your friend, nothing else."

"You want anything in your coffee?"

"Black," he answered. In the process of setting his coffee in front of him, she looked upon his face and attempted to smile. Looking at her, Steven saw that tears had gathered on her eyelashes, giving her eyes the most haunting beauty.

"What's wrong?" he asked.

Suzann whispered, "You say you want to be my friend. First you will have to get your brother's permission, and I can tell you that will never happen. But you must not tell Jay T what I said this morning or about our talk now."

"Damn it, Suzann, I just . . ."

"Please, just leave it alone," she said with a voice low and strained.

"Very well, if that is what you want," he said.

"That is the way it has to be," Suzann answered.

She placed a double serving of hot biscuits in front of him while refilling his coffee cup. She then cut open the biscuits and placed butter on them, along with some homemade pear preserves.

"Thanks," he said as his dark brown face rose up to look at hers.

"You're welcome," she replied shakily. The smile on her face slipped, as if saying, I want to be your friend too.

CHAPTER THIRTY-TWO

The summer was on and the days were hot from the sun's first rising till late afternoon. The sun steaming the ground until going barefoot was almost impossible, the earth would burn your feet, especially in the fields where the ground had been worked and was in the process of being planted. It was weather like this where long hair was inconvenient, and pulling it up off the neck let the breeze blow against the wetness of the skin. Though the breeze was hot, it still helped to cool one off. The hair seemed to hold in the heat. It was at this point where the thought of having short hair might be nice. But at night, when the work was finished, she would collapse into a tub filled with hot water. She enjoyed the satisfaction that it brought, releasing the tension of all those tired muscles; and afterwards she would sit in front of her mirror, brushing her hair until it was dry again. Seeing the sparkle in it as if it were alive and full of life made her so proud to have long hair.

Suzann had been watching Steven. He never stopped working, getting the fields ready to be planted and then planting in them. Then at night he would help with some of Suzann's work. Suzann knew that Jay T did not like that but for some reason he never said much about it. It would probably be hell to pay when Steven was gone but right now things were a little better. Steven was working on the cotton crop, which was the largest and the most difficult to harvest. The seeds were put in the ground and that was a job in itself, but that was only the beginning. After it started coming up, it had to be poisoned to prevent God's little creatures from getting too fat. Then it had to be hoed or the grass would take over. It had to be plowed at least twice, and then it would be ready to pick long before everyone was ready to do it. And the only cotton-picker seen in the field at that time was an eight-foot sack and the people dragging the sacks and picking the cotton. Jay T was always saying, "Assholes and elbows, let's get this shit done!"

The cornfields were the next largest crop. After they were planted it wasn't as difficult to harvest as the cotton was, and the corn was used to make feed for the cattle. It was combined and made into silage. After being cut close to the ground, stalk, leaves, and the corn were run through an auger that cut them into small pieces. When that was finished, everything was then dumped into a silage pit, which was a deep and wide space dug in the ground. After every load was dumped, it was run over by a tractor to pack it down tight before the next load. Once this job was started, it had to be finished, no breaks in between. After all the corn was cut and the pit was full, a large roll of black plastic was rolled over it and tucked in around the sides. Then another roll was put on top of the first one, with three feet of plastic left on the sides. Then tires were put all around the pit. The silage stayed there until winter. It was preserved in such a way that when it was opened it would be ready for feed. It almost looked like it had been cooked. The color was different and it had a smell of its own.

Then there were the bean fields. Half of them were cut for hay and the other half was combined and sold. New pastures were planted. And in the mix of pasture seed, turnip seed was added so when the grass came up there would be turnip greens and turnips all year long.

Then there was the fescue planted for hay, and straw that was used to bed stalls for the livestock. All these things had to be put in the ground one after the other. And in the order they were planted, they had to be harvested one after the other. When something was started in the fields, it was doomed to be finished; loose ends were never to be left hanging. Aside from all the normal work on a dairy farm in the late spring and summer, there were many crops to get in and put in its proper place.

From astride the tractor, Steven saw Suzann walking up the field road and was forced to smile for she was certainly worth smiling at. He knew that Jay T was being overly strict with her, or maybe he was trying to forestall her becoming a young woman but he could not stop that because she was already there in body and mind, all she needed was a little more age. The thing that he would hate to see would be for her to let someone take advantage of her before she was ready for any kind of relationship—not that she could not defend herself for she was very capable of that. But from the outside looking in, Steven could see that she would be easy prey and all it would take would be for someone to give her a little bit of attention. Even though she never said it or implied it, her eyes did. And from what he could see, she was starving for friendship, love, and someone to show her that they cared instead of how much work she could do.

What Steven had seen the night before last was still bubbling in his stomach like a volcano waiting to erupt. He had gone by the house to see Jay T and tell him that the tractor needed a fanbelt and to lay one out early in the morning so he could put it on before going to the field. As Steven passed the window he overheard Jay T screaming at Suzann to pull of his shoes and socks and wash his feet and back, treating her like a slave from years gone by. He stood close to the window and watched behind the hedges until he had to leave before he got involved in something that would make things worse for her and himself. Steven was more than starting to understand Suzann's attitude when he had first arrived and why she hated Jay T. It hadn't taken long to figure that out. Now Steven was caught up in the mystery of his own brother. "Just maybe all the talk about him in our hometown was true. And now I think that he is the reason that Mother sent me to school, to keep me away from him. Things have surely changed in all the years of me being away." Steven knew that a lot of things had been kept from him and the questions were starting to feel like a gas fire in his mind. The purr of the tractor seemed to help him think. Steven decided that the next weekend, when things slowed down some, he was going to take a ride into his mother's place and talk to some townsfolk and the sheriff and find out what had happened while he was away.

Then his thoughts were suddenly broken when he heard Suzann scream. The force of her scream split the air along with his ears. He cut off the tractor to see what was wrong with her. He climbed down and went running to her. He found that she had stepped on a snake. It was a rattlesnake but out of its normal place. Whether she knew it or not Steven, saved her life for the snake was ready to strike at her when a knife pierced it to the ground. Then he took a crowbar from the tractor and pinned its head to the ground then took his knife and pulled it out of the body and cut off the head. Then he picked the snake up and laid it beside the road.

"I will come back get it later," Steven said.

"Get it later? Why would you want it to start with?"

"I will clean it and dry the skin and make a hatband from it."

Steven took his handkerchief from his pocket and wiped her face. Then he climbed back upon the tractor and reached down to give her a hand to pull her up on the tractor with him. "Come on, ride for a while. I could use the company." He kicked the tractor into gear and aimed it up the rows that he was planting. Suzann refused to acknowledge his presence. Then he pulled on the throttle which accelerated the tractor and the noise level. There was no need to run the tractor this hard or this fast. He only did it for her benefit. With the tractor this loud, no words could be spoken or heard, thus giving her the time she needed to recover from the incident. He had finished the row and had gotten about half of the next one. Still she paid no attention. Feeling still in shock from what had just happened; she continued to look down at the passing ground.

Steven couldn't bear it any longer. Stopping the tractor, he reached out his hand and she accepted it.

"Come here," he said, pulling her to him, letting her head rest on his shoulder.

"It's all right. You are not hurt, it didn't bite you." He put his arm around her and could feel her heart pounding and her body trembling.

"Don't cry," he said in a low voice. "Here, wipe your eyes." He pulled out his handkerchief from his back pocket and handed it to her. Wiping her eyes and face, she said, "And it started out to be a good day." Teasing her, he said, "And it's going to stay that way, OK? Come on, I'm almost finished with this field. I got an early start this morning. It will only take a few minutes then I will go and help you at the barn."

"But you've got your own work to do when you finish here."

"What I've got to do will be finished when I get through with this field."

"Well, I want to thank you for what you have just done for me. I don't know what happened, I could not move. It was like me and the snake were staring each other down. What about Jay T?"

"He is in the bean field and he won't be out until he is finished, which will most likely be after dark. So you may have to do all the milking tonight, but don't worry, I will help you." Suzann pulled her hands away and said, "OK, let's spank this pig." And they both laughed.

"You do have a way with words," Steven laughed even harder along with Suzann.

Steven didn't dare question her at this point. He wanted to ask her some questions about Jay T but he didn't want to ruin the moment, so he let it go. He had seen and heard enough to know that her smiles were few and far between and he had come to enjoy those smiles. The rest of the afternoon went well. Then Handy showed up from where he was working, and between Steven and Handy, they finished just as Jay T came in from the field. Suzann heard Jay T telling Steven and Handy to unhook the planter from the tractor and to go with him back to the fields and bring in all the equipment to the barn so that they wouldn't have to do that in the morning.

"That finished the beans," Jay T said.

"Good, I finished all the cotton this evening too."

"And I got all the fields ready for the corn," Handy said.

"That only leaves the hay and corn and one pasture to be sown, then we will be done." For some reason Suzann didn't want them to be done, and it made her feel sad to know that it would not be long before Steven would be leaving.

As Suzann was walking back to the house, she heard Kate screaming. She took off in a hard run up the steps and through the door, just in time to hear, "I'm going to kill that goddamn animal." She was looking hatefully at Suzann. "That cat of yours, if I catch that cat in this house one more time . . . you better think about that!" She had been chasing the cat and her face was blotchy red with anger.

"Oh no, that cat has never hurt you. It's just a kitten. I found it at the hay barn it was almost dead. I just fed it to get it back on its feet then I was going to take it back to the hay barn so it could catch mice. I just now got it healthy enough to take back. It doesn't ever come in the house. I feed it outside and maybe it slipped in looking for me." The kitten ran out from behind the chair, like it was trying to find a way out. Suzann turned to get it but Kate beat her to it.

"Kate, don't hurt it," Suzann begged.

"I'm not going to hurt it," Kate said. Kate was shoving Suzann out of her way and making her way to the door.

"Kate, give me the cat and will take it back to the hay barn, please."

Then Suzann heard the thud against the porch post, and from the force behind the throw, she knew that it would be dead. Suzann ran out the door. "How could you? Why? Why would you want to do this?"

Steven and Jay T must have heard the commotion because they were standing on the sidewalk, taking it all in as if it was a free show. Suzann slowly moved forward to where the kitten was lying. As she bent over, her tears fell to the floor. "It's dead. It's dead," Suzann was saying in a low voice.

When Kate realized that Jay T and Steven were standing out there, she began to apologize to Suzann but Suzann knew that she was not sorry.

"You're not sorry. You meant to do this. You destroy everything that I touch and you love doing it."

"Suzann," Jay T called. "That's enough."

Suzann leaned forward to pick up the kitten, carrying it with blood dripping from her hands as she walked between Jay T and Steven. No one was saying a word. She went to the barn and got a cleaning rag and wrapped it up, and took it in the woods behind the pond. There she dug a hole and laid the still limp and warm body down. Slowly covering it up, she placed a big rock at the front of the grave, walked out and gathered some wild flowers from the pasture, and placed them upon the loose dirt.

"I know that you were just a cat but you did not deserve this. I took you from the wild and made you tame. I wish that I had left you alone maybe you would still be alive. So I guess it's my fault." Suzann sat down on the rock and gazed off through the woods. She cried, feeling like she was being babyish but she could not help it. She was trying to regroup but that guilty feeling was still gnawing at her insides. Suzann felt a sense of regret, alone with her familiar self.

"Suzann," she heard someone call her name. Having thought that she was all alone, she turned around to see who it was and there stood Handy.

"What happened, missy? I did not mean to scare you but I saw you going into the woods with the shovel." He walked over to her very slowly, slower than he had to, but he could see that her heart was breaking. He offered his hand and sat down beside her. Suzann had no reason not to tell him, everyone else knew. Suzann was finding it to be easier to tell Handy the truth so she told him what happened.

Then Suzann said something to him that she had never said before. When Handy's mouth opened, the words he wanted to say to her refused to come.

"Handy, I want to be free of them and fly like the red bird."

Handy did not need to ask who she was talking about for he knew only too well.

Looking out into the shadows of the trees, filling his lungs with fresh air, he spoke to her softly.

"And I am going to make sure that you take that flight. You just hang in there a little longer, I've got some things to do."

Suzann hugged him ever so tightly. "I love you so much, you are the only friend that I have."

"Here, clean your face and go back to the house so Jay T won't come looking for you. And you do everything that he asks so he won't hurt you, and I'll see you tomorrow and we will talk again. Suzann, don't you do anything silly. He is a big and strong man and I know you have been having thoughts about things."

CHAPTER THIRTY-THREE

Here she sat, all primed to be a young woman but she was not allowed to even be a child. Is that bad? Maybe that is a good thing. Maybe this would turn out well and have a good effect. Suzann was going to be a charming lady, no doubt, and her looks were irresistible. But her beauty she did not see. She only saw pain and felt displeasure, but she had courage and strong will on her side. Sometimes it took a moment to accept things that had happened, falling into the mud, but she always got back up. Suzann found herself singing some songs that she had made up with words that were true. She slipped on her housecoat that someone had given her and ran some bathwater to try to revive herself, or at least her smell. The days in the fields were hot, like dogwood days of summer always are. After the bath she put on some fresh clothe. Her jeans were faded and someone had already worn the new off of her western shirt. She tied up the front of the shirt so that no skin would be showing, leaving the knot hanging down in the front like a sash. She could still smell the perfume clinging to the clothes that she had pulled off when she picked them up to put them in the dirty clothes.

She walked outside and stood in the doorway watching Jay T and Steven as they were walking towards the house, probably ready for supper. Steven smiled as he spoke and Jay T was just being Jay T, he had no smile and he only spoke when he was dishing out orders. That night at the table, while everyone was eating, no one said a word about what had happened with the cat. Suzann figured it was just as well. When she raised her head and looked at Steven, a shiver ripped through her. She wondered if he thought she was ridiculous and silly like a child. But like he had said himself, if it feels right, then it is all right. And at that time, that was what she had felt like doing, therefore, she would rest her case.

After supper, Suzann had to go to the henhouse to gather eggs. Enjoying the peaceful moment, she stood outside listening to them while some sat on their nests and others were perched on the ladder at the end of their house. It sounded like they were having a nice conversation about something, only in another language. The hens never protested when Suzann came and took their eggs. They seemed to have gotten used to her frequent intrusions. Perhaps they could see that she handled their treasures like precious stones, soft gold; or maybe they liked the way that she would sing to them. Suzann had heard them when someone else gathered their eggs, and it sounded like there was a snake in the henhouse. She placed the eggs in a basket lined with a towel. After they were washed, she placed them in an egg carton and then in the refrigerator. As many hens as there were, one would think that some of them could have been sold. But it took all of them to feed all the hungry mouths running around here.

"Need some help?" Steven called out.

His tall broad-shouldered figure was planted in front of the henhouse, his hands in his pockets. He had a distracted look in his eyes. It was nice seeing him standing there, having someone like him around was for her like suddenly coming upon a dream that you had last night, a that upon waking eluded you but hung with you all day. It left you trying to capture its essence and exotic stream of its details. Asking herself, could he be a dream? But he has the wrong name, and she let the thought slip away

"Are you finished for the day?"

"I'm not finished, just quitting early," Steven answered.

Steven looked at her curiously and then squatted down on one foot, picking up a stem from a piece of straw for a toothpick. She leaned against the doorframe of the chicken house, unable to close it because Steven was all hunkered down in front of it.

"Suzann?" he asked. "Have you ever been to a movie?"

"No," she replied.

"I didn't think so. Would you like to go?"

"I'd love it, b-u-t . . ."

"No buts. I'll talk with Jay T and maybe I can take you and Dwan and Pat this weekend before I leave."

"You're leaving this weekend?"

"Yes, Sunday."

They sat there wordlessly for only a few minutes but it seemed like hours, then finally the words came back to her.

"Steven?" she said.

"I don't think that I have to tell you how I feel about you leaving." Her words made him very aware that every nerve that he had was very excited. He was also aware of her happiness from his being here, and she was so wonderfully inexperienced that he knew that she was showing him her true heart. Suzann had begun to feel like she was sinking, and the longer they stood there the more it intensified. It was like a racehorse getting butterflies just before the race was to start while waiting for the sound of the gun and the gate to open. Suzann circled his waist with her arms and pulled herself against him. "I will miss you Steven," she whispered.

Unknown to Suzann, the feeling he was getting for her and the way that she had looked at him lately was why he was really leaving. He knew that it would be best for him to go. He felt that he was much too old and she much too young, then he wondered if he was just feeling sorry for her.

Steven was biting his lip trying to think of something other than her tangled hair and rose-petal softness, and being unable to control his throbbing hardness, he knew that he had to get away. The significant and moral part of him was saying, "You can't let her see you this way." The young buck in him was steadily becoming apparent as testosterone flowed through his veins. For willing women that was OK, but this one was different. He quickly escaped from her and rounded the henhouse.

"Steven, where are you going? I'm sorry. I didn't mean anything by hugging you. I was merely saying goodbye."

"I'll meet you at the barn and help you get started."

"OK," she said, thinking nothing about it.

Suzann carried the eggs into the house and was standing at the sink washing them, when Lynn presented her with a drawing that she had made. Doing her young best to capture Suzann's attention, she grabbed at Suzann's arm. "This is for you," she said.

"Oh yes, that is very good." She continued looking at Lynn with her curly head bowed in contemplation.

Suzann said as she cupped her face in her hand, "I like this very much," wondering to herself what it was supposed to be, but Suzann appraised it as if it were a treasure. There was one thing that was for sure, it definitely had all the colors that you could want. When she had finished, she decided that she had better leave a little early to get the cows in since they were in the bigger pasture across the road in front of the house. It always took longer when they were there. It was farther to go, and when they were in that pasture they all seemed to have a contest going on to see how many could go the farthest to the back.

All of the cows were Holsteins except three that were Jerseys, and they seemed to certainly find pleasure in being the outcast of the herd. They did everything differently. They were always the last to be found, and they always brought up the rear. Coming out of the pasture, there was an opening that turned into a field road that leads back to the barn. It crossed the creek before climbing the last hill. Over time Suzann had grown to admire the bodies of water that glistened from the sunrays that fell through the trees. She would listen to the small waterfalls that slapped the rocks below. It seemed to fill her heart and mind with a peaceful feeling. The crossing site was always slippery from the moss and algae that covered the solid-rock bottom. She always focused on her footing and tried to keep her balance. Even with all of her efforts, she had still wound up with a wet bottom a few times.

She would always stop and look upstream; it was flawless, with the look of a picture of fountains, one after another, picking up speed as they traveled downstream. She was always enchanted by the view and the rainbow colors that most eyes had never seen. These were sights that had not been disturbed. Waiting for the three Jerseys to cross, Suzann would grab hold of a tail and let the cow pull her up the steep hill. After topping the hill, from out of nowhere Suzann heard Kate plunge into song "RED, RIVER VALLEY." It sounded like she had really damaged her vocal cords, and that she could blow out a lung at any time. Even the old dog that was with her was finding his way out. It was too much for his ears.

Suzann just backed up and enjoyed the performance; she never thought that Kate would make her laugh. Sneaking around and Kate not knowing she was there had done Suzann so much good. Wiping her eyes with her shirttail, she looked as if she had been crying. She had to stop because her stomach was hurting from laughing so hard. She waited until Kate was finished and then started clapping her hands. "Would you like for me to pitch pennies?" she asked. For a minute Suzann thought that she had ticked Kate off, and then there was a smile silently breaking through on her hardened face. Suzann thought that she should not have laughed but being her usual self, like she sometimes was, she couldn't pass that one up. Breaking one off on Kate had done her so much good.

Kate was standing as still as the oak tree standing beside her that she was propping on. Her face had a look of stupid or worse.

"What are you doing?" Suzann asked.

"Looks like I'm entertaining you," she answered.

"You sounded great," Suzann lied. "I just stopped to see what it was," she said, smiling.

Kate couldn't hold it back any longer and then they both were laughing.

"Why are you such a long way from the house?

"Jay T told me about these springs. He said he found them the other day while he was back here turning these fields and that they were full of cresses. So I decided that a mess of them for supper would be good.

Why are you back here?' Kate asked.

"This is where I have to come to get the cows in for milking."

"Oh, I didn't know that."

"Of course, you never get out of the house."

"Well, I have already got supper cooked for tonight, and now I'm going to go home and fix these cresses."

"This is it," Suzann thought. "This will definitely be the big one. This should be put down in Guinness Book of World Records for being a first."

"What are we having for supper?"

"We're having pinto beans, fried potatoes, boiled ribs with liver and lights thrown in, and corn on the cob. Corn bread and cresses, does that sound good?" Kate asked.

"That sounds great, but what, no desert?" Suzann jokingly said.

"Now how could I cook a meal like that and not have any desert?

All things are subject to change, including me."

For some reason Suzann wanted to believe her, but she knew that Kate would never change even if she wanted to. She had lived with so much hate in her heart that it had turned black. But it was good to see her have a good day. Not knowing how to take her, Suzann had to take off after the herd and get things started. It was good to see Kate this way, full of life and even a smile on her face.

"Should have taken a picture," she thought. "Because this is something you don't see very often. Something is not right for this has been too good of a day."

After a moment, Steven walked slowly out of the edge of the woods that flanked the opening to his room. He had hung a hammock between two of the ancient oak trees and there he stretched out, looking up through the limbs and the leaves that were so thick. He could not find an opening big enough to see the sky.

"This tree must be over a hundred years old," he thought. Even the limbs on this oak were at least twenty-four inches around. Steven had learned a lot about country living and farming, some good and some bad. But that was the main reason that he was here, to see and do things that he had never seen or done before. Then he remembered that he had left his door open and that the field mice would probably welcome the invitation to come in and make themselves at home. Rats were really bad here on the farm. He had seen some of the biggest damn rats here that he had ever seen in his life. They had tails that were at least a foot long. Some looked bigger than the cats that caught them. He pulled himself up from the hammock and walked inside his room. His back was still stiff from sitting on the tractor all day. Out of the corner of his eye he saw a cat that stayed around there that looked like it was skulking, waiting on that big catch for lunch. He rubbed his hands together waiting for the opportunity this weekend that would allow him to find his way out of this tangled disaster of a place.

The far corner of the room was graced with two small oil lamps that sat beside each other on the high corner shelf. They were most likely there to be used when the power was off. They were antiques. From their looks, they could have even come from Noah's Ark. Lighting a cigarette, he walked over to the opposite side of the room and turned on the radio. He made sure that the volume was down low. Relaxing as he sat down on the edge of the bed, it felt so good to his tired bones.

But one fact still remained. There was something tugging at his heart and messing with his mind. His insides were burning like a fire that had been shut up. Worried about holding it in and knowing that he could not, he pushed himself up from the bed and walked over and gazed into the mirror at the haunting face that was looking back at him. He stood there silently, waiting, as if the face looking back at him was going to give him some kind of answer. He had a feeling in his bones that something was going to happen here, something bad. But he did not know what or how, it was just a feeling. Fate might have broken his family apart but his spirit had not been broken. "I can't love this girl in any way other than just as a friend," he thought. "Besides, true love is only in the movies." He laughed at himself as he tried to put the thought out of his mind. So he engaged himself in listening to the music. He knew that this was his problem and that he would have to be more careful. He clenched his teeth together with a touch of anger but it really didn't help. In his heart lay many mixed up feelings. His mind was a whirlwind, searching and probing each and every feeling, and then he fell asleep.

Outside it was almost cool. A breeze was blowing off the blue-water river, inexplicably, but welcome just the same. Suzann walked down the road, pulling her shirt out because it was tight, hugging against her body, showing the contour of what it held inside. Stopping in front of Steven's room, she walked up on the porch to the door. Not hearing any movement inside, she called out.

"Steven."

His words sounded uttered from under his breath. She realized that he had been asleep as he opened the door.

"Steven," he mocked her.

"I don't have to stand here and take this," she said jokingly

"Oh yes, you do," he said in a playful harsh voice. "You're on my turf now."

"Supper is almost ready. Jay T sent me to tell you."

"You mean the sharpest arrow on your list of enemies?"

They both were laughing.

"I'm sorry," he said. "I didn't mean to fall asleep."

"Yes, you did," she replied

"No, I didn't," Steven said.

"Yes, you did," she answered.

"You trying to start a fight?" were the words from his lips.

"I might be," she said.

"Well, you will lose," he said.

"I might not," she mocked.

"I'll race you to the house."

"You're on," she challenged, and they took off as hard as they could.

"You beat me," Steven said, out of breath.

"You let me," she replied.

"No, I didn't."

"Yes, you did," she called out.

Steven grabbed her around the neck and was pushing her towards the door of the house when they ran right into Jay T.

"What is going on here" Jay T asked.

"It was a race to see who could get to the house first," Suzann answered him.

"It didn't look like a race to me," Jay T replied.

Steven put his hand on Jay T's shoulder. "Jay T, it was a race."

Jay T removed Steven's hand from his shoulder, fire in his eyes. Suzann was afraid for a minute that they were going to fight.

Suzann began to plead. "Jay T, please . . ."

"Please what?"

Kate then entered the front where everyone was.

"You all are unaware of my fine cooking; now would anyone like to eat or is everyone going to fight?"

"I'm sorry," Steven said. "But I've suddenly lost my appetite."

"Steven," Kate said. "You have got to eat tonight because I've done all the cooking. Suzann thinks that she can beat me. I want to know from you if you think that she is right."

"Hey, she's right," Jay T said. "I'm sorry, I don't know what got into me."

Jay T put his arm around Steven and walked him to the table. "Everything looks good," Jay T said. It was easy to see the resistance in Steven but he made himself stay in spite of what had happened.

Steven could see and feel the threat in his brother. It was becoming hard to swallow and Jay T's words affected him like a blow to the head, leaving him somewhat dazed, which only added to the fire that was already burning inside of him. Steven knew that he would recover but he was afraid that there were those in this house that might not.

After everyone had finished with their food, Kate, Suzann, and Steven cleaned up things and then collapsed in the living room to take in a movie that was coming on TV.

"It's going to be a hard day tomorrow," Jay T said. "I think that I'm going to turn in."

Steven's mind was still reeling from what had happened before supper and didn't even hear Jay T as he left the room.

"Is it raining?" Suzann asked, her voice soft and lazy. Kate went to the door. "It's pouring down," she said. Kate lay back on the couch with no room for anyone else to sit.

Suzann hung her head over the chair to face Steven where he had made himself comfortable on the floor.

"Ha," she whispered.

"Ha," Steven said with a smile on his face.

"A penny for your thoughts," she said drowsily.

"You can't afford them," he countered. "They would be very expensive." He lay there quietly, not moving. Everyone was silent.

CHAPTER THIRTY-FOUR

In the barn loft was lots of loose hay where the hay had come out of the bales and collected on the floor. Climbing up the long ladder to reach the loft, Steven carried her quickly across the distance of the barn and to the corner where there lay nothing but loose hay and a quilt that Suzann had taken up there to sit on when she would read or write. She dug her fingers into his shoulders and raised her eyes, giving permission to his uncertain command. They clung to each other with sweaty hands and their hearts pounded. Steven touched her soft young face with the tips of his fingers as he met her stare. He saw the glow on her face as he scanned the rest of her dressed body. She lay next to him with a curious stillness. He longed to love her tenderly but at the same time he wanted to grind her bones to him and take her savagely.

He let his hand slip down to her breast and touched them gently; he was not surprised by their large and full feel to his most sensitive touch.

Suzann read his message and answered him with one of her own.

Wordlessly she extended both of her arms and closed them around him. His skin, dark with black hair, covered his chest and the heat from his body was sensitive to her touch. She held him closer as his lips touched hers; he kissed her face and felt the upper swells of her breasts and felt her nipples as they hardened to his touch.

"Please, now," she cried out while the saliva from her mouth again pressed over his lips. In the core of him he could no longer control himself. Placing his hands on both of her hips, she helped him by arching to meet his thrust. Wanting to give herself to him in the raw, she welcomed him. She cried out suddenly and the cry echoed as he held her tighter. He moaned and the sweat was running from his face, and then he was still. He placed his hands on her shoulders and held her away from him. He had the desire for a pure heart, but he wanted her to have and keep everything else pure as well. That was one thing that no one should take from her until the time was right, and she was ready. Then they stood still.

"Steven, please take me from here. Your brother is a bad man."

He treasured her words and pondered on her statement, and somehow he knew that she was right and he believed her.

His voice trailed off. "Nooooooooooo . . . ," he cried.

"Steven. Steven, wake up. Steven, wake up. You were dreaming. You OK?"

"Yes, I'm OK," Steven answered.

"You're sweating. Your shirt is wet and you look as if you've been throwing hay up in the barn."

"Funny you should say that," Steven said.

"Why?" Suzann asked.

"Never mind. Forget it. It was nothing."

Then he left, leaving a blank look on her face as he walked out the door.

CHAPTER THIRTY-FIVE

A bright light fell on Suzann's face that woke her up to find that Kate was still standing at her bedroom door with her hand still resting on the light switch.

"It's time to get up," Kate said. "You have overslept a little."

Then suddenly Suzann realized that she hadn't set her clock before going to bed.

"Get up and get dressed," Kate said. "You're not that late. I've already got breakfast ready. I started to wake you earlier but I got busy in the kitchen and almost forgot to wake you at all."

Everyone kept watching Suzann at the breakfast table like they were expecting her to turn into some kind of creature or something.

"Why are you picking at your food?" Kate muttered.

"I guess I'm just not very hungry."

"There is some cereal over there if you want."

"No!" Suzann replied. "It's all got raisins in them and I hate raisins, they look like you should be biting into a big dog tic."

"Suzann, I was just trying to be nice and helpful."

"I was just joking, Kate. But since you mentioned the word *nice*, why are you being so nice this morning? It's just not in your nature."

Kate threw Suzann a glance then forced a smile and said, "We got a letter from Mom and Dad. They're coming up this weekend."

"Really?" Suzann cried out.

"I thought that might cheer you up."

Suzann dropped her head. "Do you think that I might be able to go home with them?" she asked.

"You'll have to talk to Jay T," Kate answered.

"You know if I ask him he'll say no."

"He might not."

"Sure, and pigs fly too."

"Don't be so hard on yourself. Ask him. If he says no then leave him alone."

"That's easy for you to say since you are not the one that's got to ask."

It was going to be a long and hot day in the field for Steven. He had started the job early that morning and felt the feeling of joy of being finished with the farm work today. But he had gotten what he came for and that was to learn about farm life and what living in the country was like. He sat in the hot sun all day on a tractor seat that sometimes had begun to feel like a part of him. Steven drew out his red handkerchief and dabbed his perspiring brow underneath his thick curly hair, then felt a certain sadness spread that was far worse than he could have imagined. A part of him wanted to go but another part of him wanted to stay. Looking forward to going back to school, but missing the schooling that he was getting here For him this was the kind of class that was not taught in school. He thought back to what his mother had said. "You will have days like this." He told himself that he was going to drive the devil out of this tractor until the engine quit; but the tractor didn't quit, it just kept on running just like it was supposed to.

When the sun rose early that morning, it had felt cool and clammy from the morning mist. Now it was high noon and hot as hell. The only cool place was under the oak that stood at the far end of the field. But now, even it wasn't so cool; it was more like a hot shade. There Steven sat on a root from the tree and funneled down the warm water that had been cold when he started that morning. He was feeling frustrated as he stepped behind a grove of honeysuckles to lighten his load by relieving himself. He felt somewhat dumfounded and furious at his brother Jay T that he had never really gotten to know. But from what he had seen and heard, Steven now believed with all his heart that all the rumors back at his hometown were true and that Suzann was right, Jay T was a bad man. He was exploring the thought that someone needed to put him out of his misery, another comment made by Suzann. And quite honestly, even though it may be out of line, he had a disturbing feeling of agreement. He still recalled the episode between himself and Jay T. He had borne the brunt of Jay T's anger. The anger itself had not really bothered him. He knew that hot weather and the frustrations of farming could bring a bad temper at any given time. What had bothered him the most had been Jay T's eyes. He had stared right back into those eyes and what he saw both disturbed and scared him. Those eyes had been cold, calculating, and soulless. He knew that there was nothing that he could do. He found little relief in knowing that someday Jay T would meet his match. His mood was as dark as his thinking. Suddenly he said to himself, "All right, asshole. That's enough of that kind of shit. You can't fix the world's problems. And even if you could, you won't be here long enough to do a damn thing!" With that, his mood lightened and he thought of Suzann. He knew that he was going to miss her, and he would pray that no harm would come to her in the time left that she had to stay in this home. As that thought faded from his mind, he suddenly realized that if it had not been for Handy, the young kids, and Suzann, he would have left the same day he had gotten here. "Of course," he thought. "It was mostly because of Suzann."

Tripping over a vine from the underbrush, he caught himself with his now hardened hands from the hard work. It was the first time that he had really noticed his hands. In an odd kind of way, he was proud of the calluses, the roughness of his hands and the things that he had learned. It felt good to be able to operate the machinery and know some real facts about hard living. He worked the rest of the day in a dead run until he finished. It was about three in the afternoon when he plowed his last row.

As he approached the barn he saw Suzann smiling brightly as she shook her head. Her hair was clean and newly brushed to a fall that snuggled into her buttocks. She stared at him appraisingly as he climbed down from the tractor. Standing in the shade of the tall trees from the other side of the road, Suzann took off her sunglasses and let them rest on her head.

Steven studied her. "That finished it up," he said, taking a cigarette from his pocket. He placed it between his lips as he dug in his pocket for a lighter. He lit it and took a draw from it, and then he decided against smoking it and threw it to the ground. He could tell that Suzann had something to say.

Suzann was having trouble finding the words, then she spoke softly. "My heart is swelling up in my throat like a rubber ball. What's wrong with me? I feel so strange, I feel like I am losing a good friend." She sounded as confused as he felt for each word came slowly and Steven guessed she was having to reach deep to find the right thing to say.

Inhaling the clean sent of her hair, he too was having trouble finding words to say to her.

"There's nothing wrong with you, and I'll always be your friend. I'm only sorry that I cannot take you to the movies like I wanted to do. But I think that it is best not to say anything to Jay T about it since he is not in the best of moods these days."

Suzann dropped her head. "I'm sorry too," she said softly. "But I understand." She lifted her head and pulled her hair back from her face, giving him a nice radiant smile. "Maybe another time." With that, she turned and started walking toward the house. He knew that she had wanted to say more, just as he had, but neither one really knew what to say.

"This is payday," Steven thought. "And I think I need a drink." Later that afternoon he got a ride with Mr. Butler into town. "I'll be back tonight or first thing in the morning to get my things. Just let me out at the next corner, I can walk from here. And thank you so much for letting me work. I've enjoyed it but it's school time again."

"You have really missed school, haven't you?" Mr. Butler said diplomatically. "But what was three months?" He reached out to shake hands and to thank Steven for all the work. "And if you ever need to work just let me know."

Steven walked in silence for several blocks and turned the corner onto Clinton Street where there were things always going on. State stores, totem stores, and the favorite hangout bars; there was traffic and sounds of horns everywhere, people shuffling to and from their destinations. And the trains making their usual clicking sound that always kept you up at night. Then Steven swallowed the lump in his throat as he realized that he had actually missed all this while working on the farm. It was about that time that he decided to settle down into the Lucky Spot Bar. He stepped inside with his mind still hanging on to unsettling thoughts. Like any other club, it had a long wooden bar with black leather padded barstools and a mirror the same length as bar that dominated the room. There was a scent of varnished wood mixed with a fresh clean scent in the air. There were tables and chairs that sat in the middle of the bar, with private booths that were sectioned off at one end. And in the middle of the room, all the way back against the far wall, sat a bandstand. The jukebox sat at the rear of the stage. He dropped in a quarter to listen to a little bit of the American Style Band. As he started walking back up front, Steven decided against sitting at a table and sat down at the bar, where he ordered a beer from the topless woman that worked behind the bar and waited on him. She had a lovely smile, in her mid-twenties with long blonde hair. Steven returned a smile gently reproachful. But he did notice that she had a fine body and glassy-blue eyes that could chase away any man's demons in one night. She kept fresh mugs of beer in front of him that she set on small black napkins as she worked in a hint of darkness with few shadows. He enjoyed the quiet moment and the sound of her soft voice. As he sat there, he listened to the last song playing and got lost in the lyrics of the song "Dark Night." Steven had lost count of the mugs of beer that he had drunk, but he now had the courage to do what he knew he had to do. Taking an extra long breath and then blowing it out, he stood to his feet and then he called for a taxicab to go back to the farm to his room where packing would be easy. He felt dissociated from reality and shrugged as he packed his one bag of clothes and a small TV. His head was expanding uncomfortably with every breath that he took.

"This is all the luggage I have," Steven explained as he stood beside the cab, looking towards Suzann's room just in time to see her lights go out.

"Hey," the cab driver said disinterestedly, shaking his hands. "The meter running."

"Yeah, so am I," Steven said. Once again he undoubtedly felt an empty spot inside him. Perhaps it was fitting to brood on this rare night.

"Back to school?" the cab driver nudged. "Do you feel underaged compared to the other students?"

Steven really wanted to just be quiet, but he answered anyway. "No, right now I just feel cold," plagued by his inner feelings of this nightmare.

"I finished four years ahead of my peers, so that makes me four years from my undergraduate years. When I'm walking around campus I don't notice that there is a difference." The conversation dropped as they drove off into the night.

The next morning when Suzann approached the barn, she found that there were no lights on. The feelings that she had would be hard to describe for she knew that he was gone. After closing the gate, she leaned on the gate post for a long time, not believing that he would leave without saying goodbye. But she knew that in his own way he had told her goodbye. With this foolish anger, she had to make herself concentrate on the work that was to be done. After getting used to having help for the last three months, she knew that she was not only going to miss him, she was going to miss the extra pair of hands.

She waited for Jay T to arrive; he was late. Suzann thought and wondered where Steven was and what he was doing, wondering if he missed being here. Why no, he's probably still in the bed and doesn't even know that he's in the world.

Suddenly jarred from her thoughts, she heard a crashing sound that came from the hay barn some distance from where she Suzann was at. Even though Jay T hadn't gotten there yet, she felt that she should go and see what the commotion was all about.

As she approached the barn, from the lights that had been turned on inside she could see hay falling from the loft to the ground. The rumbling sound went on and on and on. Suzann ran to the door; the door was so big that it hung in slides from the top. After pulling and pushing it with everything she had, she finally got it opened. Jay T was on his knees trying to help himself up with a hand grip on the side of the stable wall. As he got to his feet, he looked stunned and confused. There were bales of hay scattered everywhere around him and a big hole in the loft above him. Brushing himself clean from the hay that was clinging to his hair and clothes, he turned his head slowly and then suddenly coughed, his eyes opened as he seemed to be trying to focus.

"Are you all right?" she asked.

For a moment he said nothing and then Jay T shot her an incredulous look.

"Surely you're joking. Does it look like I've been on a hay ride? Get over here and help me brush my back off."

Her pulse began to quicken as she moved to where he was standing. Swallowing nervously, she dared not do anything short of carrying out his orders. It sounded like Jay T was accusing her of what had happened, as if it had been all her fault. The idea bothered her but there was nothing that she could do about it. Then with his sharp voice, he began to rant about the idiocy of someone putting the hay over the hole in the loft floor and then swore that there was never a hole there before anyway. And of course he was right; he was always right, at least in his way of thinking. Suzann nodded her head. She knew all too well of his insecurities, his lack of sense, and his worthlessness, and that he deserved anything bad that happened to him. After rolling his neck to loosen the tension from the fall, he just stood there waiting for her to clean the hay from him. Suzann quickly spun around, feeling silly at the goose bumps that she got as she started to put her hands on his back to brush it off. There was something there that she had never seen before. She hesitated to touch his skin and yet knew that she had no choice. There was something on his back that you wouldn't put your mother-in-law's hands on. It looked like shit; to the touch, it felt like scabbed over sores with some blisters mixed in. Circles that had a pink raw color to them. She really badly wanted to just run, but she dug in her heels just to stand there and finish the job. She pulled her hands away from him with curiosity bouncing around in that brain of hers that usually got the other end in trouble. She convinced herself that whatever it was, it had to be relatively safe because it had not killed him yet.

It was later when she did some research in the library and found out some things that Kate had told her about what Jay T had. Kate said that it was called ringworm, which was a popular name for a fungal infection of the skin. It was not caused by a worm and it was not always in a ring shaped appearance, like Jay T's was. Suzann took it upon herself to find out more about it since he lived in the same house. She found that it was caused by a group of related fungi of different types. These parasites feed on the body's waste products of dead skin and perspiration. It's usually worst in areas of folds, like under armpits and around the crotch, between the toes and the soles of feet, even on the testicles. The pictures that she saw were identical to what she had seen on his back. It is highly contagious and can be spread. This is what was so funny about this, there is a treatment for it by using antifungal drugs, but the best prevention is a matter of cleanliness. Because it lives and thrives on dirt, warmth and dampness, and smelly places; and he is all of that. After learning that, she then understood why Jay T had this mess. Even though there was a bathtub in the house, Jay T was too lazy or something because he never took a bath. The only time he went into the bathroom was when he had to. And Suzann believed that if he could that he would make her do it for him if it were possible. If he would just take a bath every day it would clear up, but Kate said that it would not clear up because he worked around water so much. But Suzann found out differently from the school nurse. According to the nurse, as long as you keep clean you can't catch it from anyone.

After finding that out, Suzann had to have the cleanest body in town; her religion became soap and water. Suzann became a perfectionist at staying clean and setting extremely high standards of cleanliness and was very displeased at Jay T's nearness.

Like ferns that grow in the dark and dampness or the tulip that opens to the sun's light in the day and closing its bulbs to the sun's setting at night, everything thrives on something.

CHAPTER THIRTY-SIX

Leaving Jay T in the barn, Suzann went back to the house, going straight to her bedroom and closing the door. Sitting down on the edge of the bed in the quiet early hour just before dawn, she deliberately redirected her thoughts from the horrible skin that she saw on his back and tried to think of one good memory from her childhood. And in those few minutes she had braided her hair and bathed herself for school. It wasn't long until the daylight fluttered into the room, shining through the window like a moth trying to spread a little color to her life. She rolled over onto her stomach, pulling the curtains back, and looked out across the orchard at all the fruit trees covered with bright new leaves swaying in the air to the silent music of the wind.

As she lay there she could hear Jim Bob crying from Kate's room and he was crying from the top of his lungs, losing his breath with each cry. Sliding from the bed to her feet, Suzann walked to the door of Kate's room. Standing at the door, she asked, "Kate, are you up?"

"Yes," she replied. "Go fix him a bottle!"

Suzann stood there undecided about Kate being up or not, and then she heard Kate moving inside, saying something to Jim Bob. Suzann hurried into the kitchen and put the bottle in a pan of heated water placed on the stove to warm the milk. Kate stormed out of her room and came out into the kitchen and grabbed the bottle of milk before it had time to even get the chill off.

"Kate, that's not ready yet," Suzann said.

But all Suzann got was a hateful look as Kate went back into her bedroom. Even after giving the bottle to him the crying didn't stop. Hearing the way that he was crying made chills run up and down Suzann's spine; something had to be wrong. Then the screaming cries stopped. Suzann ran to Kate's bedroom door and opened it to find that Kate had her hand over his face, depriving him of breath. His face was the color of blue, with extended neck veins present in his neck.

"Kate, what are you doing?"

Releasing her hand from his face, she said, "Haven't you got other things you need to do this morning besides snooping in on me! And you keep your mouth shut, do I make myself clear?"

Dropping her eyes in confusion, Suzann might have imagined this taking place with her, but not with him; he was just a baby. But he was a boy and from the day he was born, there was something different with him. Kate seemed to hate the fact that he had lived at all.

As Suzann closed her bedroom door she could hear Kate laughing inside the room. "These bastards," Suzann thought. "They love to inflict pain, but most of the time it's on me! From being slapped and kicked around and beat, the pain was sometimes unbearable and it seemed that the hurt was so bad that dying would be better. But the pain that she felt now was worse than her own. The look that was on Kate's face that she had seen before was one of enjoyment from inflicting injury and pain, with intent to hurt and do harm deliberately. It was the same look that Suzann had seen in Jay T's eyes before. "What is wrong with these people? When you look in the eyes of these two, you don't see a soul. There's only a deep dark pit filled with demons." As these thoughts of truth went through her mind, a shiver followed, going through her entire body.

Suzann sat down at the bar in the kitchen and slowly placed her hands on both sides of her face, briefly resting her cheek against them with a blank look as she stared at the bar.

Then she heard the front door as it was jerked open. "That's probably Jay T," she thought, grateful for the interruption, thinking that his being there might settle Kate down.

"Suzann?" he screamed.

"In here," she answered.

His expression was unreadable. "Get me a cup of coffee," he demanded. "And go see about Jim Bob."

"I already have, Kate's with him." She opened her mouth with the intention of telling him what she had seen and then closed it, thinking it would probably be better not to say anything at all knowing that Kate had completely gone nuts and was so disjointed and acting stranger than fiction.

Suzann stood there watching him as he pulled out a bag of Country Gentlemen and made himself a home-rolled cigarette. The smoke filled the area in the room where he was, leaving the smell that polluted the air around him, he crossed his arms over his powerful chest, his cigarette hanging from his lip.

"I want you to help me clean out all the stalls in the calf barn today," he said.

"And when we are finished doing that, we will be doing some work at the hay barn."

"What about school?"

"Your schooling today will take place in the barn."

Suzann was living in a haze filled with fear and so much depression on her from being totally cut off from everyone and everything that she loved. But despite what might happen, somehow everything would have to come out right in the end.

The stalls were so nasty; the calves were bawling and moving around nervously as they took them out one at a time to clean the stalls. They worked a while in silence, the mud and slime in the stalls almost covered the tops of their boots. Jay T coughed and spit.

"We're going to have to start cleaning these more often so they won't be in such a mess," he complained. Suzann looked up at him, saying nothing but thinking, "That will be my next shitty job I'm sure!" Jay T brought her back to earth, doing what he did best. Shouting out orders, telling her to move faster and get bigger loads in her shovel. They shoveled until they had the wheelbarrow running over with the rank shit.

"Help me with this," Jay T said. "You let us fill it too full and I can't push it by myself!" Suzann knew that he could but that he was being an ass. She struggled with the thing, tugging it away from the doorway. "You push and I'll pull," he said. They had it going well until the wheel hit a bump in the ground, causing it to tilt over and spill everything on Jay T's boots and all over his pants. The whole load was poured out mostly on Jay T. Suzann couldn't hold it; she started to laugh at the mixture of shit that had spilled all over him. "Well, if that ain't shit on shit," she thought smugly to herself. The slick mess had caused him to lose his footing and the wheelbarrow had fallen on his legs. There was disgust and anger on his face because he could see it was evident that she found relief in her laugh. He stared at her as he removed his arm that was resting on the ground.

"Hey, get your fuckin' ass over here and get the damn wheelbarrow off me so I can get up," he said roughly. His features softened when she came closer. His attention was drawn to her slightly open shirt as she bent over to pick up the wheelbarrow and get it off of his legs. He watched with an awareness of her hostility that was lightly veiled on her face. Then suddenly he threw a handful of shit at her, hitting the front of her shirt, splattering it everywhere, even in her hair.

"Why did you do that?" she asked, almost gagging.

"Why did you laugh at me?" he asked calmly, too calmly.

This change in his mood did not pass by unnoticed by her. She gave no answer, knowing that it was the best thing for her to do; after all, he would not understand anyway. His innocent words

pulled her nerves so tight that it made her feel sick, and the smell
had a lot to do with that.

Suzann held the wheelbarrow as Jay T shoveled the load back
in. After they had emptied that load, they went to the barn to spray
themselves clean of the mess that was all over them. Jay T, back to
his normal self, was cursing every breath; his voice rang out loud
and clear, accusing her of all the blame and then having the nerve
to laugh at him. He crouched down in front of her, resting one of
his knees on the ground. "I know you hate me right now but one
of these days I am going to change the way you feel about me."
Ignoring what he was saying, Suzann thought he was just running
off at the mouth like he did most of the time.

"You are so stupid. You are so fucking stupid. Just accept it. You
will never be anything. And you think that you are so smart, but
you are dumb as hell and you will always be that way! And your
grandmother and granddad are an embarrassment to the world."

Now he had her attention. There had been no cause for him
to say these things about her mom and dad; they had never done
anything to him.

"Hell," she thought. "You don't even know them, let alone what
they stand for." What he had just said was enough to cause an
overpowering pain and anger. She could never forget things like
this. It would be like a recorder that played over and over in her
head, and it wouldn't stop.

She was always so worried and on guard around him that she
was surprised to know that she could laugh at him, especially in
front of him.

The day being hot like it was, the cool water felt good to the skin
underneath her shirt. On the way back to the calf barn Suzann
noticed that Jay T was looking at her with a changed look on his
face. When she looked down at herself, she could see what he was
looking at. Having no bra on, the prints of her breasts under the
wet shirt looked inviting, but she had to save her bras to wear to
school, what few that she had.

"Jay T, I'm going to the house to change into some dry clothes."

"No, you're not. There ain't no need to do that as long as we are cleaning, you will only get this shit all over you again." As they walked back in, the straw was at the far end of the barn and had to be put down after the stalls were clean. They were walking to the back of the barn to get a bale of straw when Jay T pulled her to the side, taking hold of her shoulders with brute force.

"You're teasing me," he accused.

"What are you talking about?"

Knowing before she said a word that there was no use to trying to reason with him.

"Come on, there is a lot of work to be done," she reminded him.

Mixed emotions flickered across Suzann's face, fright being the dominant one.

"I want to talk to you," he said, now allowing her to break free of his hold. Jay T drew a sort of exited breath as he reached out and pushed her wet hair behind her shoulders.

"I can think of other things that I'd rather be doing," he said.

His eyes held a look of softness and pain, almost as if she had done or said something to cause him immeasurable hurt. The precarious knot that she had twisted in her hair had begun to unwind as she stood there listening to what he had to say. His mood swings could change quickly and could be very confusing for Suzann to interpret. This one was not!

Suzann was clearing her throat, trying desperately to swallow the lump that was growing increasingly in size, so her words would come out correctly.

"Jay T, STOP! I don't want your hands on me!"

"Is that right? Well, we'll see how long it takes you to change your mind. Maybe you enjoy being treated like you are. And you enjoy pain, do you? Well, I can oblige you as much as I can."

His voice suddenly darkened.

"When you've had enough you will beg me, you hear? Huh, you hear me?"

Suzann's next breath hung in midair, unable to force the words from her lips, while he was slapping her face from left to right, on and on and on.

"You like this? Yes. Yes," Jay T answered himself.

Hearing his voice and somehow still seeing his face, she saw that he was drowning in a strange angered excitement

"Oh, you pretty little bitch, want me to keep it up? Damn you. Damn you, you ain't a baby anymore, you're old enough. Come on, let me hear your little sobs of pleasure."

Then he placed both of his hands over her breast and the pleasure it brought him from his twisting and squeezing brought out a raging scream that she could not control, it just happened. She saw him pulling back one of his hands and making a fist. Then there was little light, it was like looking into the sky at the stars, and then there was nothing but blackness. His relief was evident from the growing wet stain beginning to show on the front of his dirty pants. He smiled and backed up, and then laughed as he left her in a tangled heap.

But for Suzann it was like a black hole, like someone had erased all the stars from the heaven. When she woke up, there was a terrible headache to go with it. Then she found a knot the size of an egg on the back of her head. She tried to open her eyes and found that the blackness and the light came off and on, so she decided to keep her eyes closed hoping that it would make the pain better. She wasn't even sure where she was. And then fear hit her that she might be blind because she could hear things, but when she opened her eyes everything was dark. The pain was throbbing so badly that sleep was completely out of the question. Then slowly she began to become aware of things. The coldness to her forehead from the cold wet washcloth which had been placed on her head by someone offered little help. And the smell around her was as if she was still in the calf barn. Then she noticed that the clothes she had on were still wet, and she knew now that the smell was coming from her. She tried to sit up but the pain that shot through her head was so intense that it caused her to grab her head as if she had to hold it on her shoulders, and she had to lie back down ever so gently. Everything was clear now except for the lump on the back of her skull. When Suzann opened her eyes and looked up, she saw Kate standing over the bed looking down at her, shaking her head.

"Kate, will you help me get myself cleaned up?"

"You got yourself into this mess, so you can get yourself out!" Kate's obvious enjoyment at Suzann's pain and misery registered on Suzann when Kate turned to leave. As she walked away, a strange eerie giggle came from her lips. Then she turned and looked at Suzann and openly laughed out loud, and then she left the room.

"Kate, please, don't leave . . ."

Suzann squelched the rising feeling of panic and clutched at her stomach as the convulsive gagging reached her throat. With one movement Suzann went from the bed down the hall and into the bathroom, with the room turning and spinning out of place. She finally found the commode and hugged it for dear life.

Suzann thought that she must have lost her toenails because everything that had been down came up, and she began dry heaving until there was nothing more left. Immediately she snatched a washcloth from the back of the commode and wet it with cold water, washing her face. But the longer she stood there, the worse the spinning got until she could feel herself going limp. When she came to this time, Handy was holding her and washing her face.

"Shhh," he said in a soothing tone, "don't fight it. Just relax and take some long deep breaths and another and another."

"Handy, please help me get into some clean clothes. The smell of these is not helping the way that I'm feeling.

"Suzann. Suzann,"

Jay T called out to her. "Look at me. Look at me, Suzann."

As she looked up this time, she could see that it was Jay T in her face.

"Where is Handy?" she asked.

"Handy is not here. I'll help you get your clothes off and clean you up a bit," Jay T said.

"NO. NO!"

Suzann could see Jay T's face in between the lights when she was herself and in the darkness when she wasn't, but she could not tell for sure what was going on. She knew that he was doing something, but she was not sure of what. At some point Suzann could hear Jay T and Kate talking but she could not make out what they were saying.

Jay T picked her up from the bathroom floor and carried her into her room and put her in the bed. Suzann remembered positioning herself and was determined to remain there until she fell asleep.

CHAPTER THIRTY-SEVEN

Suzann alternated between feeling ridiculous and energized. Dressed in pale green bell-bottom jeans and a dark green western shirt with pearl snaps and her hair pulled back in a Farah Fawcett do to help cover the large swelled knot on the back of her head, she stood there listening. She could hear Kate and Jay T talking and laughing in the living room. They were saying something about cleaning out the stalls. There was no telling what kind of lie Jay T had told Kate about what happened to Suzann. As she listened to them, she could not imagine how there was anything funny about that kind of work. Then she overheard Kate tale Jay T that she was pregnant again; her voice was loud and clear. Suzann felt weighted, consumed with disappointment. Not believing that Kate would let herself become pregnant again. Hell, she didn't want the ones that she already had and she sure didn't love them. Suzann had to take care of Jim Bob most of the time and the rest had to do for themselves with a lot of help from Suzann.

Other people that she had met and those in school always seemed to have love or were able to find love. But Suzann's life found no such harmony. It was better for her to make a good life on her own than to count on anyone in this house for something that they could not give. Suzann was thinking that she had to get away from here for what had just happened with Jay T And she knew what he was after, and next time she might not be so lucky.

So she made up her mind and decided that she was going to tell Handy what had happened. A shiver took over her body from the thought of Jay T touching her in any way. "Maybe he needs the opportunity to really cut loose and go into town. And now would be a perfect time since he was so damn horny. He needs to discover a wild woman, one who doesn't care. Maybe if he got lucky he could make her feel all warm and gushy inside—if she kept him in the dark, with the darkness being for her benefit." With all the thoughts running through her head, she suddenly noticed that there was no longer anyone talking in the living room. Jay T must have left to go back to work. "Maybe he will fall down the cliff on one of his trips to unload the barrels of shit."

Although the day sun seemed immensely bright outside, her room felt dark and closed in around her like a trap with no way out. She was sliding back down in her bed, pulling the covers almost over her head, when she heard her door slightly open. She pretended to be asleep as the door started to close she caught a glimpse of Kate before the door was completely shut. Lying there so very still, Suzann had the sense that someone was watching her. As she turned to look out the window, she saw a familiar pair of blue eyes outside. Suzann raised her window. "Handy," she said in a whisper. "What are you doing here?"

"I got your note that you left for me."

"Oh yes, I had forgotten that I left you one."

"Are you OK?"

"No, I need to talk to you desperately but not here. If Kate should see or hear us I would be in a lot of trouble."

"Suzann, are those bruises on your face?"

"Yes."

"Why do you have bruises on your face?"

"I'll tell you later. But not now, things here are not good."

"I know," he answered. "I can see that. Will you be all right? Can it wait until tomorrow because Jay T has got to go with Mr. Butler around noon to look at a new bull that he is wanting to buy. They will be gone most of the evening because Mr. Butler has asked me to do the milking tomorrow evening."

"Yes, that would be perfect. I'll find you after lunch tomorrow."

Handy left her window and Suzann lay back down to try to get some rest because she knew that tomorrow would be a long and hard day. And she had some talking to do. Suzann uttered a rueful little laugh to the fact that Handy was overwhelmed to see her so unprepared and forgetful. He was used to seeing her running wide open and on top of everything. Handy didn't know but he had a way of picking her spirits up when she was feeling down. He didn't know but that was exactly what he done today. Suzann fell asleep thinking about all the things that she was going to tell him tomorrow.

Awakened from a dead sleep from the sound of Jim Bob; it was a blood curdling scream, then another and another. With concern, Suzann was trying desperately to get to him. As her feet hit the floor, the room began to spin again, leaving her with the feeling that she was going to throw up again. Holding on to the sides of the wall, trying to make it to the door, finally she got it open and slowly walked down the hall where she could hear Kate talking to Jim Bob. Not believing what she was hearing, she stopped at the entrance to the room where Kate was and looked around the corner of the door. Suzann's mouth dropped open, not believing what she was seeing.

Kate was changing his diaper with a clean one. She was taking the pins and sticking them all the way in his butt, leaving one there and taking the other one and probing it as a surgeon would do in an exploratory surgery of some kind.

Talking to him, in a manner of rage, saying, "I hate you. I hate you. Why didn't you just die while you were being born?" She took pin and pulled it out and then poked it back into his butt again and then again. And then she said to him, "If I knew that you were going to be another boy, you would be resting next to your brother." As Suzann stood there, trying to back up a little so Kate wouldn't know that she was there, and she sure didn't want Kate to know that she had heard what was said. Suzann felt like she was going to melt to the floor, her body was trembling and her hands were wet from sweat. And her head felt like it was going to explode. There was a twofold sense of fear and anger that gripped her insides as she stood there hearing what was said and watching Kate enjoy the brutal pain that she was inflicting upon Jim Bob, piercing into the flesh of this baby who had no way to defend himself. The only thing that he could do was lie there and scream with the breath leaving his small defenseless body every time she pushed the pins deeper into his buttocks. A little blood was oozing from the puncture wounds in his little butt and hips. Suzann's mind was spinning faster than the room. "Kate has lost her fucking mind. There has to be something bad wrong with her. There is no mother in the world that does a baby like this. How can Kate find pleasure in this cruelty? How can her face have such an expression of immense pleasure and a sick sort of relief? What do I do? What do I do?"

Suzann knew that what Kate was doing was not uncontrollable; she meant to do these things. "She is as mean as Jay T, and they deserve each other." Normally, this thought would have brought at least a small smile but it did not help today. There was nothing funny about this. Not prolonging the suspense, Suzann could not allow Kate to continue what she was doing. She licked her dry lips.

"Damn you," Suzann shouted as she jammed her fist into the upper wall over her head. Even the feel of the hard wood that peeled back the top layer of skin from her knuckles brought no pain. Feeling the room spin, Suzann let herself slide down the wall until she was sitting on the floor on top of her feet. Not feeling any pain from her torn hands, she placed them over her face. Tears mixed with blood were running down both of her arms and onto the clothes that she was wearing.

"There's no help for anyone here," she thought agonizingly.

Suzann burst into another deluge of tears. When she moved her hands from her face, she saw Kate out of the corner of her eye, standing over her like a big bad ass who liked to beat up people who could not defend themselves.

"Damn you, you're back and you're snooping on me again, aren't you?" She began kicking Suzann in the side with her foot knocking her over onto the floor from where she had been sitting. The force behind her foot was hard and had a lot of weight behind it. Suzann whirled around to block her kicking foot, weaving her hands to prevent Kate from kicking her in the face.

"That's right, hurt me. Go ahead. Hurt me but don't hurt him anymore. You think you are so big and bad. Here, take your anger out on me."

Suzann dreaded what she might encounter after saying what she did, but at this point she didn't care anymore. Taking every bit of the energy that she had left in her body, she swallowed her fear and begrudgingly got to her feet. Now she was looking Kate face to face and seeing the fire in Kate's eyes. Her look said she would like to kill Suzann where she stood. Suzann's voice was beginning to break. "Don't hurt him anymore. I'm begging you, please. Why do you want to be like this?"

"Let me tell you something. If you can't handle what you see, then don't watch. Go into another room or leave the house. I don't care what you have to do, just don't ever interrupt or try to tell me what to do and don't you ever curse me. Girl, and one more thing, if you ever breathe a word of what goes on in this house, I'll kill him. I won't have to worry about killing you because Jay T seems to be trying to do that. Dwan, get in here and clean up this fuckin' mess."

Dwan came in and picked up Jim Bob and put his diaper back on and tried to get him to stop crying. But the crying wouldn't stop, so Kate jerked him from her arms and took him in her bedroom and threw him in his baby bed. Then she turned and walked out and slammed the door behind her then stormed out of the house, saying as she was stomping out,

"Leave him alone. He'll shut up when he shuts up."

Suzann's lips formed Dwan's name as she closed her eyes from the bloody tears and pain inside her head. There had been so many experiences that led her to this moment; she simply had to find the courage to take the next step. Keeping up was exhausting to her, and the only thing that kept her going was praying that the reward would be well worth it.

"Dwan, could you please help me?" Her hands were on the floor to help push herself up. With Dwan's help and the walls, Suzann was able to stand. She slowly half walked and half staggered to her room. There she sat down in a chair next to her bed that sat against the wall. Dwan went to the bathroom and got a wet washcloth and cleaned the blood from her face and hands.

"Here, hold this rag around your hands until I get the blood off the floor in the hall, then I'll come back and we are going to have to wrap something around your hands. You skinned them up pretty good."

Dwan thought for a minute and then looked up at Suzann with a faint little smile. "Heavens," she said. "Things are bad with you and Mom, why does she hate you so much?"

They stared at each other for a moment in stiff silence; Suzann drew a long deep breath and exhaled the air that filled her lungs, loudly. There was no answer. Suzann was going to have to practice a new balancing act just to keep herself from going insane. Emotionally, and slowly overwhelmingly, Suzann was being forced to let go of some of her own desires and allow her life to flow in whatever direction it might take her. But her adventure in this move to this home had never been a good one.

"Well, I'm going to clean up the mess before Mom gets back so she won't be mad."

Suzann sat there holding the rags in place and then she began to feel the pain pulsing throughout both of her hands. Thinking back over the nightmarish event that had just happened, she began berating herself repeatedly for allowing herself to let Kate do this to her, but it would have been hard to defend herself with the room spinning out of control and everything feeling out of place and not being able to focus. But she would rather be a whipping post for Kate to take out her frustrations on than that little boy in there. Suzann was in no way prepared for moments like these. There were no possibilities, only responsibilities that were enormous. Sniffing back the runny nose, with tears blurring her vision, she lowered her face down into her hands wrapped with a washcloth so full of blood that it was once again dripping on the floor. The sound of the spattering blood and the mess it was making went unnoticed by Suzann. Her mind and almost her whole being had retreated to somewhere dark and hidden. She knew that she would have to climb out of this hazy place that she was in and face reality. That reality would hold nothing for her but pain, pain from her torn hands and even worse would be the pain and suffering of the small infant added to her own sufferings. As she started her mental climb, another dark thought stormed into her already delicate state. It brought such fear and horror to her that her mental voice screamed in anguish. "WHAT IF I TURN OUT TO BE LIKE THEM?" Her mental state suddenly fell into an even darker abyss. Her self-will gained control and she pushed the fear aside. She recalled and reviewed her actions in several events in her life. She was satisfied that she had handled each happening as correctly as she could have. This satisfaction caused her full consciousness to awaken. But the opening of her eyes caused her thoughts to come even quicker. "There is no room for another person like Kate and Jay T on this earth. They are two moles that surely have a need to be destroyed." Suzann stared off with her expression troubled and so very grim because there were so many doubts in her mind and unanswered questions. She found herself talking to the heavens above, thinking that all questions and answers should be simple. It's supposed to be the human way to grow, learn, and share thoughts to make everything in life better. Maybe God is deepening and patiently waiting for the day that all these things are noticed. She pushed away her feelings when her door opened carefully; it was Dwan. She had a white cloth that she had cut out from a tee shirt, and then she went back in to the bathroom and got the bottle of alcohol. When she returned, she closed the door and then it was just the two of them. Her long slender fingers went to work cleaning and trying to pull the skin back in place. Working quickly and quietly, she wrapped the rag tightly around Suzann's hands to the best that she knew how.

Suzann saw the sweat that had collected over her face and that the color was leaving her natural brown tone.

"It's going to be all right," Suzann assured her. "You should think about being a nurse, you would make a good one. It looks worse than it actually is." She thought it best not to try to get up and walk, afraid that she might pass out again and knowing if that happened Dwan would not be able to get her back up in the bed. Suzann turned her tortured eyes up to Dwan and tried again to speak.

"What . . . what . . . about Jim Bob? How . . . bad is he hurt?" Her voice was stammering and sounded wheezy from all the crying.

"He is going to be all right."

"Did you see what she was doing to him?"

"No, I didn't see her doing anything to him, but I slipped in there after Mom left and gave him a fresh bottle. I took off his diaper and looked at his bottom, and it looks really bad. Whatever she was doing, she had been doing it for a long time because his butt is so bruised, really bad, and there are fresh marks everywhere. It looks like needle marks, and his bottom end is covered with them. I put some bacon grease on it, but it looks like he needs to go to the doctor. There are sores and scabs, and some of them had stuff running out of them. I cleaned them the best that I could, but he would start screaming when I tried to touch them. It has to hurt really badly. Suzann, his butt looks like a pin cushion. And that place on his foot looks awful."

"What place on his foot?"

"It looks like teeth marks, and it is cut in the skin pretty deep."

"Do you know when this happened?"

"Yes, the other morning, after you had left to go to the barn, he woke her up crying. He must have been wet or hungry, but anyway she got all mad and just went crazy or something. I stayed in my room. It's my fault, I should have done something."

"No, it's not your fault. Don't ever think that. You done the right thing. There was nothing that you could have done."

After hearing all of this and seeing what just happened, a cold shaky sensation invaded and hovered over Suzann, leaving her feeling weak inside. She slowly undressed and cleaned herself up, changing into some clean clothes. In the silence, Dwan helped her get back into bed.

"Suzann, you need a doctor. That place on your head feels soft and mushy."

"Both of them are a worthless pieces of shit!"

"Shhh . . . don't say that too loud. You know how they are." Her hands were interlocked in her sleeves, as she talked. It was obvious that she was nervous and scared.

"Suzann," Dwan said slowly. "I'm scared that someone is going to lose their life from things that are taking place here. There are too many accidents and I'm scared of death."

Suzann could hear the fear in her voice and tried to give her an answer that she could understand. "You should have no fear of death. Your desire and instinct to stay alive are always the strongest, but death is a condition the no one has any control over."

Dwan gave her a grateful look that radiated a certain look of relief that helped release her fears. In the conversation, they both heard Suzann's stomach growling over what they were saying.

She had not eaten since the day before and was starting to feel weak.

"Come on, let me cover you up and I'll go and fix you something to eat."

"No, my appetite is gone."

"Well, you need to eat something so you can get your strength back. I'll be back in a little bit with something for you to eat."

After lying there for a while, her mind began to drift off again. Mulling over all the things that had happened and trying to find some sort of key that could make everything better. There had to be an answer to all of this.

She turned her head cautiously, trying to find a position where it wouldn't hurt, but that position was not found. Her mind had begun to badger her, beat her up, with words that she could not turn off. Afraid to analyze the meaning of her presence, her purpose in life, and the absence of love and needs were backward here; there was none. Being frightened and not understanding why this was happening to her left her feeling so distant and alone. While staring at the top of the ceiling, she remembered Handy's visit. Tomorrow was going to be a challenge, yet she welcomed the opportunity to meet with Handy. She had to start somewhere, and whatever happened would just have to happen. "It doesn't matter. It cannot get any worse than it already is," she thought to herself.

CHAPTER THIRTY-EIGHT

Morning came and caught Suzann looking out the window and watching the rain drizzle to the ground. Watching the curtains flutter from the breeze that was coming through the windows that were slightly raised somehow gave her a tremendous sense of relief with the thought of talking to Handy. And at the same time, knowing what she was going to say was causing her to get butterflies in her stomach. Her tears weren't going to change anything around here no more than the rain was going to change the color of the dirt after it was dry again. Telling herself that she would have no regrets; things had been going on far too long and she was going to make a stand.

Dwan came into her room with a bowl of chicken soup in her hands.

"You feeling any better?" she asked.

Sitting up in the bed, Suzann placed the bowl in front of her, taking a bit then smacking her lips together. "Mmmm, very good. You would make a good cook also."

"This is a change," Dwan said.

"What are you talking about?" Suzann asked.

"Well, you are usually the one that is waiting on everyone here, and I'm enjoying waiting on you for a change even though the circumstances aren't the best."

"It smells so good."

"You just eat it. It will make you feel better. You want me to get you some bread or crackers to eat with it?"

"No, the soup is just fine. Thank you so much"

Dwan moved aside and sat down and watched as Suzann ate the soup.

"Can I ask you something?"

"Sure."

"What happened yesterday? When Jay T brought you to the house you were unconscious I thought that you were dead."

"I don't know. I can't remember," Suzann lied."

"Jay T said that you fell and hit your head on something."

"Well, if you knew that why did you ask me?"

"Well, after seeing you, if you fell that would explain the knot on the back of your head but it don't make any sense how you would have those bruises on your face. So I think that he lied."

She had a gleam in her eyes but there was doubt in her voice. Suzann's fingers loosened their grip on the cover of the bed as she was talking.

"Well, maybe I need to build up a little more immunity to not feel pain so much," Suzann said with a smile, ignoring Dwan's opinion on truth.

"I don't think that your immunity is working at all," Dwan answered.

"You know, I think you are right." The words had barely left her mouth when Jay T walked into the room, saying, "Don't you think that you've been in that bed long enough? You've been asleep for sixteen hours or longer. Come on, it's time to get up."

Trying to get her eyes focused, she could see him through blurred vision although he seemed to be in a tunnel a long distance off.

"I want you to get up and take a good hot bath, put on some clean clothes and some of that smelly good stuff that you wear, and then eat something. And then I'll walk you to the barn so you can get some fresh air, that will make you feel so much better." He smiled.

But Suzann could see right through his shitty ass smile and knew that it didn't mean shit. She had learned the hard way that when he was nice to her, it always would lead into something bad. His smile was like the face that it was on, cold and dead. "What a loser," she thought. "I'm gonna set you up for a bigger fall than the one you had in the hay barn," she was thinking.

Sitting up in bed, she felt a little lightheaded as her feet hit the floor. Standing up beside her bed, trying to pull herself together, she could still feel the pulsing in her head. Standing in front of the mirror, she could see that there was a little bruising on her face. She began to unwrap the bandage from her hands that Dwan had put on yesterday, or the day before, she wasn't even sure what day it was. After Suzann had finished, she went into the kitchen where the smell of something good cooking caused her stomach to do flip-flops.

"Sit down, I'll fix you a plate," Kate said.

Suzann sat down at the table and Kate brought her a plate that had enough food on it to feed at least three people, along with a glass of milk.

"And drink your milk," she ordered.

Suzann ate until she could hold no more and poured the glass of milk into the sink while no one was there to see her like she always did with all other glasses of milk. All finished, she put her plate in the sink and went into the living room.

Standing there looking over little Jim Bob who was lying on the floor on a pallet, sleeping ever so soundly, a feeling of sorrow swept over her for him.

"Are you ready?" Jay T asked.

"You've been waiting on me. I'm sorry."

"That's all right," he said. "I'm in no hurry.

How's the hand?"

"Better than my head," she answered.

"Kate told me that you went out of your head and tried to beat the wall down before she could get to you."

"What a lie, wonder how long it took her to make that one up," she thought in silence.

"Let me see your hands. My god, Suzann. Who did you think that you were beating up?"

"I don't remember," she lied again. She let her thoughts backtrack to what had happened, Jay T had not a clue what Kate had been doing to Jim Bob.

"Well, I have got to go with Mr. Butler today. And while we are out I'll stop and get something to put on this. It looks like it could have used a couple of stitches.

Kate, why didn't you tell me it was this bad?"

Kate walked over and looked. "Well, it didn't look that bad when I wrapped it."

Suzann was standing there listening to all those lies, trying to figure out which one was the best at what they were doing. What a big front. They work so well together. They both had on a face that would make any judge believe what they were saying. Suzann could not believe what she was hearing. They had to have gotten together and rehearsed this act for hours, they were so perfect.

What Suzann really wanted to say when he asked was that it had been his face that she was beating up but she didn't. She kept all her thoughts to herself and under her breath, just like all of her prayers. And why the sudden concern? Suzann looked up and saw Dwan standing there and listening to what was said, dropping her head as she turned and walked out of the room.

While walking to the barn, Jay T informed Suzann that she would not be going home with Jim and Mary tomorrow when they got there, saying "I know that is the only reason that they are coming. The only reason that they come at all is to take you back home with them, do you hear what I'm saying?"

She heard him, but then asked, "Why can't I go back home with them? It's the only time that I get to go to church."

"Yeah, and that's another reason. When you go to church, you come back home different, hard to get along with. It drives you away from what could be a good relationship with me."

"You are swirling in a whirlpool of selfish desires and you are wrong. You are a bad and mean man, you have a bad heart," Suzann said.

"I've made my damn decision so don't question my ruling no more. And you have said quite fuckin' enough. You don't know a thing of what you are talking about. This is some of that fuckin' dumb shit that I'm trying to get out of your damn head."

Suzann was thinking, "You are the dumb shit. You are a bastard, both of you, and I hate you so much. I repent and give my heart to God and pray every night, alone in the dark, and ask him to forgive me of my feelings and the way that I use my mouth, my thoughts, but things seems to be getting worse by the day. I try so hard but I feel like I'm walking alone and sometimes I would rather be dead than walk this path of life that I'm being forced to live."

Her thoughts were interrupted by Jay T when he bumped her hand with his hand, swinging it back and forth as they walked. Then he grabbed her hands and squeezed them with his large hands which put her vigorously to the ground from the pain that he was forcing her to endure. Tears stung her eyes as he knelt, letting his knee rest on the ground. Suzann closed her eyes and felt the blood being drained from her body and heat being the replacement. She turned her sad eyes up to his face "Why, Jay T? Why?"

"You still like pain, don't you? And I've not heard you begging yet, and you know what I'm talking about."

Releasing the pressure from her hands, Suzann regained her composure and concentrated on her hate for him instead of the pain in her hands. It worked. Everything inside her died. It was like she had been injected with Novocain to the point of numbness, all she could feel was hate. "I hate you. I hate you," she was saying over and over and over in her mind

The seal had been broken again where the cuts were on her hands, causing them to bleed once again. Ignoring the blood that was soaking through the clean bandage on her hands, he looked at her and waited for her to answer his statement with no trace of relief in the expression on his face. She stood in silent disbelief at what he wanted her to do. He turned and looked behind them and then said gruffly, "Let's walk." They were walking on towards the barn when he suddenly said, "Sit the fuck down." She sat down on an old dead log that was lying next to the corral where the registered bull was kept for breeding. Jay T started rolling another one of his nasty smelling cigarettes.

"Jay T?" Suzann asked. "Will you give me some time to recuperate and get my strength back?"

"Meaning what?" he asked.

"Meaning nothing, just a little time to think about what all you have said."

"Then what?" his voice was full of suspicion.

Worriedly, she knew by her words that she had said too much but she could not stop now, she had gone too far. "I'm pretty banged up right now and you know why I'm in this shape. But that is not all that is bothering me.

Don't misunderstand me, but you have got to stop Kate from mistreating Jim Bob. Please, you can stop her from hurting him."

"She's not hurting him; it's all in your mind, you're just making that fuckin' shit up," was Jay T's answer. "Well, I'll do like you said that you would do, I'll think about it. When you give me an answer, I'll give you one."

"Why would you do that? You just said that you didn't believe me."

"Now you need to go to the house and clean up your hands. I've got to stay here and meet Mr. Butler and go with him. You won't have to do anything the rest of the day. Handy is going to take care of the work." He had completely ignored her comment. Jay T scanned her face; she saw the look on his face and could tell that he thought that he was finally breaking her down.

"I want you for myself. You will never let it be known. And any time that I want it, you will give it up to me with no argument. Think about that, Suzann. It's up to you, now go."

Suzann knew that there was no reasoning with him, so she started walking back to the house. Suddenly, her voice spoke a thought that seemed to fill her body and mind with a renewed strength. "Before you fuck me, you mother fuckin' son of a bitch, one of us will be dead and I don't aim for it to be me! Oh, and by the way, Kate, you just made the same list!" She was almost there when she saw Mr. Butler picking up Jay T. Then she made a ninety-degree turn and went back to the farm to try and find Handy.

CHAPTER THIRTY-NINE

Silence followed her walk, with plenty of time to wonder as Jay T's words absorbed in her mind completely. She could not forgive him for the things that he had done, things he had said, and the things that he was asking of her. But after all it has been said that time does allow for compensations. Suzann had but little time and she knew it. But no one had a clue or knew the real perpetrator, which was the problem. He would probably be the least suspect even though he was not that intelligent. "He does hate his mother and his god hangs in the Bible belt that he uses and I'm a hundred percent convinced that Jay T is capable of doing anything and getting away with it." She closed her eyes as she walked and in a strange way his attack on her had energized her, leaving her with no choice but to fight back knowing that she would not have a chance physically. "But there is more than one way to kill a goose." Without so much as a blink, Suzann now felt that she could calmly take a gun and kill him. But Jay T did not own a gun for some reason, and would not have a gun in his home. Suzann knew that all life was precious, her emotions stirred and she dared that son of a bitch to try and take her virginity, that was the one thing that she held sacred and the only thing that he had not scarred in her life. Now he was after that. Her insides turned to jelly with the thought, and her heart wrenched within her chest.

Suzann had prayed and prayed, hoping and asking God to show her the way to reduce the pain and suffering to those children that had no chance, they had to take whatever was dished out to them. They had become, by no choosing of their own, victims of a bad circumstance. And they had to suffer for no reason; Suzann shrugged her sore shoulders and thought, "Maybe God is showing me the way." He is life itself but she could not understand why God would let such little innocent lives be tortured. There had to be a comeback. If it was to be, this is one comeback that would be embarrassing, especially for Suzann. Too many people knew too little and in her semi-brainwashed condition, she was embarrassed and at times blamed herself for many of the incidents.

The sun flamed across the sky as she wet her lips anxiously worrying about all the unanswered questions running through her head on her search for Handy.

Then she heard a voice saying, "You are going to wear yourself out thinking so hard," drawing her momentarily out of her nether world of doubt and pain. She reached out her arms and ran to him with all the strength that she had, hugging him, and preparing to open her soul and not seal it again. Tears traced down the warm lines of her cheeks. Even through the tears, she smiled gently.

"What is the reason for you tearing yourself apart? Why are you shaking?"

He held everything that precious to him, for Suzann had become a big part of his life, as he held her tightly to comfort her. His expression stayed curiously calm, taking out his handkerchief to dry her face from her tears.

"This is not a good place. Come on, we will go to my room and talk. There, no one can see or hear anything. Does anyone know that you were coming to see me today?"

"No, no one knows."

"That is good, and we will keep it that way."

Suzann watched his heavy form as they walked away. She felt a knot in her stomach and began to tremble, thinking to herself, "Is this what I really want to do? I've got to make up my mind. I've got to do this for little Jim Bob's sake if nothing else. She was lost in her worries as Handy opened the door to let her in.

"Shhh," he said, holding her tight. "It's all right now."

But he already knew that things were not all right with her, there was something badly wrong.

"Let me look at you. What . . . your hands, your face . . . What is going on, Suzann?"

Then Handy noticed the back of her head while he was pulling her hair back from her face.

"Oh my god," Handy said.

He felt his pulse begin to race. He bent forward and kissed her on the forehead. Telling himself that he was just going to listen to what she had to say, thinking that if he interrupted her she might stop talking and this was one time that someone was going to hear what she had to say.

Suzann reached the edge of his bed and sat down, holding her hands still with the blood soaked rags around them. Handy snapped the radio off and went to the kitchen sink and fixed some warm water. "Come here and let me take a look at your hands and clean them up. I saw Jay T a little while ago and he was holding your hands. You were on your knees. He was hurting you, wasn't he?"

"Yes, Jay T has been impossible lately." Tears glittered in her baby blue eyes as Handy placed his hand on her shoulder while taking off the bandages from her hands.

"Damn, girl. Did he do this to your hands?"

"No, this was my doing."

"Are you sure?" Then he whispered to calm her, "Talk to me."

"Things have changed so much, I am not sure where to start and don't know what to do." They both were quiet. She cleared her throat, smiling reluctantly, knowing that she felt the safest in his presence. Handy shot her a sidelong grin and allowed her time to get it together.

Handy put some medication on her hands and rewrapped them. "You don't need to have your hands in water for a couple of days, give them some time to close up and start to heal."

Suzann was now ready to talk. "Handy, from the first day until now, all of this time and what has been going on is tearing me apart. Remembering all the talk when I was smaller about never giving up and things being good, being able to make anything in my life that I wanted. Things happen for a reason, is what I have been told, and it will lead to a good thing. No one knows the truth. And I'm starting to believe that these things are not meant for me."

"Suzann, I want to know the truth and we will go from there." What Handy was hearing from Suzann was far more then he could have ever imagined.

Suzann told Handy everything, leaving nothing out. For hours, only the groan of wind disturbed the spilling of her soul. Suzann finally dropped the shell that had been weighing so heavily on her chest. Handy extended his hand to her with his chest rising and falling swiftly under his shirt. With a red face filled with the blood of anger. Suzann braced her elbows on her knees as her hands covered her face and once again tears flooded down her cheeks. She was filled with embarrassment and now ashamed to look him in the face.

But Handy was not dumb and he could see through what she had to be feeling and could understand, and he knew that she had every right to feel this way. But Jay T had no rights; he had none whatsoever. The only right he had left was to die. He clamped his hands around the collar of his shirt, pulling it tightly around his neck as he stood there looking at Suzann while she sat on the edge of his bed with her head held down in shame.

"Suzann, you have no reason to be ashamed of what he has done. It's not your fault. Now, you get that out of your head. For your sake, don't even think that."

Handy bowed down on the floor in front of her, respectfully trying to hide the irritated look on his face, desperately worried, but he knew that this was not over. Handy reached up and removed her hands that were covering her face, letting his head fall to the side as he looked at the shadows of bruises that covered her checks. Her hair straggled around her small shoulders and gave off a sweet fragrance. He touched her hand that still showed a nervous movement. His mouth twisted as he dipped his head in acknowledgment and said,

"Your sense of honor is shining on your pretty little face." Then he asked,

"Does anybody know any of this, anything at all?"

"No, only you," she smiled as answered him.

"I am the one that should be ashamed. I knew that Jay T was violent but I didn't know that he would do things like this, I knew that he was mean to you and I hated that but he has gone too far this time. And Kate, I can't believe that she would be as mean as him."

Handy seemed so surprised, annoyed. And it was easy to see that he was not pleased at all with what she had told him. Handy made that low sound from deep in his throat. "I used to think that Jay T was all right. Hell, I've been pretty damn close to him until I started seeing and hearing things that he had said to you. It was the way that he talked to you. The worst was the way that he makes you work. Hell, you work as hard as any man around here. Now I know what you mean when you say that no one would believe you. They would take his word because he is so good at putting up a front." Handy's mind was blown just contemplating this. "I can tell by the way you talk that he has made you hard, and you are such a beautiful young woman." He tried hard to hold on to his grip, but feeling sorry for her was not going to help her from this situation. Her being tired and frightened entered her voice when she spoke.

"Handy, I'm scared; I'm scared for Jim Bob. I cannot stand by and let Kate hurt him anymore. I've got a bad feeling."

Handy stared at her troubled face as she talked about being intimidated by a rank, smelly, and dangerous women. He listened to every word and read between the lines where he saw was so much hurt inside her. Handy held her head against his shoulder when he heard her say, "I would not wish my life on anyone."

He stood perfectly still, hearing her conversation as it traveled around the small room that he lived in. His face reacting to everything that was said, his eyes glassy as he spoke in a low different voice, trying to find the right thing to say that might give her some relief. Thinking to himself what was he going to do to help her, he didn't know for sure but he was going to do something.

Then at just that moment, they heard steady sprinkles of rain that had just began to fall, and the sun was still shining. But in the company of the rain there was a desolate sound, a secret sound that closed her secret now around two. Suzann no longer stood alone. Suzann looked up at him, searching beyond his eyes deep into his soul for answers, then she said, "I have no regrets in telling this dark secret to you, but I can't tell my mom and dad because . . . well, you know why."

The rain had stopped. Handy shook his head, then sighed. "I promise you that Jay T will never know that you even talk to me, and I also promise you that this is going to stop."

"How?" she asked.

"I am not sure yet. Let me think on this tonight and see what I can come up with." But Handy had an idea, and if that didn't work he had better one.

Suzann was reluctant to see the evening end, wanting to hold on to the fatherly closeness that she felt in him.

"Suzann, don't do anything to make him mad. Do everything that he asks you to do, and I mean work. Keep your distance as much as you can from him. I might be taking off work on Monday. Now, you said that your mom and dad were coming tomorrow, right?"

"Yes."

"OK, you will have them here with you all weekend and that will give you some time to heal."

Suzann said in a relieved tone as she stopped in front of his door, "Thank you for being a friend." Standing there, she looked awkward for a minute. There was something guarded about her eyes. Handy could see it as he too had that shell-shocked look in his own.

She rolled her eyes to the ceiling, taking a long deep breath while Handy stepped outside to make sure that no one was around to see her come out.

Suzann felt like a ton of bricks had been removed from her shoulders as she was walking back to the house but she knew that what she had done had not changed a thing in this home.

CHAPTER FORTY

It was Saturday morning when Jim and Mary arrived; Suzann was standing in the backyard, looking out at the views of the land knowing that she had left dirty dishes on the counter and would have to admit that she hit the snooze button and overslept this morning. With the tips of her fingers stuck in the pockets of her faded jeans, she was still annoyed with confusion and pained emotions from feeling guilty, trying to remodel and shield the shame that she felt. After all these years, the ground beneath her feet was shifting; leaving her with a twinge of wonder at what she had gotten herself into. Enjoying the uncontrolled wind that was blowing against her face, Suzann knew that something else, something unnerving, the worst, was still to come. Then out of nowhere came a voice.

"Come to me," someone said behind her in a gentle, most perfectly audible voice.

"WHAT?" Suzann asked as she was turning around.

"Surprise!"

"Mother, oh, Mother, I'm so glad to see you."

"Did you not hear us drive up?"

"No."

"We saw you standing down here; you looked like you were in another world."

"I guess that I must have been. I didn't hear anything."

Mary noticed Suzann's face was bruised and she could see that there was something deeply wrong. Suzann was very much aware of the way that Mary was looking at her and her smile faded little by little.

Reaching out, Mary took hold of Suzann's hands. "It's so good to see you. Look at you. And you are all grown up. What happened to your hands?"

"Oh, it's nothing. I just skinned them a little." Mary nuzzled her cheek as she slipped some money into her back pocket. "I have missed you so much." Suzann gazed into her mother's agonized face and saw the lines that etched the corners of her eyes followed by a look that she might cry.

"Don't worry, I'll be fine."

Feeling frightened and uncomfortable and a little embarrassed for having to lie to someone who didn't deserve to be being lied to, she continued,

"Where is Daddy?"

"He's talking to Jay T over by the truck. Come on, he can't wait to see you. He has been talking about this day all week. We have been worried about you, wondering how you are doing."

Slowly they walked back across the yard in the direction of the truck. When they arrived there, they found that Jay T had just left.

Her daddy was standing there with open arms and Suzann walked directly into them.

Stroking her hair, "God, it is so good to see you," he said.

"How have you been doing? Are you all right? Still doing well in school?"

Her answer was yes, yes to all the above.

"I'm fine," she reassured him.

"But she looks so pale and thin," Mary said.

"You know your mother, she is always worrying about you."

Then Mary pulled out a folded quilt and held it tightly to her heart, saying, "I made this for you and I wish you to have it. It is very precious to me. It belonged to my grandmother; I had to redo it a bit." Suzann watched as she unfolded it to show her how there were no unbroken bands through the pattern in the whole quilt.

"It's so beautiful, but I think that you should keep it."

"No, I want you to have it and pass it down to your children. Come on let's go show it to Kate."

"NO, I mean not right now. Can we do that later?"

The morning was passing quickly as Suzann tried to find a way to get her dad somewhere to talk to him in private, away from everyone. She was starting to feel quite ridiculous, sitting there listening to everyone talk about things that were nothing but lies. Her mind and body felt as if they were two different entities as she continued to watch them drink coffee and tea, with Kate putting up another front, laughing and telling how good things were and how happy Suzann was there. She went on saying that Suzann had done a lot of spoiling the kids. But there was nothing said about how hard she had to work or anything bad that had happened. Suzann could tell by the way that her mom and dad looked and their response that they were soaking in everything that Kate was telling them.

Suzann's chance of getting Jim alone was looking slim to none. Sitting there for what seemed like hours, hearing words being passed back and forth but not knowing half what was being said, Suzann was in another dimension, another time, another place, and wishing that she truly was.

She sat there patiently waiting. Kate and Mary got up to go and start dinner. Hearing that brought Suzann back. At last her vigil had paid off. This left Suzann and Jim alone at last; here was the chance that she had been waiting for. But suddenly she found herself without words. Her mind searched frantically to find them but they wouldn't come. How could she start this conversation and what was the best way to reach him? All of her senses were going haywire as her heart began to pound in her chest.

Then Suzann got up unexpectedly as her mouth tightened. She wanted something. She needed to talk to her dad, knowing that if Jay T caught wind of what she was doing, well . . .

"Dad," she said in a voice throaty with a little anger. "Come on and let me show you around the place. I would like you to see the old graveyard that I found. You will be absolutely astounded. There are things there that you won't believe and it's unreal. It's completely unimaginable how old some of the rocks are, but yet it feels peaceful as if it still had life."

As they made their way out the door, Kate called out. "Where ya'll going?" she asked.

"We're just going to the barn," Suzann answered.

She caught a look from her dad, lined with wonder of why the lie, but not saying anything about it.

"Do you go there often?" he asked

"Yes, I walk there quit often. It's a good walk to clear the mind and find a little peace sometimes." They walked slowly down the road. Jim was pretty sure she didn't know how obvious she was, but he was concerned by her mood and her eagerness to get him alone.

She tried to put her thoughts together, knowing that this would be the last time that she would be able to talk to him. Hoping that he would believe her and help, she tried to speak clearly with a guarded caution, not wanting to tell any more than she had to.

"What's wrong, Suzann?"

"I've got to talk to you," she answered.

"Dad, do you care what becomes of me?" she asked

"Of course I do. Why in the world would you ask me such a question like that anyway?"

There was a pause.

"What's the real reason that you wanted to show me this graveyard?"

But the words wouldn't come to answer his question. She could see the frown furrowing his forehead and could tell he might be brooding over the mental image of what she might be going to tell him. He gave her a brief, wistful smile. They walked until they were at the site.

"It's beautiful here, isn't it?"

"You might be able to say that," he answered with a stoned look on his face.

"Remember that haunted house that was talked about when we first came here?"

"You're talking about the house with all the hedge bushes around it."

"Yeah, that's the one. This is where they are buried, and the words on their tombs are weird." Jim nodded as if this was a complete explanation to the reason they were here.

"Suzann, what are you thinking about with such a sad face?" he asked.

Suzann breathed hard, acutely aware of the hurt and anger that had embedded deep within her. Her mind was trying to drift away, but in all the drifting she knew that she had to stay in control.

"This is hard for me say, but I want you to know that things around here are not what they seem and Kate and Jay T are not the same people that you think they are."

"What do you mean?"

"I mean that I want you to take me back home to live with you and Mom, and you have got to promise not to tell Jay T or Kate what I'm telling you.

Promise?"

"OK, I promise."

There was a pause.

"Well, now what is the problem?"

"The problem is, they don't want me and they don't care about me or anything that happens to me. As far as that goes, they don't even want that baby up there, and Kate's pregnant again. All they want from me is to cook, clean, work, and take care of the other kids. Dad, things are really bad here."

"That's some pretty big accusations."

"These are not accusations! It's the plain truth, you just don't know." She ended her rage with a bitter sob and felt sudden remorse and some embarrassment at having bared her soul to him and then getting the impression from him that she was just making all of this up just so that she could go back and live with them.

Jim did not know what was really happening here and Kate's lies and carefree attitude had lulled him into feeling that everything was all right. He was a bit shocked and confused by what Suzann had said. He had no way of knowing that Suzann was looking for peace of mind, a sense of freedom, seeking help, crying out to the only ones that she thought would listen, someone who would understand, and for her sake, help.

Jim dropped his head but continued staring up at her, she had a look that he had never seen on her face before. He felt himself waver, what was she doing? What has brought all this about? Never before has she said anything at all about things being bad or anything about Kate or Jay T. Suzann simply stood there looking at the ground, thinking of her willingness to take this risk. She was afraid of putting Jim's life in danger and knowing for her this would be a suicide mission. Fury boiled inside her, her eyes widened and then she found herself saying hotly from the heat of the day crashing down on her, "Dad, I need your help."

He stepped away feeling uncertain, thinking with certainty that she was overreacting She had probably been scolded or gotten her hands slapped for something she had done and coming to him would be quick a fix. He wondered, "Is this my fault for spoiling her from birth? But I didn't spoil her. You can't spoil someone that never asks for things, and she never asked for anything. The only thing that she has ever asked for is to live with us." But when Jim looked at her he saw hurt, a change in her, anger coming from her in waves and it seemed that she was becoming a totally different person.

Suzann cleared her eyes, trying to bring his face into focus. But Jim seemed so far away, to be so close, different somehow. She blocked everything out of her mind except this man who raised her, taught her right from wrong, held her when she was little and never intended to let her go. Now she felt like all of a sudden he was letting go. His eyes were big; he had his lips pinched together, looking incredibly hard and grim.

"Dad, my hands, they are hurt because of them. You see the blue on my face, bruised because of them. Look at this place on my head. It's there because of them."

After a moment's silence, he looked up at her again. "Can I ask you a question?" For an instant she paused, taking a breath, and then said, "Yes." Then he asked her what was on his mind.

"Why is this happening now? Everything has been fine all these years, why now are things going wrong? Maybe you are going through, what they call, growing pains."

Being scarred from the past by his own daughter, Jim was thinking that something here sounded familiar.

"Things have never been fine, not since the first day that I was here,"

Suzann added.

"You have never said nothing and I've never seen anything."

"I know."

Jim looked at Suzann and said "I love you" over and over, his voice fading to a whisper. He felt terrified by the sudden sadness that he saw on her face, almost sick. He did not understand and was unsure if she was telling the truth because she made him promise not to tell Kate or Jay T what she had told him. Yet she seemed so serious, but there was something missing. Jim wanted to take her in his arms, thinking maybe all she needed was his promise that he loved her and some reassurance, but he was suddenly afraid to ask. Something vague yet haunting was trying to speak to his troubled mind.

"Suzann, give them another chance. I think you will find out differently. You have to stay here. I know that it's been hard on you, but Kate is our daughter and you are . . . her daughter. And the law would say that you belong with her, not us."

"The *law*? You want to talk about the law? The law would protect those maggots up there. From the outside looking in, one would think that Kate and Jay T were an endangered species, they're so phony."

"Suzann, you're thinking wrong. I have never seen you like this. What is wrong with you?"

"You ain't seen nothing and I'm trying to tell you. Please hear me."

Jim ran his hands through his hair and whirled around. He was usually funny, charming, and she made him feel like the best part of his day, but not this day. Her voice got low and husky, so low that he had trouble hearing her even in this place of death and silence.

"Come on, I think that we should be getting back to the house. They will be wondering about us.

Suddenly, Suzann knew that she was on a collision course; she was damned if she didn't and damned if she did. "I am fucked no matter what," she thought to herself.

"Dad, remember the promise that you made about not saying anything about this conversation we just had?"

"I remember." he said in a voice just above a whisper. Not a word was passed all the way back to the house. Both of them walking slowly as Suzann let her mind run wild. "Why would he not believe me? Was it because he didn't want to get involved in such a scandal like this? Maybe it would jeopardize his career as a preacher, which made a small living for him and Mom. Maybe he had no money to hire a lawyer, or he didn't want people talking, starting rumors of him taking a child from his own daughter. No one would believe me over Kate and Jay T; it would be their word against mine." Suzann fought to remember who she even was and to remember who her company was, the man that she loved with all her heart more than anything in the world. But Suzann felt like he was treating her like a person who cries wolf all the time, this was a lot different. But he had no way of knowing that her cry was demanding, requiring immediate action because later would be too late.

Her thoughts and heartbeat became frantic, and although her words stung, she kept her voice even.

"I'm sorry, Dad, but I had to try. And I think it's time that you knew the truth."

She dipped her head with the pretence of something in her eye to avoid making eye-to-eye contact with him. She was embarrassed, ashamed, and this time, let down. But at least someone else knew a little more about things going on here. Another stand that she had made and she was glad that she had told him. She was starting to feel like she was coming out of her shell. Her newfound confidence was beginning to grow even though she knew that all hell was going to soon break lose. What she couldn't know was that vengeance was the biggest part of her strength. Its darkness was slowly consuming her and she welcomed it, unaware of the demanding price that darkness may require. She was having trouble controlling her thoughts as neither of them spoke. An awesome and intense silence had fallen between them as they trailed on to the house, afraid to breathe, let alone speak, for the fear of adding to the already explosive situation.

Suzann felt lonesome and deserted, swimming in the old feeling of abandonment. She didn't need to have these feelings with her dad, she encountered them often enough with Jay T and Kate.

When they got back to the house, everyone was sitting around the table.

"Suzann, fix your daddy some coffee," Kate said.

"Sure."

Suzann glanced back, watching Jim as he sat down with them smiling as if nothing had been said at all.

"Suzann has been showing me around the place. It's quite a spread."

"Yes," Jay T answered. "She should know it better than anyone since she is always getting lost out looking around the spread, especially when there's work to be done."

Suzann's ears did not miss Jay T's insinuating comment which implied laziness on her part, nor did she miss the smiles on everyone's faces after the untruthful comment had been made.

She had been stirring Jim's coffee when a cold fury of anger and hate almost took completely over. "You lying son of a bitch, and you too, you fucking whore. This is going to change. You are going to wish that you'd left me somewhere and never saw me. You are going to . . ." her thoughts were interrupted when she felt hot coffee on her fingertips. The cheap but sturdy spoon had been bent almost double. She glanced around but no one had noticed, so she grabbed a tea towel and wiped up her mess and straightened out the spoon, telling herself to calm down. Any such behavior would certainly look bad on her part and be taken as such.

"I imagine there's a lot of work here with only one person such as you having to keep up with everything," Jim said, being very conversational.

"It's not so bad. We get extra when it's time to put in the crops and then again when it's time to harvest them."

Suzann took Jim his cup of coffee and set it down without speaking. His coffee was hot, with a little milk and heavily sugared. As he took a sip, he said," Ah, you remember how I like my coffee I see."

She stood there rather uncertain. "Well, I'll let all you grownups do the talking. I'll go and feed the chickens."

"Hold up," Mary said. "I'll go with you. I need to stretch my legs anyway; the ride was rather a long one."

"OK, when you're ready."

"I'm ready if you are."

"Then let's go," Suzann said.

When they got to the henhouse, the door was stuck. Suzann tried to open it but it would not budge. Getting a board to use like a crowbar, she was prying on the door to force it open when the door released all of a sudden, causing her to hit her knuckles against the outer henhouse wall. The pain was more than bad; she could have slapped her great-great-grandmother.

"GOD bless," she yelled in anger, holding back what she had almost said.

"Oh, Suzann," Mary groaned. The expression on her face was as though she was in more pain that Suzann.

"Here, let's have a look at that hand; I thought you told me that it was nothing."

"It isn't."

"You don't act like it isn't; now let me look at it. Suzann, you act like you are afraid for me to look at your hand. What are you afraid of? How did you say you done this? This should have been sewed up."

"We're not taken to doctors around here unless you're having a baby."

Mary let out a half laugh and said, "Well, that's once a year."

Mary wrapped her hand back up and in a low voice filled with anger, she asked, "They aren't talking care of you are they? Never mind, it's obvious. I can see that. Kate didn't do anything?"

Suzann stared at her and felt uneasy once again; her eyes darkened with unspoken thoughts. "I tried to tell Dad some things and he didn't believe me so why should you?"

Then Suzann softly said, "Kate could not care less."

"I think someone needs to say something to them."

"Mother, please. Don't say anything to them.

Look, in a little while, you and Dad will be leaving, right?"

"Yes, but that ain't got nothing to do with this."

"That's got everything to do with this. I have to stay here. I won't be leaving. And if you say something to them, when you and Dad leave I will be in big trouble.

Look, I didn't want to come and live here to start with. You and Dad went along with it. You could have stopped them, but you didn't. I don't know why, but it's a little late now, isn't it? So don't try to raise me now. For the last years, it has been hell here so don't make it worse! You don't have a clue as to what goes on here."

"Suzann, you don't understand."

"I don't understand? I understand that I am the result of a one-night stand. I didn't ask to be brought in this place, but here

I am and no one cares. No one gives a damn about the way I feel. What about my needs?"

Her face was sweating; she reached out to open the door, when it swung out, almost hitting her in the face. Placing her face in the bend of her elbow, leaning into the wall, with tears that filled her eyes. Suddenly, a hand reached out and wrapped around her waist, pulling her gently. Mary's invitation was like an angel from heaven. Suzann's eyes softened as she pulled away from the arms of her mother.

"This accident is typical of the way things have been going lately for me. Mother, I'm sorry for screaming at you. I didn't mean to take this out on you."

A flush was slowly creeping up Suzann's face; they were silent for a moment while Suzann tried to convince herself that everything was all right.

"Oh lord," Mary groaned, not knowing what to say to offer comfort.

"Come on, let's get your face all clean so no one will know that you have been crying," Mary cautioned.

"Mother, I just want you to know that all these years it hasn't been a night passed that I haven't prayed and wished for some reason that I could come back and live with you and Dad for the rest of my life. Remember the wallpaper that we put up in my room? It had the red rose print on it."

Mary smiled. "Yes, I remember," she said.

"Well, sometimes when I go to sleep I dream of waking up in the morning and seeing those red roses staring me in the face. And sometimes just before I open my eyes, I pray that all of this is just a bad dream, a nightmare, and when I open my eyes I'll see those roses smiling back at me and I'll know that I'm really home. But every time when I open my eyes, I see those cold creepy hardwood walls, and I always feel let down when that happens. Does that sound stupid?"

"No, it doesn't. Oh, Suzann, what have we done to you?"

As they walked with no destination in mind, laughing and talking about old times, it felt so good to laugh even if it was only for a little while. Then they noticed that they were a good distance from the house on the dirt road.

"We better get started back to the house. They'll think that we left the country," Mary said.

Even with all the laughs, there was an anger that was deep and hard to cover up. It was to the point that Suzann's smiles were just a front, a cover-up. For if she struck out with these two, it would be her last chance at bat.

After returning to the house there was something that Suzann had to do without anyone seeing her. With everyone tied up in talking, this was her chance. When she politely said, "I'll be right back," she acted like she was going to her room. And she did but there was something else she had to do. Finding a pen and paper, she wrote, "I used to think that I hated being poor and being made fun of, but now I know that there are worse things in the world. Like being unhappy, knowing pain, being hurt, being sick, having no friends and living in a home that has no morals or decency. I am putting this quilt back in your truck and asking you to keep it for me, because I know that you don't know this, but Kate and Jay T destroy and burn everything that you have given me just because they know that it breaks my heart. Please believe these words I say, I swear to the good Lord above that I am telling you the truth." She signed it and wrote, "I love you." She grabbed the quilt and attached the note to it and placed it back in the truck.

The rest of the day passed quickly until it was time for them to go. Jim had said that they wanted to get back home before dark because he could not see well enough to drive after dark. And with the way that he was squinting through his glasses, Suzann knew that he was having trouble seeing.

"But I thought that ya'll were going to stay all night," Suzann asked.

"Maybe next time. Maybe next time you can come back home with us. I don't know why you couldn't come this time." With that being said, he looked directly at Kate.

All the goodbyes were said in the house; Jay T had already gone to work. Suzann excused herself one more time and ran back to the truck and placed the money that her mother had slipped in her pocket with the note and added, "Dad, use this money to get you some new glasses. You need them, I don't need the money." With a smug smile, she returned them back where they were. Suzann walked them to their truck with tears in her eyes, trying so hard not to cry but that was not happening. Heartbroken, Suzann was left standing in the road, watching them as they started to pull out. Then something bit her right in the butt as she called out, "Daddy. Daddy, wait." Running to catch up to them, out of breath, she leaned in the window with her arms crossed.

"Dad, if you don't believe what I told you this morning, there's someone else that knows the truth, only one person." Mary sat quietly and listened.

"Suzann, lets don't start that again!"

"At least take his name. I have never asked anything from you, but I am asking you for this. I just want you to know that I am telling you the truth."

With a long sigh, he dropped his head. Suzann could see Jay T out of the corner of her eye, standing, watching from the barn.

"His name is Stephen, it's Jay T's brother; I don't know where he lives."

"You want me to talk to Jay T's brother about . . . I can't do that!"

"His brother is not what you would think. He is nothing like Jay T."

"No, Suzann, Absolutely not!"

Mary was very still, studying him. The tone of his voice had caused Mary to lose her smile. This was not normal for Jim to speak with such temper, and especially not to Suzann. With a warm blush reddening her skinny cheeks, she pushed herself back into the truck seat, acting as if she was perturbed. Letting out on the clutch, they drove away, not even looking back to wave a last goodbye. Suzann could see him and her mother talking to each other until they were out of sight. Then there was nothing but dust as far as she could see.

CHAPTER FORTY-ONE

Jim and Mary had driven about twenty miles when the rain descended from an almost clear sky. As one mile turned into another, his thoughts haunted him. He could still hear Suzann's words. Her statements and accusations had been very unsettling to him, yet the old adage kept returning to him, "Where there's smoke, there's fire!" As he continued to drive, his methodical mind started dividing the whole afternoon into sections. He went through each one piece by piece, trying to make some sense of the day's happenings.

"JIM!" Mary screamed as the truck headed down into a shallow ditch and off the road. The incline towards the ditch was covered with holes and loose rocks which bounced them roughly around in the truck. Mary's face was a contorted mask of fear as she held on to the windowframe and the dash of the bouncing truck. Jim let off of the gas and finally maneuvered the old truck back up onto the side of the twisting road.

"DAMNED I AM," Jim said loudly and roughly as the truck came to a stop.

"Jim, your language. We're not hurt. We're OK. Let's just sit here a few minutes and calm down!"

"Mary, I wasn't cursing about anything. Are you all right?"

"Yes, I'm fine. What is it that you're upset about?"

"It's Suzann, all of the things that she was saying. It's like I was cursed and couldn't see, hear, or understand anything that she was trying to tell me. All of a sudden, I'm starting to think that there's truth in what she was trying to say! Not only that, I know now what was bothering me the most. It's her demeanor or personality or something in that way if that makes any sense. She seems to have some kind of darkness about her and a determined one at that. I think that maybe she was asking for more than even she realized!"

After sitting there for a few moments, silence filled the air as he tried to recuperate. He pulled back up on the road and the miles seemed to slowly melt away. Jim slowed down to make the last turn for home. He shivered at the memory of his little girl begging him for help. His heart pounded with the thought of, "What if I was wrong, and she was only being honest?" He wanted to cry. Tears stung his eyes, but he held them back ever so forcefully. He didn't dare let Mary see how helpless he was really feeling. It was beyond a doubt that Suzann was more like his own daughter than Kate would ever be or had ever been for that matter.

Slowing down, for their trip had ended and home was in sight, he turned his head to face Mary then he turned back to stare straight ahead at the driveway.

"What are you thinking?" she asked. "You've been way too quiet. You haven't said hardly a word all the way back and you have already admitted that something's bothering you. I've been married to you for many years now and believe me, Mr. Jim Banks, I've learned how to read that handsome face of yours." Mary felt her frustrations mounting. "You have no right to keep what she said to you from me. We've shared our thoughts far too long, all good and bad. This may take the both of us to figure this out."

"Aye," he boasted. "You know me too well."

Her love and her comment about his looks brought a momentary smile and lightened both of their moods. But it was only momentary.

Now, not really knowing what to do about Suzann stuck in his throat and made his insides tighten. After shrugging his shoulders to loosen the tension, he turned again to look at Mary. Her frustration had been overcome by uncertainty. She wasn't sure what she had seen in his face at all.

"Well," she said cheerfully. He gave her no answer.

"It's Suzann, isn't it? I don't know what she said to you but I know what she said to me and what I saw. I feel that there is something wrong; it was in the look of her eyes, the sound of her voice. There's something going on there. And her hands, I also got the feeling that she lied about how she hurt them."

"Why do you think that she would lie about that?" Jim asked.

"I don't know, but she made me promise not to say anything to Kate about them not taking care of her. And did you see her hand?" Mary asked.

"No."

"It looked really bad. It should have been sewed up but she said they didn't even take her to the doctor. I'm really worried about her. I think that we should try to do something."

Jim shook his head as he glanced up at Mary and moved off into the living room.

Mary smiled her best and phoniest smile just before bursting into tears. Then after a moment her cry escaped her as she clamped her hand over her mouth and took in a few deep breaths while waiting to hear what Jim had to say.

"I agree with you. But what can we do? We have no money to hire a lawyer, and you know that we would have to take Kate to court. It could get nasty. And you know that she would be unwilling to give her up without a fight. And from what I've heard about Jay T, he's a hard worker and does not give anyone a problem, so he would have a good career reference to start with. And if we lose, we might not be able to see her again."

"Yes, you're probably right. But, Jim, I don't like repeating myself, but we've got to do something!"

"I don't know what we can do . . . yet. I . . . I need to just think for a bit, OK?"

"All right," she said, trusting his judgment. She turned and walked into the kitchen. Mary distracted herself, working in silence, doing a little cleaning, racking her brain trying to make some sense of what had taken place. She was wiping the counter when her hand hit the sugar bowl, knocking the bowl off of the counter and the top in another direction. Somehow she caught the bowl without spilling much of the sugar. She had just barely finished cleaning the mess when Jim fairly yelled, "MARY," which caused her to hit the sugar bowl once again, knocking it to the back of the counter. It was the last straw that her shattered nerves could take. She leaned onto the counter with her head lying on her arms, fighting the need to scream and cry.

Jim walked into the kitchen, saying, "I'm going to get up early Monday morning and drive into town to see if I can find this Steven that she was talking about."

"Are you serious?"

"Yes, I sure am. You pack me a bag. I may be gone a few days. Mary, are you all right?

"Jim, let's go and sit out on the front porch for a while. My nerves have just about had it."

Jim sighed with understanding and followed her out the door. Sitting down on the old swing, feeling the warm night air as it brushed by them with a whisper of fragrance from the rain that had come earlier, leaving cleanness in the air as they held on to each other's hand.

Mary looked up at Jim like he was her favorite hero especially now. Jim paused for a moment, then pulled her a little closer to his side. He could not stop looking at her. In his eyes, she was still the most beautiful woman that he had ever seen in his life. Fifty years and he felt very proud and pleased every time she slipped through his mind. As he looked into her eyes, he could see the worry that was lying there. He took her into his arms and kissed her on her forehead ever so gently. Mary laid her head on his shoulder and held him tightly. This man had been her rock and she trusted his judgment. With the love they had for each other and a lot of help from God, they had faced, survived, and conquered many situations. But what she had seen today was a picture she'd never thought she would have envisioned when they arrived to see Suzann.

They left the old porch swing and went back into the house, stopping in the hallway and looking at all the pictures that had been taken of Suzann in all the years that she lived with them. Mary politely smiled at him; he could see was trying very hard not to cry but the tears found their way to the corners of her eyes.

"We've got to find a way to make her smile again like she is in all of these pictures, she looks so happy."

Jim went on ahead of her to shower and shave while Mary went and packed him a bag for the week and laid him out his clothes for church tomorrow. When he had finished and came out, Mary dashed into the bathroom to clean herself up for it had been a long day.

It was well after sunset when they settled down for the night. Jim sat there remembering Suzann when she was little and how she would watch him when he would shave and how she would sit on his foot and he would rock her and she would say, "Ride the horse, Daddy." He could not escape the visions from long ago, and that made what happened today tug even harder at his heart. His mind was made up. He was going to find Steven and he was going to try to get her back. He knew that it was going to be trouble and that it would be difficult, but if it was God's will then it would happen.

CHAPTER FORTY-TWO

It was in the late evening on Sunday night when Handy packed himself some clothes and was headed out to find Jim Banks to talk to him about Suzann and her well-being. As he was packing his car, he could hear the bobwhites and all of the tree frogs singing out behind his little house. And in a far distance, he heard the call of a whippoorwill's cry. It was such a peaceful sound that it could lull him to sleep in just a heartbeat if only he could get rid of the angered knot that was lying in his stomach. But he couldn't sleep if he wanted to, there was too much on his mind.

Handy had gone to the bank on Friday and checked out enough money to give to Jim to get a good lawyer and try to get Suzann out of this place of hell that she was in.

Handy had only driven a short distance down the road when he came upon a car that was stopped in the middle of the road, blocking both lanes. The driver was standing beside the car. Handy stopped and asked if he could be of any help. The older woman who answered sounded older than dirt and tougher than a bag of nails. But she was none too anxious to receive his help.

"You're lucky that I came along. This road is not traveled on that much." The old lady closed her eyes to slow the dampness welling and then she swallowed over the lump in her throat, and said, "I'm sorry. I don't know what happened to my car. It just stopped, I've been here quite a while."

As Handy got a closer look, her back was stiff, jaw clenched, and her gray hair braid was draped over her right shoulder. She resembled a woman walking to her death. Handy's broad face lined with concern. "What are you doing out this far from nowhere?"

"I have family and friends that are buried down in the in the old cemetery."

Handy could tell by her shallow hard tone that she was wounded in the soul.

"I thought that most of the graves were as far back into the eighteen hundreds."

"My last name is Lucifer. My family tree started its roots there, what's left drifted southward. I come here as often as I can. All of this land used to belong to Mr. Lucifer, and I'm here to tell you that this land is spoiled. Things happened here, bad things, always has and always will."

Handy dipped his head and raised the hood of her car to see if he could see what might be wrong. After looking around and wiggling wires, Handy took a deep breath and rocked back on his heels and said, "I need to get a flashlight from my car but I think I know what your problem is."

"Do you live around here?" she asked.

"Yes, I live and work on the dairy farm which you passed a few miles back."

"Yes, I know it very well," she added.

"How far do you have to go?" he asked her.

"Oh, I have to drive all the way into town. I have to live there because of health issues, close to my doctor and there things are more convenient for me."

"Maybe you know someone that I'm looking for. I think they live about twenty or thirty miles from town. His name is Jim Banks."

"Why yes, I know Reverend Jim. He is the pastor where I go to church, been preaching there for . . . lord . . . I . . . don't know, about twenty-five years or more. They are the nicest people that you could ever know, everyone knows Brother Jim."

"Do you know where he lives?"

"Yes, you take highway 72 east, turn right on county road seven, then take the first right. They live in the first house on the right."

"Thank you so much, now I know where I'm going. Well, I think I've got you up and running. Get in your car and see if it will start."

The old lady got in her car and put the key in and it started right up. "I will follow you into town. I got something to do there tonight and tomorrow I will go and find Brother Jim. But you might want to take your car in to the shop and get some new battery cables, I think that is what your problem was."

"OK," she answered. "Well, it's been good to meet you and I thank you."

Handy got in his car and followed her all the way to town. Handy decided to go ahead and check himself into a room for the night and then went to visit an old army buddy with whom he had served time overseas. He knew all the tricks of the trade on how to put someone down. Handy was raised with Paul, gone to school together and then to war; they had fought side by side for years. Handy would never forget the last day before they were to come home. They had gotten pinned down and Paul had placed himself in harm's way to save Handy's life. Handy hadn't seen it coming, everything happened so fast. They crawled in every direction with Handy dragging Paul with him, trying to work his way around the enemy. Shoving sagebrush aside to peer under the branches, searching and trying to get in a position to take out the sniper and being quiet was a problem, for the pain that Paul was in was unbearable. Handy knew that he had to do something so he stuffed his handkerchief in Paul's mouth so his cries of pain could not be heard. They were pinned down with no way out; after hours of gunfire, when the fight was over, Handy had carried Paul out over his shoulder with most off his Paul's legs blown off. And for all of this, Handy was awarded a Purple Heart and Paul got new legs and a sweet retirement. That was another day in that dreadful place that Handy would never forget.

Paul ran a gunsmith shop from his home, which kept him working full time. Paul's specialty in the war had been making bombs and setting boobytraps. And he had a good sense of feel when something was not right, that was what had saved Handy's life.

It was very late when Handy returned to his room, but he had had a good visit and picked up some things that might come in handy to him later.

The next morning, Handy got up early and went down to the coffeeshop and had some breakfast and coffee to help get him awake and his mind working for he had a man to see that day.

CHAPTER FORTY-THREE

It was early Monday morning when Jim and Mary got up. Mary had everything ready for him to take on his trip to look for a man called Steven.

Mary walked him to the truck, holding his hand and wishing him the best of luck and warning him to be careful.

Mary stood there and watched him as he drove out of sight. Jim took a deep breath and slid himself back in the seat and got comfortable for the drive. Placing his elbow out of the window, he was feeling good about what he was going to do. The morning was wasting away by the time that he got into town. He was feeling a little hungry so he stopped at the greasy spoon restaurant, this would be as good a place as any to start his search. As Jim walked in and sat down at the table, he saw that this was a busy place. Jim was thinking that since there were a lot of people there that the food must be good. The waitress was dressed in a fitting white dress that was belted with a deep raspberry apron, with her long blonde hair put up neatly away from her shoulders. Ignoring one and all, he began to partake of the food that he ordered. When he had finished and gotten the waitress's attention for the check, he asked, "Do you know Steven Blanking, by any chance? I'm looking for him and it's very important"

"Does he come here?"

"I don't know.

What does he look like?"

Jim smiled a little, "I'm afraid that I don't know that ether." His voice was anything but relieved.

She apologized. "I'm sorry, but there are so many that come in here. Some are regulars, some you see every once in a while, some only one time and you don't see them anymore."

Jim turned his head, his eyes darkened; he paid his bill and thanked her anyway. Jim was thinking to himself this was going to be like looking for a needle in a haystack. He walked farther down the street where he saw the ladies of the night standing on both corners, looking for a ride with someone. Jim was mindless of pursuit, not really wanting to ask them but thinking they might just know. In a smooth voice, he said, "Excuse me, ma'am, but do you happen to know someone by the name of Steven Blanking?"

"Look, mister, I only take their money, not their names."

He ignored her and went on, gripping his hand into a fist in his pockets. When he heard her voice draw him back, her voice held a measure of kindness. "I'm sorry, mister. I didn't mean to sound sarcastic, but it's not been a good day," she said with a warm smile. Jim stiffened at the sound of her voice. "Forget it," he said. He turned and left her standing alone with her amazement and charms, if that's what you would call it. He could see by the look in her eyes that was welcoming him. For Jim, it was rather infuriating for he had not done anything to cause it. She would be leaving with someone else, not him.

Jim walked furiously from door to door, person to person, asking the same question. He recognized his own determination; perhaps even more so, it was an upsetting realization. Monday had passed quickly with no luck, but Jim had seen a lot of things firsthand—expensive cars, hotels, trains—and he felt like he was traveling in time. He had been more than shocked at the call girls working the streets who had more skin showing than they had clothes on. The blind man standing on the corner begging for money, kids walking up to him begging for a dime, he couldn't believe it. But then again, here he was asking total strangers if they knew a man that was a stranger to him. Jim stopped in the middle of the walkway, held his head back, and loosened his tie. "Man, it's hot," he said to himself. He must have asked a hundred people, but everyone gave him the same answer. But he knew that he had to keep searching. Jim was hot and a little frustrated, but he was hungry too so he walked into a place, not even noticing the name of it. But it was impressive, that pleased him very much. It had a big fireplace with a rock hearth in front that looked very country. The tables were oak with padded cushions on one side while the other side had wooden benches. The silence was pleasing. The waitress was extraordinary, dressed in a simple dress which fit her very loosely. She was a little on the heavy side with a homely face.

After a pause, she dropped the order book she had been holding. When he knelt down to retrieve it, she saw his hands shake as he handed it back to her. She frowned as she pulled the pin from her pocket. "Why, Brother Jim, what in the world brings you into town?" His breaths had gone shallow with his chest rising and falling beneath his white shirt.

"Well, hello there, Miss Ann. I just saw you yesterday in church. I didn't know that you worked here."

"Lord yes, I've been working here for fourteen years."

"How's the food?"

"The food here is what you will like, home cooking."

"Good, I'm starving."

Jim ordered a plate of next-to-the-best food he had ever eaten, it was not Mary's but it was close. When Jim had finished, Miss Ann came and cleaned his table and sat down. "Well, what did you think about the food?"

"It was excellent," Jim replied.

"Next time you are in town you know where to eat. By the way, it's on the house. Where is Sister Mary?"

"She is at home."

Jim sat and talked with her for a while and told her who he was looking for, but she did not know Steven.

That night, Jim went to the hotel where he had rented a room for the night. He fell into the bed, fluffing the pillow to suit his head, grateful for the rest and his feet said thank you. He closed his eyes briefly to say his nightly prayer. "Maybe tomorrow I'll have better luck," he thought. It was getting late when he turned off the light and rolled over for the night. Tuesday came and went just like Monday, no luck. Jim came upon a city park and sat down on an old wooden bench, stretching his legs, watching the sun through the low-lying clouds. He walked to the water fountain to drink and found that the water was indeed cold and tasted awfully good. He filled his hand from the water spigot and splashed it on his face but it did not diminish his thoughts in the least though it felt very soothing to his skin. His few minutes of privacy drew to an end, when he noticed a couple of men arm in arm, sitting on a bench to the left of him. One of the men was biting the other one on the ear. Jim could see him running out his tongue and following the contours of his ear and neck. "Oh lord," he thought with surprise and shock to see such things. "Something here is just not right," he thought to himself. Then he eased up from the old stiff bench, leaving them the whole park to romance in. Jim turned quickly, trying to get out of there when he ran right into another man. "Oh, excuse me," Jim said.

"Why are you in such a hurry?" the man said in a low soft squeaky voice. He or it was chewing gum, and Jim noticed that it was wearing nail polish and moved like a woman. "Is something wrong?"

Jim was unable to answer this time. As he watched this person play the part so well, flashing his eyes like he was unable to stop the desiring look that he was giving Jim. Jim looked away, frustrated; this was ridiculous, drooling after another man. What in the world could force or drive this man to be like this. Jim felt his pulse pick up, swallowing his own saliva with difficulty.

"Look, mister, I'm not your type and I don't have any money. And you wouldn't like me very much if you make me mad. I might hurt you and you would not want me to scar your pretty little face, and

that's not half as bad as what God would have to say!" Jim had not
gotten all the words out when the queer spun around and started
walking in high speed across the park. He did not look back. He
was only moving forward. The warm, rushing feeling was fading
although his hands were still shaking. He did not know where he
had found the words that he had spoken. "I guess that there is a
first time for everything and this was my first time and I pray to
God that it will be my last time for that kind of . . . ungodliness,"
he thought to himself. "Now I know why I live in the country and
not the city. I wonder what my congregation would think of this."
The thought brought a small surprising chuckle. His anger slowly
subsided but his face was still the color of crimson as he found his
way out of the park and back to the beaten path. His amusement
was short-lived and turned into something very near frustration
as he continued his search with no results. By the end of the day,
he was so exhausted that he did not even stop to eat. It had been
all that he could do to just open the hotel door and fall into the
cheap bed.

He was starting to feel like a recorder as he was having a cup of
coffee at the coffeeshop early Wednesday morning. He sat there
wondering where he was going to begin today and starting to feel
like he was not going to find Steven at all, and he knew that he
could not stay but one more day because he was running out of
money.

When he heard a voice call out his name, Jim looked up to see
who it might be. To Jim's surprise, it was the sherriff.

"Brother Jim," the sheriff said as he walked over to the table
where Jim was sitting.

"Well, Mr. James Campbell," he spoke as he got up to shake his
hand.

"Or should I call you Sheriff James Campbell?"

"Oh, it don't much matter what you call me. I've been called
about everything," he said in a deep serious voice that ended with
a laugh. Jim was excited to finally bump into somebody that he

knew. Jim had known James since childhood and had grown up with him.

"I still can't get used to seeing you in a uniform," Jim commented.

James was the sheriff now and had been for the past eight years; prior to that, he had been a door-to-door salesman for many years.

"Well, how have you been doing?" James asked, still shaking his hand.

"I know that you are still preaching. I hear my wife talk about you quite often."

"I'm doing fine," Jim answered.

"What brings you into town on Wednesday? There's nothing open hardly after twelve o'clock except the bars and pool rooms."

Jim sat there knowing that those were the only places that he hadn't looked, but he was planning on hitting them today before he left.

"James," Jim said in an exaggerated drawl. "I wonder if I might ask you something."

"What's wrong? You know if there is anything I can do all you have to do is ask."

"Do you know a young man by the name of Steven Blanking?"

James repeated the name. "I can't recall the name right off."

"I've got to find him. That's why I'm here. I've been here all week looking for him, but I've not had any luck."

"Has he done something to you or your family?"

"Oh no, nothing like that, but it is urgent that I find him. I've got to talk to him. I don't think that he is working a steady job because he works various places farming, maybe some mechanic work."

"Sounds like he would be a hard one to catch up to, being that he moves around like that. But if he is here, we will find him."

"Well, I know, or at least I think, that he lives here in town somewhere," Jim assured him

"Tell you what I'll do, I'll give the name to all my deputies and have them to ask around and I will personally check the files and see if he has been picked up for any reason. And if I find anything, I will come out and tell you myself. I will let you know whatever I find out. I heard about Kate coming back and taking that little girl, I was sure sorry to hear that."

"We were sorry to see her go, and still miss her," Jim answered.

"I just could not believe that Kate married that man." He paused, "Oh, I can't even think of his name. Some of the deputies were talking about him just the other day."

"His name is Jay T," Jim told him.

"Yeah, that's his name. Anyway, one of my deputies' father is the judge here and he recalled the case that sent Jay T to prison. In this profession, sometimes the nights can get long and we talk about things that have happened, things that we've done and or seen. That's how Jay T was brought up."

Jim was rubbing his hands over his mouth.

"You knew that he had been in prison?" said the lawman in a questioning tone.

"No, I'm afraid that I did not know that. Why was he in prison?"

"What little that I can remember, there was a lot of things going on, bad things. The townspeople were terrified of him. There were barns burnt down, cows killed, break-ins. Everyone knew it was him but would not talk, and the law never could catch him or prove that he did anything. And then there was that young girl that was raped and beat to death but there was no witness, no proof that he did it. Then he stole a car and got caught and the judge threw the book at him. After Jay T was sent off to serve his time, everything went back to normal. And then the same year that Jay T got out, the judge's wife was raped and killed. But no one knows to this day who did it, the case is still open. You know, sometimes the law protects the wrong people because of some kind of technicality. But I have talked to Mr. Butler on several occasions and he says that Jay T is doing a fine job for him. I do know this, there were several men killed in the prison and Jay T was always around. But every one of the deaths was made to look like it was an accident. So the prison officials could not prove otherwise. Maybe he didn't do all these things, maybe he did. I guess only he knows the truth."

"James, what you just told me makes it even more important that we find Steven. I think now that he can tell us some things that would help."

"Jim, I've know you for a long time and you're not telling me something."

"I'm sorry, but I'm not even sure myself. That's why I'm looking for Steven, maybe he can help; or at least, Suzann thinks so. I have reason to believe that she might be in danger. But like I said, I'm not sure. I'm sure a man of your religious convictions can appreciate that."

The sheriff was a man of his word and not a bullshitter. If he told you that he would do something then you could consider it done.

"Jim, I will get started on this right away."

"James, Steven is Jay T's brother. Just to let you know."

"Oh my goodness, you know, I remember their mother. So Steven was the young boy that she sent away to school. He did not grow up here. That's where we will need to look. I will check out the college. If he is still in school, that's where he would be. We will keep this thing under our hats until we find Steven and then we will take it from there."

Jim was speechless, flabbergasted at this man and his attempts to help and his humor. James got up to leave. Jim turned completely around and stared at his friend and said,

"From the bottom of my heart, I thank you."

"I will be out at your place Saturday with or without Steven. If I can find him before then, I will bring him out there and we will find out what he knows. I'll do everything in my power to find him.

If he is in this town I will find him, I promise you that. But in the mean time, I want you to go home. I want you to promise me that you won't do anything until you hear from me. Don't go out there and confront Jay T until we have something. If there is something going on, this time there won't be any technicalities. I want this man."

"We're talking about Suzann's well-being, may be even her life."

"I know that, but if we don't do this right he will walk again free. Was Suzann all right Saturday when you saw her?"

"Yes. Physically, she had some bruises on her face and her hands were skinned up and bruised. I'm not sure about her mentally."

Jim reached out to shake his hand and thanked him again.

Normally, a chance meeting of an old friend would have left Jim excited and happy. But today's encounter had left him with a growing anxiety full of fear and worry. After hearing all this, it confirmed his feeling from the past weekend, and he wished that he could let Suzann know that he was going to help her, and having now a gut feeling that she knew enough to help herself by telling the truth to the right people. Maybe Steven could do that, if he knows anything. This time, Kate had gotten in way over her head. Jim's mind was even more determined; and now he sensed that something was definitely wrong. So he prayed for a spirit, a spirit of God, to give him the strength and guidance to carry him through this and find Steven, and most of all, to protect Suzann who might be in the hands of something wrong and something bad. Then Jim thanked God for answering his prayer while on this journey. When he raised his head and looked up, he saw that the waitress was looking at him but his expression was unreadable. Then unexpectedly he grinned. She shifted her gaze away from him as he walked out the door. Jim left with his head high for all these things had been on his mind constantly, but now his confidence had been restored by an old friend. Walking back to his truck, he was ready to go home. It had been a long three days and he was missing Mary. Jim slid into the truck seat. His frown darkened when he thought of what he was going to have to tell Mary, for he knew that she would be worried sick for her baby when she learned of the news that he was bringing home to her.

CHAPTER FORTY-FOUR

After Handy had finished with his breakfast, he got into his car and started out of town to find where Jim and Mary lived. He would be following the directions that the old lady had given him the night before. Her directions proved to be perfect and led him right to their driveway.

Handy sat in his car looking around and admiring what he saw. Everything was so clean, and the yard was so well manicured. The house was old but it had a warm and welcoming face. Handy took a long deep breath; his chest rising and falling swiftly underneath his white tucked shirt. As he stepped out of his car, only the breeze of the wind disturbed the peaceful quiet.

He combed his fingers through his hair as he now stood at the front door and knocked three times, lightly. Not a sound was heard. Handy got the feeling that no one was home when he noticed that Jim's truck was gone.

Then from nowhere Mary stepped around the corner of the house, with her straw hat over her head and gloves on, holding a hoe. "Can I help you?" she asked with uncertainty.

"Yes, my name is Handy and I am here to see Brother Jim."

"He's not here at the moment; can I be of any help? Is this a church matter?"

"No, I am here on behalf of your granddaughter, Suzann."

"Is something wrong with her?" Mary's voice was now filled with fear.

"I'm not sure exactly how to answer that but I will try."

"I'm sorry. Please come over and sit on the porch swing. Can I get you a cold glass of tea?"

"Yes, ma'am. That would be nice."

Mary looked away, thinking while walking into the house. There was an awkward silence; he slid down into the chair that sat on the front porch. Her expression turned into a little distrust and wariness, not knowing the stranger who was sitting on her front porch. Returning with two glasses of tea, she sat down on the swing facing him.

"Look, I know that you don't know me but I have come to know Suzann very well, and I think of her as if she was my own child. I have watched her grow into a young woman. I don't know if you know this or not but you and Mr. Jim need to get her out of that home. Suzann is not being treated right. She is abused, she's not allowed to have friends. It is so bad that when she needs to talk to me we have to hide from Jay T and make sure that he does not know. I can tell you this, she has wanted to tell you and Jim about all of this but she has been afraid to. She is scared that Jay T will hurt you. I love that little girl with all my heart, and if you can't get her out of there then I'm going to do something about it. I'm not going to stand by and see her hurt anymore. And just so you know, it is not just Jay T. Kate is just as bad. Do you know when Jim will be back? I would like to talk to him."

"No, I am not sure when he will be back home. He left Monday, going into town to look for a man named Steven, trying to find out what is going on. We want to get her back but we are not sure how we can make that happen. We were hoping that Steven could help us. Suzann has not told us anything until this last weekend, and she only asked if we would help her. All she said was that she wanted to come back home."

"Please understand she can't tell you," Handy answered.

"Then how is it that you know so much about her?" Mary asked.

"Because I have been there. I live there, work there, and I have seen things, heard things, and Suzann talks to me. She tells me about things that I have not seen, but I know that what she has told me is the truth. Jay T is a bad person, and so is Kate. I could tell you things that you would not believe."

"Then tell me."

"I think it would be best if I could talk to Jim. I have something to offer. If you would please take this. I know that you have no money, but there is more than enough here to get a lawyer, and a good one. And you don't have to worry about paying me back; just getting her out of there would be the only way you could pay me back. Tell Jim I'm sorry that I missed him but if he needs to see me you know where I work. But I think that it would be better if he needs to see me to let Suzann know and she can let me know, and I will come back out here to see him. Jay T does not need to know anything about this until Suzann is out of that house."

Mary took the advice from him and gave him credit that he deserved. But still she had a feeling of being uncomfortable, like guilt nagging at her, as she stood up; she accepted the envelope that was filled with money. Then she walked with him halfway to his car before she softly spoke.

"I don't know what to say. But thank you, thank you for being there for her. I hate this so bad, we should have been there."

"You had no way of knowing. Don't blame her, she was right for not telling you."

Handy then got into his car and wished her the best in saying goodbye. His trip home was silent, partly because the windows were down and the wind whipped through the car. He knew that his volunteering was somehow going to put him in the middle of this. But he had had some time to think about what he was doing and his conscience pleased him.

CHAPTER FORTY-FIVE

Suzann was a bit sleepy, or so she thought. But as a matter of fact, when her feet hit the floor, she was wide awake to the thought of what she had on her mind of doing that morning. She saw no reason to withdraw from her plans.

Her jaw clamped tightly shut as she jumped into her clothes and hurtled out the door, leaving everyone still fast asleep at two o'clock in the morning, which would give her plenty of time to carry out her mission without getting caught. Suzann was praying to God for some kind of help to clear out the dark energies that now nested with a disturbed spirit deep within her heart. It did not matter that anyone could see or feel it, she knew it was there and it was driving her, wishing that it could be passed into another dimension where it could find a happier place and not be enslaved within her.

Suzann was feeling like something was trying to tell her something, but the situation she was in was a violent one. She knew that it was wrong to take the life of another, and deep inside she held this true in other circumstances, including capital punishment like death row, the electric chair, but she was smart enough to know that these situations should not be taken from an emotional standpoint. Having these thoughts only proved that she cared, but the feeling of need to be apologetic was gone.

Suzann could feel a huge rage radiating from within like the heat from a raging fire. Walking and thinking was all she seemed to do these days. Then she found herself standing outside of Handy's window, knowing that he would not have left it locked because it was their way of communication by her leaving notes inside of the window. Suzann pushed up on the window and could hear the sound of it rising as it echoed in the distance. Climbing through into Handy's room, she could feel the hole in her stomach where a case of nerves had moved in. Deliberately, she tried to avoid making any noise while having to feel her way around the walls to find the light switch. In the pitch dark, she could not see her hand in front of her face. After finding the light switch, she looked at the clock on the wall; it was already two thirty. She knew that she would have to hurry up and get things done and get back to the house before anyone got up. Not knowing really where to start, she stopped and gazed around the room. But she knew that Handy had several guns. On the wall were three guns in a rack, but those were the ones that he used to hunt with and they were not what she was looking for.

Suzann started pulling out drawers and found nothing, but she knew that he had a couple of handguns somewhere in here. Suzann had a worried look on her face that held a frown between her eyes. She grunted under her breath and replaced the frown with a half smile as she looked at his bed. "Under his mattress," she thought. "That's got to be where they are."

She was trying hard not to make any mistakes by leaving anything out of place, so Handy would not know that she had been there. When she gave the mattress a nudge and held it up with her shoulders, yes, there they were.

Suzann pulled all of them out to see which one she thought would be the best to fit her hands. As she opened the cylinders, she found that all were loaded. Each had six rounds in them, and she thought to herself, "Now that ought to be enough to do the job." Not knowing one brand from another, she chose the one that felt the best. It was a little heavy, but with two hands she could handle it.

She wished that she could do something to calm the wild heartbeat that she felt in her throat. She fought against the panic and doubt that she now felt. The hard twisting knots inside her were the effect that was drawing her. "Lord, what if I am wrong?" Then she dropped her gaze and continued staring at the guns. She simply stood there and watched the clock ticking down. Looking at what she had in her hands, she couldn't ignore the fact that it gave her something to focus on besides her problems and feelings and her adrenaline as it added a little spice to her morning.

Then she remembered the places that Jay T was most likely to corner her, which were in the hay barn and in the feed room. "Now which place should I hide the gun?" Suzann wanted to be ready for him this time. "So now what do I do?" she thought, talking to herself. "There's a solution to this problem; I'll get two guns instead of one."

Looking at the clock and seeing that it was going on three o'clock, she felt the danger with a confidence that could make her vulnerable to venture into a messy territory. As she made her way to the window, she placed the two guns on the ledge, looking exactly at where she laid them, knowing that when she cut off the lights it would be pitch dark. Knowing that, she could not afford to make a single misstep or misjudgment with two loaded guns which lay there so dangerously.

Suzann walked to the light switch and took one last look before cutting off the lights. Then there was absolute darkness. She felt her way back to the window. With the light of the moon, she could barely see what she was doing. Climbing back out of the window wasn't easy with the guns lying in her way, but she made it out. Taking the guns, she went to the milk barn and put on the lights and placed one gun in the feed room in the corner and covered it with feed sacks so it could not be seen. She knew that no one would bother the sacks because they were saved through the year to help kindle fires in the winter. Picking up her pace, she turned out the lights and ran to the hay barn and climbed up and placed the gun in the little corner where she studied.

Suzann tried to cover her tracks but she didn't realize that she had forgotten to let down the window in Handy's room. She did not thinking about anything now but making her way back to the house, and hoped that no one was up.

Suzann was terrified as she slipped in the back door, hearing only the wind's voice talking ever so low in her ear. All of the lights were still off as she walked over to the kitchen and put on the lights as if nothing had ever happened. She walked over to the sink and ran some water to make the morning coffee, then filling her hands with water and splashing on her face, she took a long deep breath of relief. She felt a little breathless as she quietly went to her room to get ready for the morning milking. Then she immediately felt guilty as she went past Dwan's room and saw all the little ones lying so peacefully, sleeping in their bed. Holding her hand over her mouth as she stood there staring at them, Suzann frowned with her eyes searching her increasingly worried face, momentarily distracted from her efforts to avoid any more pain.

That morning when Jay T arrived at the barn, Suzann had made sure that he would not catch her in the feed room for she had gotten the feed up first thing before she had done anything else. His face was unrelenting now,

"Well, looks like you are on the ball this morning," he retorted. He was cold and arrogant and every bit as aggressive. But Suzann had nothing to say to him as she finished up with the cow that she had just brought in.

"What? The cat got your tongue this morning?"

Then she spoke. "I want to go home with Mom and Dad this weekend."

"Oh, you do, do you? Well, you can want in one hand and shit in the other and see which one fills the fastest. How dare you," he said.

"It's been three months since you let me go, and there was no reason."

"Boo-hoo-hoo, cry me a handful."

"I don't have to listen to this," she hissed as she ran out the barn door and kept running until she got back to the house.

"Get your ass back here," he screamed.

But this time she did not listen.

Jay T walked back in the barn, thinking to him elf, "That little bitch will pay for that one, and soon. I ought to go to the house right now and beat the hell out of her, but that would be too easy, I'm going to fuck her until the last breath and beat her to the point where no one will recognize her and then leave her in the woods like I left the last one. And I will take my slow time in doing it."

This morning the air was cool, deliciously so, and Jay T saw no reason in rushing to follow up on his thoughts. He was forced to delay his thinking when he saw Mr. Butler pull into the barn drive, and Jay T wondered what he was doing out here so early this morning. Jay T paused while standing in the doorway as Mr. Butler approached the barn.

"Good morning, sir," Jay T said in the well-mannered voice of a gentleman.

"And a good morning to you, sir," Mr. Butler answered.

"How are things going?" he asked.

"Things could not be better," Jay T answered back.

"I . . . ," he hesitated. "Well, the truth is that I will be going out of town for the week. I'm taking my wife to Florida, a long deserved vacation, and it is all because of you. You have done me a good job here. There has been no problem. Milk prices have gone up, and the price of cattle. So therefore I'm giving you a ten-dollar-a-week raise and a beef calf a year. We are leaving today but I wanted to come out and tell you this morning before we left."

"I don't know what to say," Jay T said.

"You don't have to say anything, just keep up the good work."

Jay T mumbled, his words had indistinct sounds down with the volume to a respectable level, and Mr. Butler definitely knew that he would keep up the good work. He shrugged as he turned to walk back to his truck.

"Oh, Jay T, have you heard from Steven lately?"

"No, I haven't, why do you ask?"

"Do you know where he lives?"

"Yes, I think that he is staying somewhere near the college, I know that this is his last year."

"Well, I got to get going. See you when I get back. Hold the fort down."

"Oh, I'm going to do just that,"

Mr. Butler detected something in his voice but let it go as he drove away.

CHAPTER FORTY-SIX

Jay T finished the work at the barn and decided that this night after milking he was going to celebrate his good fortune. He thought that he really did have the damnedest luck, and it was all good. The day passed quickly, and in the late evening Jay T slipped into his whisky jug and started sipping on it. Suzann was staying out of his way because she knew that sometimes when he started drinking things could get bad. The situation might have been easy but this night Kate was on her warpath, raising hell about everything.

Suzann walked very slowly, more slowly than she had to. Even at eight in the night, the heat from the sun was still powerfully hot. She was just walking around trying to stay out of the limelight of Kate and Jay T. She ended up sitting on the porch swing then stretched out her legs and tilted her head up to study the stars in the sky. When her silence was interrupted, she heard Kate making a point that must have been convincing to Jay T.

"You do what the hell you want and the hell with me. You don't give a damn about me and I don't give a damn about you. And I will reassure you that I won't hesitate to tell the law everything that I know about what you have done in the prison. You told me that you had no choice but I bet the law will see it different. And why is it that all you want is girls?"

Instead of him addressing the sentiment, he focused on the way she presented it. Jay T stared at her for a moment, unbalanced by the shift in conversation and that last drink of whiskey was helping.

"Don't tempt me. I'll do it," she said in a rage of anger.

"You and what army?" he asked.

"Fuck you, you bastard."

Then there was a sound like someone hitting the floor, and then Suzann heard the backdoor slam shut, and there was silence in the room except for the sniffling from the girls. Suzann went into the house. Kate and Jay T were not there so she went into the girls' bedroom and found them all sitting on their bed crying.

"Don't cry. Dwan, you take care of them and keep them in here. Lock your door and don't come out."

"What is going on with Mom and Dad?" Dwan asked.

"I don't know. They're just fussing. Don't worry, they will stop sooner or later."

"Suzann, I think you need to check on Jim Bob. I saw Kate doing something to him and she was saying some things to him that were not good." Suzann felt the sweat that penetrated through the pores of her skin, finding its way to the outer layer, leaving it damp and wet.

Dwan's hands clung to her arms for a moment as the sweat grew into a chill across Suzann's back.

"That's what started this with Mom. Jim Bob was crying and would not stop, I think that she might have broken his arm and it was not an accident. I saw her; she put his arm in front of her knee and pulled back as hard as she could. I know that it is broke, all because he messed in his diaper and it run out and down his leg. She just went all mean. Then she fixed him a bottle and in about twenty or thirty minutes he stopped crying."

"OK, you stay in your room. Lock the door. I'll check on Jim Bob."

Suzann went into the kitchen and saw that Kate had fixed him a bottle of milk, but something was not right because she had taken the time to heat the milk and that was something that Kate did not ever do. She just gave it to him cold, she did not care. Then Suzann saw something on the countertop that looked different. It was remnants of rat poison; the powder was still on the countertop from where she had mashed it up. The bag was still under the sink. Suzann knew that this had never been there before; this was something that stayed at the barn, in the shop.

Suzann hesitated with suspicion in her eyes as she slid around the bar in a dead run out of the kitchen, through the living room down the hall, and halfway to the door before she disregarded her own assurance as she turned the doorknob to open the door. The room was very quiet, too quiet.

"OK, OK," she said, her voice was unsteady. Suzann cleared her throat, drawing both of her eyes to the baby's bed. She skimmed both of her hands over her hair and pushed it down into her collar. Then she walked up to the side of the bed and slid her hands under his thin shoulders to lift him. When she saw his head fall back, she jerked her hands back and she dashed to the light switch to put on the lights so she could get a better look in this dark, now scary, room.

Her hands began to shake and her heart was racing. She turned his head and placed her first two fingers on his neck to see if she could feel a pulse, there was none. She shook him violently but nothing. She placed her ear on his chest where no sound was heard. Then Suzann noticed his arm that dangled to his side and lay in a puddle of blood. As she lifted his arm, she saw that the bone was sticking out of the skin between the wrist and elbow. Then Suzann noticed that she had blood all over her hands from lifting him up.

Suzann rolled him over and saw that he was lying in a puddle of blood and the blanket that he was lying on was soaked.

"Oh my god," she cried as she fell to her knees on the floor. With her hands holding the side of his bed and her head hanging between her arms, the tears raced from her face and fell to the floor.

"Why, Lord, why would you let this happen? Not to him, he was just a baby. Why did she poison him? From the looks of all the blood, she didn't have to poison him."

Suzann pulled herself up and stood there looking at this little boy that was brought into this world unwanted, unloved, and suffered so much pain that was brought to him by Kate. Suzann's heart was breaking to see what she was looking at. Little Jim Bob lay there with nothing on, guess Kate hadn't wanted to dress him after he messed himself.

Suzann picked up a diaper and cleared her eyes so she could see a little better. She saw all the bruises on his little body and pin marks all over his privates along with cigarette burn marks. And the foreskin on his penis had been pulled back, and the head was swollen so big and the color of purple, it looked like it could burst.

"Oh my god, oh my god."

Then it hit her as to why Kate hadn't wanted her to bathe or take so much care of him. Kate had let on like she was taking good care of him herself. It had all been a lie. She just hadn't wanted anyone to see what she was doing to him.

Suzann was picking herself up shakily, looking at all the blood on her hands. Then she ran to the girls' room with her heart in her throat.

"Dwan, open the door. It's me." When the door opened, Suzann grabbed all of them and took them to her room because she knew that there was a hasp and lock on her door where Jay T had locked her in her room so many times. And there was only one key and Suzann knew where he kept it.

"What's wrong?" Dwan asked, and by now they all were crying with fright.

"Nothing's wrong . . . well . . . I'm going to find out what is going on. I want you to stay in this room; I'm going to lock the door so no one can get in here. And you keep everyone as quite as you can, don't make a sound. No one needs to know that you are in here. You will be safe here."

"You're shaking," Dwan said. "Oh, Suzann, you be careful. Don't let Dad hurt you again."

"Never mind that, he won't." Her answer was rougher than she intended. Suzann was struggling to keep as much of her composure as she could. She hugged them and give them a kiss on their foreheads. "I will be back. Keep quiet."

Suzann left the room and locked the door behind her and put the key in her pocket. Going back into where Jim Bob was, looking down upon him, she said a few words.

"Jim Bob, I know that you can hear me, and I promise you that she will pay for what she has done. She will burn in hell for this." Suzann drew a sharp breath and inadvertently tightened her hands around his. She took one last long look and felt the rage of anger that ripped through her. Suzann broke down on the floor and cried so hard. "Why, God? Why?"

A deep nonhuman sound burst from her with an undeniable rush of anger as she fled out the front door to find Kate and Jay T. Running crazily, a temporary insanity set in as she went from place to place looking for them. She stopped and placed her hands on her knees to catch her breath. Her muscles were rigid in trying to keep her thoughts focused, along with the fact that she did not have not a clue as to what she was going to do.

Suzann picked herself up and started running. She ran as hard as she could until she found herself at Handy's door. She kept beating on the door with her fists but there was no answer. Then she noticed that his car was not there.

"Shit. Shit."

Suzann started walking back towards the house, then she heard voices; it was Kate and Jay T. Suzann started screaming and running to where they were.

"Why? Why, Kate? Why did you do it?"

Suzann was screaming as loud as she could. Jay T took the back of his hand and hit her in the face, knocking her to the ground. Then reaching down and picking her up by the nape of her neck, he drew back his fist drew.

"Go ahead. You can kill me but you can't eat me."

"What the fuck is your problem?"

"Go look at your son and you will know what my problem is."

"What the hell are you talking about?"

"He's dead!" she screamed.

"What the fuck you mean *dead?*"

"Yes. And she done it that's why I'm upset," Kate said as she pointed her finger at Suzann.

"Then why haven't you told me?"

"I was scared to," Kate answered.

"You liar!" Suzann screamed.

Jay T turned Suzann loose and looked at the ground.

"I'm going up there and my son had better be just fine, you hear me, girl?"

Then Jay T stomped off towards the house.

"Is this your way of not feeling responsible, blaming this on me?"

"That sounds perfect," Kate began.

Suzann moistened her lips and wiped the blood that was running from her nose.

"You are not going to get away with this, I promise."

"You mean *you* won't," Kate answered in a laughing tone.

Suzann's voice tightened. She exclaimed angrily, "I can't believe you. You are a sick person, and somehow you will pay for what you have done."

"Get the fuck out of my face, bitch. I think before this night's over you will be the one to pay. Just who do you think that Jay T is going to believe?" When Kate reached out to push Suzann aside, Suzann caught her arm in midair and shoved it back at her. "Don't you touch me," Suzann warned.

"Oh, you so bad."

Kate turned and headed for the house. In that moment of silence, in the dark night, a blood-curdling scream came from the house. Suzann knew what it was. The scream came over and over, sending chills down her back. Suzann bowed her head in prayer, asking God to place his hand upon her and give her strength to survive this night, and not let anything happen to the rest of those babies up there. She walked to Handy's porch and sat down. Placing her head in her hands, she wished that he would hurry back home.

CHAPTER FORTY-SEVEN

After the shouting was done, there was a single moment that Jay T knew that he didn't need this kind of attention focused on him. It took him a while to work his way out of the house. Finding the steps and sitting down, he then decided to have another drink.

"What the fuck, Homer?" And that thought was drowned by, yet another drink. His stomach gurgled and growled with displeasure and the feeling of being slightly deranged. He sat there with his thoughts running through his head, trying to figure out who was telling the truth. He knew that he had caught Kate in several lies, but to be honest with himself, he had never caught Suzann telling him a lie. He thought back and asked himself why Kate would threaten him by telling the law things that he had done in prison.

"She killed Jim Bob and she was going to put the blame on me, that's what she is up to. Well, that ain't fucking going to happen. If she thinks that I am foolish enough to fall for that, she will have a bad awakening."

Kate was standing at the corner watching and hearing him talking to himself. She was feeling a little abandoned as she spied on him. Her heart fluttered wildly even as she placed both of her hands over her mouth to keep from laughing at him. She could see the anger on his face and the red in his eyes.

She stepped silently out so he could see her, her urge to laugh had subsided by the time he looked up and saw her. She smiled but avoided looking into his eyes. Through grimly pursed lip, and the heat from his breath along with spit flying from his mouth, he shouted as he slowly was starting to get up. Kate opened her mouth but words refused to form; she could not get anything out. Before he could reach her, she acted on her impulse and turned and started to run. Jay T attempted to make a quick dash to catch her but missed, and the race was on. From the dark of the night, with only the moon for light, Kate felt her stomach throbbing against the hard ground. She tried to get herself up but felt Jay T with his knee on top of her. With one hand, he cupped her head and slanted her backwards, releasing her without undo haste.

"Going somewhere?" he asked. "What the fuck have you done?"

"No one will ever miss him, no one will ever know."

"I FUCKING KNOW!" he screamed.

Kate tried to hide an expression of pleasure, but not quickly enough, and it didn't take Jay T long to see it.

"You bitch," he said.

"And right back at you," she answered.

Kate was now standing on her feet, face to face with him. She turned to walk away, leaving him standing there looking at the ground. After she had walked a few feet from him, she turned around and said,

"Now what are you going to do, Mr. Inmate Killer?"

With everything that had happened, that was the wrong thing to say, and Jay T flew into a mad rage.

Kate fell helplessly as Jay T flung her to the ground. Her body bounced off the ground. Her breath heaved from her body from such a hard blow. She was grabbing at him and trying to get away when Jay T spun her over and slammed her face into the hard dry ground.

Kate managed to roll over. Reaching down, she pulled her knees up into her chest and grasped them for dear life. Looking out across the open space, she saw flashing lights while disembodied tree limbs floated in midair. She could hear a voice calling out for him to stop but did not know that it was her own voice. The blood ran down her face, drenching her dress, but she was unable to wipe it from her eyes. Confused, she tried clutching at his hands that were wet with sweat along with her blood. His feet stumbled as he knelt down on top of her and he caught himself upon the uneven ground with one hand. The other hand was reaching into his pocket and pulled out a long bladed jackknife. Her heart was racing wildly and her head felt as if it was twisting into knots. She knew that this was happening to her but in her dazed state, she felt as if she were a bystander watching the whole scene. She could hear Jay T laughing as it echoed in the air. The echoes seemed to continue over and over.

"You won't be having another baby, bitch."

"Jay T, you know that I am pregnant. Don't hurt the baby."

"Since when do you give a shit about a baby? This is one baby that you won't hurt."

Jay T stood up and started kicking her as hard as he could, cursing her each time he landed a kick. "Yeah, I killed them motherfuckin' sons of bitches in prison and now I'm going to kill you, by God. That will keep you quiet."

Kate tried to push her body up off of the ground. He laughed once again and his ham-sized fist hit her in the face, breaking her jaw. Even that blow did not render her unconscious. Her heart filled with terror and her eyes filled with blood. She knew that he was going to kill her. With blood-curdling screams from Kate, he took the knife and ripped open her stomach. Jay T then pulled out the unborn baby and laid it on the ground beside her. Then he ripped off her panties and picked up the knife once again. He looked into her terrified eyes and saw that she was dying. A hellish giggling growl came from his throat as he drove the long blade between her outstretched legs. He watched the life leave her eyes and face. He smiled and then stuffed the unborn up inside of her. In doing all of this there was no remorse, it had become total enjoyment for Jay T who laughed as he worked. It had now been a while since Jay T had had a drink, and he decided that it was time for another one, maybe two or three.

Jay T felt giddy with anxiety as he stood up, adopting a stance and trying to steady himself. Wiping the blood from his hand on the tail of his shirt, he had other ideas on his mind. He reached down and got part of Kate's dress and wiped the bloody knife with it, not even looking at her dead body. He suddenly turned and started walking to the house. He had taken only a few steps when he smacked his lips and said very softly, "Where you at, Suzann dear? I've got something for you. In fact, I've got two somethings for you. And they're both long and hard. Oh baby, you're gonna like the first one but you ain't a-gonna like the second." Stopping only to take another slug of whiskey, he unsteadily continued his trek towards the dark house.

CHAPTER FORTY-EIGHT

Jim's gaze traveled hungrily upon his wife when he returned home and met Mary at the door with a welcoming hug. She could see that his old bones were tired from the trip. The looks in his eyes was completely different.

"Jim, you look like you have lost some weight," she said. Jim made a sudden growl, indicating that she might be right.

Jim knew that Mary had been worried and the curiosity that fed her instincts definitely wanted to sit down and hear about his trip. Jim could not stop grinning as his head shook, looking at her. He knew that she was dying to find out. She took him by the hand and dragged him to the dining room table, sitting him down in the chair.

"I'll get you some coffee and fix you a bite to eat." Jim went along just to humor her for he knew that she had been alone these last few days and he knew that she was going to tell him everything that she had done since he had been gone.

"OK, tell me what happened. Did you find Steven?"

"Hold on, let me catch my breath and I will tell you everything."

Jim scooted up to the edge of his chair to unlace his boots and give his feet a rest. He felt thoughts of his trip soaring in his mind. He tried not to ignore her but had to deal with some overheated emotions. Jim was just trying to cool them down. Jim then started telling her everything that he ran into, saw, and everyone that he talked to. But the best part had been running into James. That pleased her, she was so thankful for that.

"You know, I don't know why we didn't think of him to start with," Mary stated.

"I know, I guess we were just not thinking," Jim answered.

"But he is the best one to find Steven, and he will!" Mary answered.

"You know, James knows everyone in this county. I'm surprised that he didn't know Steven," Mary said.

"He did know Steven's mother, where she lived, and a little about Steven. He knew more about Jay T, and the things that he told me about him were not good, I think that Jay T has a very dark side. I think that, knowing what I know now, Suzann might be in danger. But we have got to let James handle this; I promised him that we would."

Jim looked up and saw Mary's face and could see that she was trying to hold back the tears that were targeting her eyes.

Mary left the room for a moment and then returned to where Jim was sitting and handed him the envelope.

"What's this?" Jim asked.

"Open it and look inside," Mary answered.

Jim opened the envelope and looked inside.

"What . . . in the world . . . where did you get this? There is a lot of money here."

Mary explained to Jim what had happened and told him all about Handy and what Handy had told her.

"Oh my god, Mary. There is something bad wrong out there. I've got a bad feeling." Jim was running his fingers through his hair, with a hard look of worry on his face.

"Maybe we just need to go out there and get Suzann," Mary said.

"No, we can't do that. I was asked not to go out there until we heard from James."

"What if something happens to her before we hear from James? I could never forgive myself if that happened."

Her voice sounded worried as she stated what she was feeling. With each word she spoke so slowly, Jim guessed that she was having to dredge deep to find them but he knew that it was all coming from her heart. Jim tugged her face up and gave her a kiss on her cheek. Even though he too had the feeling that he was being turned inside out.

"Oh no, no," Jim murmured. He held her close to him as her gaze stayed fastened to his face, not allowing herself to see anything else.

"We need to pray, and pray harder than we have ever prayed before for Suzann's sake," Mary suggested.

"Baby, I'm wearing God's ears out with prayer," he answered.

"I tell you what, if we don't hear from James in a couple of days I will go back into town to his office and talk to him again. But right now, I need to lie down for a little while and get some rest. I am really tired."

"I know that you are," Mary said.

And so Jim went into the bedroom and lay down his weary body along with his thoughts and fell into a troubled sleep. Mary closed the door and left him to rest. Mary had no misunderstandings and complimented Jim on all of his efforts and success. Mary did not know why this all had to happen, and she was reluctant to change her thoughts. She shrugged her shoulders beneath her country dress and apron but that couldn't hide the narrow bones that moved under her skin. When she picked up her pace, and went into the kitchen to bake a black berry cake, being one of Jim's favorite. Thinking that might cheer him up.

A couple hours later Jim got up to the pleasure of the aroma that lingered in the house. He knew exactly what she had fixed, and the cake that sat on the table was not unnoticed. After a fine supper, he went into the bedroom and studied his Bible while Mary was cleaning up after their meal. Then in a instant her face froze when she heard the knock on the door and saw that it was James, and saw the sheriff's car in the driveway.

James remembered this part of the county very well for the next-door neighbors had a son who was nicknamed trouble because that is what he stayed in. James remembered picking him up on more than one occasion for starting fires in the old folks' mailbox and burning their checks that came on the first of each month. The last time James had heard from him was when he was sent to reform school. That had been a few years ago.

Mary went and got Jim to answer the door.

"Hello, again, James. Won't you come in? How has your day been?"

"So far it ain't been too bad, staying busy as usual."

"Won't you come in and have a seat?" Jim asked.

"Sounds good, don't mind if I do."

"Would you like some ice tea? Or I can make some coffee. And we just finished supper and there is plenty left if you would eat," Mary asked.

"No thank you on the food. If I go home not hungry, my wife will whip me after she has cooked a big meal for me. But I will take some ice tea."

James sat down in an old rocking chair. "Now this is what I call home. I haven't rocked in one of these since I was at home. I can remember my mother, God rest her soul, rocking me when I was a small boy." He took a box of matches from his breast pocket and lit up his old pipe. He looked at Jim and Mary, guilty and fascinated and a little excited to have some good news for them. He placed one arm over the arm of the rocker, holding his tea, and the other hand around his pipe. He smiled vaguely. "Well, I told you that when I found out something that I would come out and let you know."

"Did you find Steven?" Mary asked, being somewhat impatient to hear what he was going to tell them.

"Mary, just relax and let the man talk," Jim said as he smiled at her.

"Well, I did find Steven. He lives over in the next county, going to college. I met with him and asked him several questions about

Jay T and Suzann. And this is what he told me, he said that there was something wrong out there on that farm. He said that he worked out there this past summer break for three months. Steven told me that he felt like Jay T had another side to him. When there were people around, Jay T could not be a better person, but he said that he thinks that Suzann is scared to death of Jay T. And Steven thinks that she has good reason to be. Steven said that he had overheard words from Jay T that were threatening to Suzann, and he also said that he saw Jay T one night making her take off his boots and making her wash his feet and his back. Jay T was very mean about it because Suzann did not want to do it. He also said that he was concerned about her well-being out there with Jay T. He told me that Jay T was his brother but . . . well, I don't think Steven is proud of that. Steven stated that if Suzann has told you anything that it would be the truth and he thinks that someone called Handy knows a lot more than he did. So with all of this being said, I think you did the right thing by checking into this matter. I also think that Suzann needs help. There is something else I think you should know. Steven told me that Jay T works her like a dog, that she does most of the work there and that her day started at three o'clock in the morning until very late at night, or whatever time it was when she got done. One other thing, Steven is willing to testify or do whatever he can to help us. I think he too wants to see Suzann get out of there."

There was a moment of silence which filled the room; it was as if everyone was thinking.

Then Mary spoke up. "Jim, we have got to go out there and get her. I've got a really bad feeling about this. I've had this feeling since we left from there last weekend."

Jim looked at Mary and then looked at James. "We have both been scarred by the past when they took her, and now we are scarred by the present."

James could relate to them, at least as far as the worried and scarred part. For he had had a sister who had been killed by her husband, and no one had listened to her when she told them that she needed help until it was too late. There was concern on everyone's face.

"Jim," Mary said. "Tell James about the money." When Jim told James what Handy had done, that was enough.

"OK, this is what I'm going to do. I am going to drive out there and just have a look around and make sure that everything is all right for tonight. And while I'm there I will have a talk with Handy, and Jay T won't have to know the real reason that I'm there. I don't want to put Suzann in any more danger. I will come back tomorrow and let you know what I find out, and then we will go into town and get the judge to give us papers, temporary custody so that you can get Suzann out of there, and also see if the judge will give you restraining orders to prevent Jay T from coming around her and you. And if Suzann will tell the truth, I think that I can pick Jay T up and put him back where he belongs. If I have to I think that I can pull some strings with the prison officials and do some investigating and if we can prove that he had anything to do with the murders there you won't ever have to worry about him bothering her again."

"James," Mary asked. "Would it be too much trouble if I ask you to come back by tonight and let us know if Suzann is all right?"

"Of course not, but it is already after ten. It would be at least twelve before I will make it back."

"That will be just fine; we won't be able to sleep anyway. We will wait on you," Jim answered.

"Well then, I will see you in a couple of hours," James replied.

Jim and Mary stood in the doorway and watched as James pulled out of the driveway. After he was out of sight, Jim and Mary went back into the house and sat down on the couch, facing each other, holding hands, and thanking God for this man and the people that were willing to help.

"Do you want to get her room ready?" Jim asked.

"No, it's been ready since she left. I've always kept it ready and waiting for her to come back home."

So Jim and Mary sat there waiting for the sherriff to come back and were looking so forward to the homecoming of their baby girl, this time for good.

CHAPTER FORTY-NINE

Suzann sat there with her eyes tensed shut and her hand placed tightly over her ears to block out the shouting and cursing coming from Jay T and Kate. Hunger gnawed at her belly when she silently slipped down to the ground with an elbow on each knee keeping her ears covered and rocking herself back and forth. Not knowing how much time had passed, only that somehow something was different. She removed her hands and heard no voices. Suzann was still a little reluctant as she pushed herself to her feet, looking down at herself and seeing the blood splatters all over her clothes from the licking that she had taken from Jay T earlier on. Then out of nowhere she heard shouting coming from the house, followed by a pounding sound. Her shoulders sagged and once again she could feel her anger start to rise when she remembered Jim Bob lying up there dead and nobody had seemed to care. Then her thoughts went to the girls that she had locked in her room.

"Oh my god, I've got to get up there and make sure that they are all right. I promised them that they would not be hurt, and I will make sure of that if it cost me my life. They are not going to hurt them."

Suzann hesitated, wishing once more that Handy would drive up. She looked down the road but everything was dark. She was looking for headlights but there were none. Once again the pounding broke her concentration and she took off running to the house to see what was going on. As she got closer she could hear Jay T shouting her name. With her eyes focused on the house, Suzann found herself lying on the ground. She had tripped over something. She knew the path so well and was just expecting flat ground. Suzann got herself up and was wiping the small pieces of gravel from her hands when she saw something in the light of the harvest moon that made it look so light out. Her face froze with a look of horror when she saw that she had tripped on Kate.

Suzann walked over and touched the body of Kate that lay on the ground. But Kate didn't move. As a small cloud moved on by, Suzann then noticed there was blood all around her, she looked like she had bled out. Suzann felt herself stepping backward, holding her screams inside. Nodding her head, she could not tear her eyes away from the mangled body. Suzann slowly bent down and lifted up Kate's arm that lay beside her on the ground and found that it was limp, there was no sound no pulse. Then she noticed that Kate's stomach had been ripped open. The torn flesh was ripped apart, looking like something that a wild animal might do but Suzann knew that this wasn't the work of any four-legged animal.

Suzann's arms clung to herself for a moment as the sweat grew into a chill throughout her body. She left Kate where she lay, knowing that she could not move her, thinking that it would be best if she didn't let Jay T know that she had found her. Suzann got up and took off running for the feed room at the barn and got the gun that she had hidden there. "Just in case," she thought. Then she ran all the way back to the house. She eased into the house through the front door and placed the gun under the cushion of the couch without Jay T seeing her. He was down the small hallway and around the corner, still pounding on the door and shouting her name, saying, "If you don't come out, I am going to kick in the door. And where is my damn key? This is your last warning. I ain't asking again!"

"You looking for me?" Suzann asked. She could hear all the girls crying and knew that they were scared to death. But even with everything that had happened, she had a feeling of relief to know that they were still safe.

Jay T turned around and stared at her as he hit the bathroom door with his fist and caused it to rattle in its own frame. Then after hitting it again, the door swung open and banged into the wall, taking out the latch that held it shut. The house was dim with only the kitchen and bedroom lights on but Suzann could see the look in his red bloodshot eyes, and the expression on his face was one that she had never seen before. Suzann did not know what to do except maybe try to talk to him and see if she could calm him down. She knew that whatever happened she could not leave him alone in the house with the kids after what she'd seen outside in the yard.

In a loud booming voice, he said, "Where the fuck have you been?" Suzann caught a vision of Kate in her mind and her disfigured face with one of her eyes rolled looking up, like the eye of a calf in a slaughtering pen. Without waiting for her answer, he stormed into the kitchen and found a glistening wet place on the floor and almost slid down. Catching himself on the corner of the bar, he found his bottle of whiskey and downed another good long drink.

Suzann walked to the doorway. "Jay T," she asked. "What are we going to do about Jim Bob?"

"Well, just what the fucking hell do you think we should do about Jim Bob?"

Then the smile faded from his lips as he started walking towards her. It was at this point that she knew talking to him was not going to help but she was still going to try; she didn't know what else to do.

Then there was another moment of brief silence before she answered.

"I don't know, but we've got to do something," she answered, not that it mattered because Jay T wasn't listening anyway.

Jay T was now starting to feel a wonderful warm sense of satisfaction. Suzann could hear the echo from his voice as he called out her name. "Come here."

She felt the blood as it rushed through her veins and her knees became weak. Her hands began trembling. His eyes were abnormally big, filled with the look of rage. He reached out quickly, grabbing her by both of her arms, and pulled her to him. Looking her right in the face, he asked, "What did you tell them?"

"What did I tell who?" But it came out so low that she had to clear her throat and say it again loudly.

"Who? Hell, you know exactly who."

Suzann looked up with a start, her mouth open. His large hand slapped her across the face.

"Let me see if that will jog your memory."

Her strong resistance to the pain that he brought surged within her as he was drawing back his hand to hit her again. The skin on her face felt like a thousand ants were stinging it.

Suzann knew what he was referring to and she felt no guilt that she had said something to them and wished now that she had told them a lot more. But Jay T would never know that she had said a word to anybody even if he killed her. She remembered his threat to kill anyone that she might talk to.

"Have you thought about what we talked about?" Jay T asked.

"Yes, I've thought about it. Like I had a choice," she answered.

"Oh yes, you have one choice." Jay T raised his hand at her once again.

"Wait, don't hit me anymore," she pleaded with him through all the tears and the swollen eyes.

"Sit down," he demanded.

Suzann just stood there watching him.

"I said fucking sit down!" Not giving her a chance to move, he shoved her from her feet into the chair. Sitting there in the quietness, he rolled a cigarette, spilling tobacco all over the floor. He stared at her while he smoked with a smirking grin on his face. "I'm still waiting for that answer," he said in a mean harsh tone that filled up his voice. Suzann's expression told him that she did not understand why he would want to go through

with this, and the whiskey was making him indifferent to her
pleas. And he was damned if he was going to sit there and listen
to her whining ass. He lifted his broad shoulders. He jerked
her abruptly to her feet. Then he placed his hands around her
arms just above the elbows, holding her arms clamped tightly
to her sides.

"What are you thinking about?" he shouted into her face. He
was in an ecstasy of rage now, screaming into her face over and
over.

"Goddamn it, you look at me."

Looking directly into his face, the words were uncontrollable.
"You fucking bastard," she said.

His hand slapped across her face again and again until the pain
no longer hurt.

"Now, let's hear you say that you're sorry and that you did not
mean it."

Suzann was now trying to fight him, trying to get away from him,
but hitting him was like hitting a brick wall. Her tears had flushed
the blood from her eyes, but the swelling was so bad that she could
barely see. He pinned her down on the floor. She had fought
him until there was hardly any fight left in her. Her arms were so
weak that she could hardly lift their own weight. He laughed and
laughed and laughed. Playing with her like a cat would play with a
rat just before the kill. His hooded eyes toured her body, her shirt
wet from fighting and blood and sweat from him and her.

"Take your clothes off," he ordered.

"NEVER," she answered. Then she could see the devil that was
looking back through his eyes.

Her hair had been confined in a long plait and the way that
she had it pulled back from her face should have added a lot of
severity to her face. But it did not, it only showed the perfection
of her jawline. And underneath the bruised and puffy surface
and the sweat there was still the innocent curve of her cheeks. He
was disgusted when his eyes drifted from her face to start at the

start of her breast, and the emotions of a different kind started to surface.

"Take off your clothes," he ordered again.

"Fuck you."

"OK, then I'll take them off and then fuck you."

Then from out of nowhere there was a clap of thunder that shook the whole house and a bolt of lightning flowered right behind it.

"Now, that's weird," Jay T said. "There's not a cloud in the sky." Suzann was fighting still and trying to wiggle her way to where she had put the gun, but where he had her pinned down she could not reach it. Rolling her over onto her back, he was trying to rip off her shirt. She was screaming now with all the voice that she had left, and kicking, trying to get lose from him.

"Go ahead and scream. No one can hear you. I like it that better that way, makes things more exciting."

He picked her up and sat her up on the floor. He ripped what was left of her shirt completely off her. Suzann crossed her arms across her breast, trying to cover them from his gawking eyes. Unzipping his pants, Jay T pulled out his hard dick that looked like something that would be found on an ape's body.

"Ever seen one of these before?" he asked. "Let me guess, you have only read about them. Then you should know what they are used for. Rub it."

She held her arms even tighter to her breast.

"I said rub it." Then he took her hands that she had clamped. as tight as she could make, into a fist, refusing to open her hands. Jay T forced her by taking her hand and placing it on himself. From the blood on her hands, he was having trouble keeping them on himself because of them being so slick.

"So you want to play a little rougher, hey? That's the way that I like it." Then he took hold of her other hand that she also made a fist with, cupping it in his large hand and started to squeeze it as hard as he could until the pain was unbearable, making her feel sick to her stomach. Blood had begun to run down her arm and elbow where he had scratched her with his long hard fingernails. He had broken her will-power, and at last she gave in and opened her tight fist and placed her hand around him just like he ordered her to.

"Now that's better," he said, still holding her by the other hand. "Now I'm going to let go of your hand, but if you disobey me again I promise you the next time I will break it. Do you hear me? Answer me, damn you."

"Y-E-S."

"There are so many things that I want to do to you that I don't know where to start first."

"Please, no. No. No."

The words came over and over and over from her busted lips. Shoving her back onto the floor, Jay T undid her pants and pulled them off and flung them over to the side. Then placing his hands around her breasts, he started pinching her nipples until there were blood blisters present.

"You bitch!" he uttered. Suzann cried out with pain and fear, not knowing what he was going to do next. Her fingers scraped nervously at the floor, digging her nails into the wood breaking them off to the quick. Her cries echoed. She stiffened and her tears flooded her face, mixed with her blood while she feared for her life. Jay T seemed to be trying to find a more comfortable position as he dragged her to the couch. For Suzann, that was the best move that he could have made.

CHAPTER FIFTY

Handy made the turn into his driveway, glad to be home but it had been really good to see his old army buddy and spend some time with him, something that Handy felt he should do more often.

Handy got out of his car and started walking to his door where he tripped over a rock. He fought to keep his balance and stay on his feet, which ended him at his front steps. He sucked in a breath and started to unlock his door when he noticed something that was on his door that was not there before.

"Shit, that's blood marks and they are still wet."

Handy went ahead and opened the door and put on the lights. He then noticed that his window was opened. He looked for a note, thinking that maybe Suzann had left him one and forgot to close the window. Then he thought, "She never opens the window all the way up just to leave a note.

Something is wrong, something is not right."

So Handy decided to run up to Jay T's and look into Suzann's window to see if everything was all right. Then he noticed that the corner of his bedspread was tucked under the mattress. He ran to his bed and looked under the mattress and saw that two of his guns were missing. Taking the one that was left, he headed out to find Suzann for he had a gut feeling that she was in trouble. As he stepped out on the porch he heard a commotion coming from the house. He opened his mouth and squinted his eyes, trying to see and hear what was going on. "Hell, that was a scream," he said excitedly to himself. Even before his thought had time to end, he took off in a dead run. When he got to the house, he saw Kate's body lying there on the ground. Once he got closer, he stopped for a second, waiting for his heartbeat to slow down before he trusted his eyes to look and see who it was. His relief and horror was seeing that it was Kate and not Suzann.

"Ho-ly shit."

Then there was another clap of thunder that rumbled the ground.

CHAPTER FIFTY-ONE

Suzann lunged, frantic to escape, but her efforts were useless. She struggled to get away, she couldn't. Jay T had her arm pulled around to her back and then he placed his hand on her hips and picked her up onto her knees and had her bent over the front of the couch. He was pulling her legs apart while Suzann used her only loose arm to try and feel for the gun. She knew where she had put it and was trying to get it in her hand. Then she got a grip on it. Her cry echoed. She stiffened, her tears raging down her face from the pain that Jay T was inducing.

Now that she had the gun in her hand, she was trying to figure out how she could use it when he had her lying face down and he was at her back. Then she heard him spit on his hand, she knew she had to do something. So she pulled out the gun, squeezed her eyes shut, and pulled the trigger. The only place she could fire it was toward the front door, but in doing that maybe this would get his attention and get him off of her.

Handy ran up the steps and kicked the front door open just as the round went off. He was hit by the round that she fired.

"What the fuck," Jay T shouted as he backed off and grabbed for the gun, trying to take it from her. Suzann's last bit of adrenaline was rushing through her veins, when she managed to roll over and kick Jay T right in the balls with both of her feet.

Then the worst thing that could have happened, did. Jay T was gasping for his breath but still had his hand on the gun, trying to take it from her, when the lights went out. He jerked the gun from her hand and hit her over her head. And then there was another round fired, Suzann could see the fire that came from the end of the barrel and then another. And then she was unconscious, falling over onto the floor.

At the same exact moment, Sherriff James Campbell pulled up and he heard the gunfire. Turning on his red lights, he grabbed his radio and called for backup. He pulled his gun from his holster and ran up the steps. He stood beside the door, trying to see who was doing the shooting. But it was too dark and there was a deafening silence, no sounds at all.

Then there was another big clap of thunder and on came the lights.

"What the hell," James whispered to himself. Then he heard a moan. It was Handy and he was holding Suzann in his arms, rocking her back and forth.

James saw that Jay T was lying on the floor with his pants down and a gun in his hand, with a gunshot to his head. James went to where Handy was sitting and holding Suzann. "I'll be right back."

James went to his car and called in for more help and an ambulance. As he started back to the house, he thought, "Hell, I might as well call for the coroner too because there's one that will not need any medical attention. Old Jay T has finally met his Waterloo."

James went back into the house and told Handy that there was help on the way.

"Sheriff, Kate is lying out there on the ground next to the house."

"Are you all right?" James asked.

"Yes, I've been shot worse than this. It just got me in the shoulder." James's knelt down beside Handy to look at Suzann.

"Oh my god, how could anyone do this?"

A guttural sound escaped from her throat as she tried to tell Handy something.

"Shhh," Handy said. "I've got you. You are going to be all right."

"No, Jim Bob . . . Kate killed him," her raspy voice tried to say.

Wrapping her only good arm around Handy's shoulder, she tried desperately to hold her cries. With a message of prayer and her good arm extended toward heaven, her cries were loud.

The sheriff went into the bedroom and brought back a blanket to cover her and looked at Handy. "The baby is dead. It's a good thing that you got here when you did."

"I didn't get here soon enough," Handy answered as he looked down upon Suzann.

"Yeah," the sheriff replied, shaking his head and rubbing his hand across his mouth. James was standing out on the porch, watching, and he could see the other deputies and the ambulance coming around the bend. "They are here. Get her and put her on the truck first. Can you walk?" James asked.

"I'm going with her. She has nobody, Sherriff. If you would, could you get a hold of Mr. Butler? He will need someone to take care of the milking. I will be with Suzann. I will not leave her alone, she's had enough of that in her life."

CHAPTER FIFTY-TWO

Jim and Mary paced the floor as James did not return like he had said he would. Mary was in tears with worry.

"It's not as bad as all that. Maybe James is just running a little late, you know how he is when he gets to talking."

Jim's conversation was a struggle and Mary was relieved when he ended by saying, "Come on, we're driving out there."

Jim was not one to speed but this was one night that he exercised his will to break the law. The truck held silence on the way, and it was no time until that they topped the hill to see all the red lights flashing. He eased the old truck onto the shoulder to allow the ambulance to get by them. Jim's heart rate increased with a quiet nervous desire to know what in the world had happened. He reached over to hold a familiar hand that he knew needed holding. Her day had been filled with worry and unwarranted guilt. It had left her weak and shaken. He had heard her gasp from seeing what she was looking at. Tears stung Jim's eyes but he held them back ever so forcibly. He didn't dare let Mary see how helpless he really felt. He knew something bad had happened. Mary sat in the truck in silence as Jim pulled up into the drive. Then they saw that the whole house had been roped off. A deputy met them at the truck before they had time to even get out, informing them that they could not get out.

"You need to stay in the truck. I'll go get the sherriff."

James was wondering how Jay T could have done what he had, but the fact remained that this was a mystery that would never be resolved. His thoughts were interrupted when he heard that Jim and Mary were there.

James walked out to where they were in the truck, and Jim could see that there was something distasteful on his face. Jim and Mary sat there quietly watching and waiting for an explanation. The sherriff looked down at the ground and cleared his throat. Jim could wait no longer.

"James, what has happened here?"

"Brother Jim, I hate to be the one to have to tell you but right now I'm not sure myself what all has happened here tonight. I know that I have three dead bodies, one in really bad condition, and another one shot. Kate is dead"

"Oh lord, she was pregnant."

"Really, then I have four dead people.

"Suzann, is she all right?"

"No, she's not all right but she is still alive and she has been taken to the hospital."

James stood there once again looking at the ground with a strange look about his face.

"Is there something that you are not telling us?" Jim asked.

"No, I've told you about all that I know at this point. There'll be a whole lot more investigating to do before we actually know the whole story. I guess you could say that tonight I've become a believer. I've always heard strange stories about this part of the country. Well, what I heard from an old-timer when I was a kid is true, I guess. These hills and hollows seem to fill people's minds with *evil notions*."

PHOTO GALLERY

This is a picture of the farm house
and what remains of it today.

This is a picture of the graveyard
that was said to be haunted

This is the cover of the album that
Suzann and Billy did for our troops.